MW00399244

COCKY ROOMMATE

BOOK BOYFRIENDS BOOK 2

CLAIRE KINGSLEY

Always Have LLC

Copyright © 2017 Claire Kingsley

All rights reserved.

No part of this book may be reproduced in any form or by any electronic or mechanical means, including information storage and retrieval systems, without written permission from the author, except for the use of brief quotations in a book review.

This is a work of fiction. Any names, characters, places, or incidents are products of the author's imagination and used in a fictitious manner. Any resemblance to actual people, places, or events is purely coincidental or fictionalized.

Published by Always Have, LLC

Edited by Elayne Morgan of Serenity Editing Services

Cover by Cassy Roop of Pink Ink Designs

ISBN: 9781548835453

www.clairekingsleybooks.com

❀ Created with Vellum

To my first roommate, who was not cocky, and will probably never read this, but was still the absolute shit.

ABOUT THIS BOOK

He's such a bad idea.

This roommate thing is not going to work.

Kendra is a messy-haired, pajama-pants-wearing little ball of sass. The first thing she does is try to make friends with my random from the night before—giving her all sorts of bad ideas.

I don't date. I don't use words like girlfriend, or I'll text you later. F*ck that. Relationships aren't for me. I'll give a woman a night she won't forget, but once it's over, I'm out.

I keep people at a distance, and I have my reasons. But Kendra starts getting under my skin. And when my life crashes and burns—literally—Kendra is the only person I can count on.

I'm not built for relationships, and Kendra is not a one night stand. But living with this girl sleeping one room away might just be the thing that kills me.

1

KENDRA

*T*he early morning sun glints off the hood of my car and I adjust my sunglasses. It's a gorgeous day for a drive, which is good because I have a long one. It's been a great weekend away, although technically it was a splurge I can't afford. But I couldn't afford *not* to go. Not when I'm just striking out on my own.

My phone dings with a text and I swipe the screen. It's from my brother Alex's fiancée, Mia.

Mia: K-Law! Are you home yet?

I giggle at her nickname for me. My last name is Lawson, and Mia cracked herself up for five solid minutes when she first thought of it. I picture her laughing as she typed it just now. Since she started dating my brother, Mia has become one of my best friends. She's a little awkward, but once you get to know her, she's hilarious and super sweet. Alex did good.

I tap the screen to call her back. She hates phone calls, but I'm not going to text and drive. Plus, I'm bored and I still have another hour on the road. She better answer.

It rings once. Twice. *Come on, Mia. It's a phone, it isn't going to bite you.* Three times.

"Kendra, why are you calling me? You know I don't use my phone for that."

I laugh. "Mi, I'm driving. I can't text you back."

She groans. "Fine. How was your weekend?"

"It was good," I say. "I made some really good contacts."

"That's great," she says. "Pick up any new clients?"

"No firm commitments," I say. "But I got a lot of names and contact information. It helps that I can say I'm Lexi Logan's editor."

"Yeah, I bet."

Alex secretly writes romance novels under the pseudonym Lexi Logan. I helped him get his books off the ground, and I've always been his editor. For a while, I was the only one who knew about it. Now, Team Lexi consists of me, Mia, and our brother, Caleb. Most people think Alex is a consultant who works from home.

I've worked as an editor since I graduated college with an English degree. My last job had me working primarily on non-fiction for a small press. I decided I couldn't stand the thought of editing yet another self-help book. So I quit.

It wasn't a decision I took lightly, and it was a long time coming. My boss was a jerk and honestly, who has time for that? I'm not getting any younger, and I decided it was time to take control of my life.

My brothers both gave me an earful when I told them. Alex wanted to know how much money I had in savings (not much). Caleb wanted to know if I had a business plan (not really). All I know is that I love editing fiction, and it's time to take a chance and do what I love.

Hence my weekend away. I went to a writer's conference in Portland, about four hours from home. It wasn't cheap, especially because I had to pay for three nights in a hotel. But it gave me the chance to meet tons of authors and get my name out there. I really need more clients—fast. My clout as Lexi's editor helps, but a reputation doesn't pay the bills.

"What's up with the roommate situation?" Mia asks. "What happened to that one girl who answered your Craigslist ad?"

Getting a roommate is on my list of *things to do to make this work.*

"Which one?" I ask. "The tarot card reader who wanted to set up her psychic services business in my living room? The college student who asked if I'd be okay with leaving the house on Friday nights so she can throw parties? Oh, or the chain smoker?"

"That's what you have to choose from?" she asks.

"Pretty much. Luckily, I found someone else."

"You did? Who is she?"

"Well, to be honest, I don't know much about her yet," I say. "It was a really last minute thing, but she's someone Caleb knows. I don't know the details. He called me on Friday, right as I was about to go into my first session at the conference. He said one of his colleagues was looking for a place to stay, temporarily. Probably just for a few months, but needs to move in right away. I figure, if Caleb suggested her, how bad can she be, right?"

"True," Mia says. "Sounds awesome."

"Yeah, I think it will be," I say. "It's a little weird, but what's the worst that can happen? It won't be for long, and that will give me a chance to find someone who'll stay longer. Or maybe my new freelance career will take off and I won't need a roommate anymore."

"That would be great," Mia says. "Speaking of, I'm telling all the authors I know about you. So hopefully a few of them are looking for a new editor."

"Thanks, Mi, I really appreciate that," I say. Mia is a popular romance book blogger and she has a lot of contacts.

"Of course," she says. "So when does she move in?"

"I think she's already there," I say.

"Wow," she says. "You're braver than I am. I don't think I could agree to live with someone sight unseen."

"Yeah, but if Caleb knows her, I'm sure it's fine," I say. "Who knows, maybe Caleb has a thing for this girl. That would be fun, wouldn't it?"

"Oh my god, I would die of happiness," she says. "Caleb really needs someone in his life. As long as she's awesome."

"Well this will give me the chance to find out," I say. "It's perfect."

"So perfect," she says. "You have to tell me everything about her."

"Obviously."

"Okay, you've used up my phone call quota for like the entire week."

"Fair enough," I say. "I'm about an hour out and I think I need a nap when I get home. I got up at like five so I could get on the road early."

"Yuck," she says. "Okay, text me and tell me what she's like."

"I will."

I turn up the music after I hang up with Mia. I'm getting a little drowsy and I don't want to stop before I get home. I stayed last night so I could attend one last informal meet and greet in the hotel bar, but that meant I had to get up early to get back. It's Monday, and I have an edit due tomorrow. It's one of my first new clients, and the last thing I want to do is blow a deadline.

An hour later, I'm pulling up to my house. I have a little two-bedroom cottage style house near Sand Point. It's not very big, but I don't need a lot of space. It was built in 1910, so it has all these amazing details. Little storage cupboards, beautiful molding, original hardwoods. It's a bit creaky, and the list of things I need to fix or replace keeps growing. But I love my little house.

There's a sleek, black Mercedes in the driveway. Wow. I don't know much about cars, but I'm sure that's not cheap. Caleb is a surgeon; maybe my new roommate is a fellow doctor. That could explain the nice car. In any case, what she drives doesn't matter. And maybe if she likes nice things, she won't be a messy person.

I grab my bag out of the back and head inside, careful not to make too much noise. It's still early. I have no idea when she works. If she has a schedule anything like Caleb's, she could work all sorts of crazy hours. I don't want to wake her if she's sleeping.

By the time I set my bag down and head for the kitchen, I'm already rethinking my nap plan. What this day really calls for is coffee so I can power through. I'll just go to bed early to make up for it. I have a lot of work to do.

The floor creaks behind me and I turn, gasping.

"Oh, I'm sorry," I say. "You startled me."

A woman with bleached blond hair and huge boobs stares at me with her mouth open. I guess I startled her too.

"Hey," I say with a smile. "I'm Kendra. It's nice to meet you."

"I'm Lana," she says, her eyebrows drawing down, like she's confused.

"That's a pretty name," I say. "I couldn't remember if Caleb gave me your name or not. Which is weird, I know, but I had to get off the phone, so I cut him off. This whole roommate thing happened so fast."

"Oh," she says, her face brightening. "Roommate."

"Yeah." I glance around because I'm not quite sure what she means. Who else would I be? "Anyway, I'm making coffee. I got up so early and I think this is the only way I'm going to get anything done today. Can I make you some?'

"Sure," she says. "That sounds great. I didn't get a lot of sleep last night either."

"That's too bad." I pour some grounds into the coffee maker.

"The house is kind of noisy. It creaks, but you'll get used to it. I don't even notice it anymore."

"Hmm." She sits down at my small kitchen table.

I get out two mugs and lean against the counter while the coffee brews. I try to be cool about it, but I'm totally scoping her out. Her long manicured nails are painted pink. She's wearing a white crop top with shiny red lips on the front, and a pair of high-waisted skinny jeans. I glance at her feet—bright red stilettos. It's a weird outfit for early morning. It looks more like a going-out kind of thing, but maybe she's just not into comfy clothes.

The coffee finishes brewing and I pour us each a cup. "Cream and sugar?"

"Yes, lots of both," she says.

I add sugar and cream and hand her the mug, then take the seat across from her.

I'm having a really hard time picturing her with Caleb. Even if they're not a thing yet, would he really be interested in her? Her makeup is a little smudged and faded, like she slept in it, but she's still wearing a lot. Blond hair bleached even lighter, judging by her roots. She flicks a manicured finger across her phone screen, one leg crossed, her foot bobbing up and down as if she's listening to music. She just doesn't seem like Caleb's type.

Not that I really know what Caleb's type *is*. My brother got married young, when he was still in med school, but unfortunately his wife died in a car accident a few months after their daughter, Charlotte, was born. That was five years ago, and recently my brother and my niece moved back to Seattle from Houston to be closer to family.

Maybe Caleb's isn't into this girl, because he's really careful about who he lets into Charlotte's life. I don't see this Lana chick as being *meet the daughter* material.

But what do I know. And I'm being awfully judgey, now that I think about it. I hate that I keep thinking *bimbo* when I look at her. For all I know, she could be crazy smart and just has mildly slutty fashion taste. Caleb said *colleague*, so she must work at the hospital.

"So what do you do, Lana?" I ask.

"I work at Cowgirls, Inc.," she says. "It's a bar downtown."

I blink at her. "Yeah, I've heard of it." That's so weird. How does working at a bar make her Caleb's colleague? "Are you a bartender?"

"No, dancer," she says.

I have no idea what to even say to that. Does she mean stripper? But I don't think Cowgirls, Inc. is a strip club. "Oh, really? Um, what's that like?"

"Oh, it's fun," she says. "I do mostly bar top stuff, and it's good because I earn tips, but they can't touch. And I keep some of my clothes on. It's totally classy."

She seems very pleased with herself. This is one of the strangest conversations I've had in a long time. Where did Caleb meet her? I didn't think he hung out at bars, like, ever. He's been having so much trouble finding a good nanny to take care of Charlotte while he works, I can't imagine he has time to go out to bars.

I open my mouth to ask how she met my brother when the back bedroom door opens and someone comes down the hallway. My heart jumps and I realize I'm staring—but I can't help it.

A tall man with an utterly exquisite body walks out wearing nothing but a pair of dark blue boxer briefs. Sleepy eyes blink a few times and he yawns. He has a strong, chiseled jaw and full lips. Piercing gray eyes. My eyes drift down his broad chest, across a set of rippling abs that belong on a book cover, to the bulge in his underwear.

I rip my eyes away and force myself to look at his face,

feeling my cheeks flush. I just looked at his dick, and I can tell by the look on his face that he knows it.

Shit, I'm ogling my brand-new roommate's boyfriend.

"Oh, I'm sorry," I say. "I didn't realize you had someone over. I mean, it's fine, of course. I just wasn't expecting..."

I trail off because I can't think of anything else to say while I stare at this hot piece of man candy standing in my house. Damn it, why does my roommate have to have such a hot guy? This could get awkward.

I start to talk again, but so does he. We both stop and my phone chooses that moment to ring. "Sorry, let me just check." I grab it and look at the name. Caleb. "It's my brother. Excuse me for a minute." Hopefully Caleb will help me make sense of this weird situation.

2

WESTON

*T*he smell of coffee wakes me up.

I stretch and glance over my shoulder at the other side of the bed. Empty. That's good. The last thing I need is Laura wanting to make morning conversation. I probably could have fucked her once more for the road, but I'm not really a morning sex kind of guy. Probably because I almost never let girls stay over. I'll chalk last night up to laziness. I was falling asleep after I banged her the second time, so I didn't bother telling her to have a good one. She fell asleep next to me, and I let it go, the voice in the back of my head telling me I'd probably regret it in the morning.

Do I regret it? Depends on how long it takes to get rid of her, I guess.

But why the hell do I smell coffee?

That thought wakes me up a little more and I stretch again. She isn't out there making us coffee, is she? There is no fucking way I'm going to sit and chat over a mug of joe with Linda. Or was it Lena? Fuck if I can remember, and it's not like it matters anyway.

The floor in the other room creaks, like someone is walking

around. This house isn't all Caleb made it out to be. When he told me his sister Kendra was looking for a roommate, he said she lived in a charming craftsman style house in Sand Point. Maybe my definition of *charming* is different than his, but this place is practically falling apart. The floors creak, it's drafty as hell, it gets freezing at night. Kendra needs to do some serious work on it.

But I guess I won't be living here long anyway. It's just temporary while my house is being remodeled. The scope of work kept getting bigger, and there have been so many delays. I've been living in hotels for weeks now, and that was getting old. When I complained to Caleb that I needed a new living situation, pronto, he mentioned Kendra. Apparently she's been looking for a roommate and striking out with weirdos answering her ad. He called her, right then and there, and she said I could move in the next day. Seemed like the perfect setup.

Caleb met me here Saturday morning to help me move my stuff, but Kendra wasn't here. Out of town for the weekend or something. The place is small, and there's only one bathroom. But I got my shit settled well enough, and it was nice having the place to myself for a while. Gave me a chance to get comfortable without worrying about some girl.

Voices carry down the hallway. Is Lisa talking to someone? Or is it Lana? Whatever the fuck her name is, she's either talking to someone, or she turned on the TV. I hear another woman's voice.

Oh, shit. Is that the roommate?

I get up and drag on some boxer briefs. I hope Lauren isn't lounging on the couch like she's welcome to hang out for the day.

Lois? Fuck, was I drunk last night? Whatever.

Still blinking the sleep from my eyes and running a hand

through my hair, I wander down the hallway and stop dead in my tracks.

Two women are sitting at the vintage kitchen table. One is my lay from last night. She's dressed, thank god, but she's got her legs crossed and a cup of coffee in her hand.

The second woman must be Kendra. She looks like Caleb. Brown eyes that are slightly almond-shaped. Can't tell how tall she is, but she's thin—maybe even willowy. Her hair, though. It's up in this messy bun thing with all these little pieces sticking out everywhere. Did they not have a mirror wherever she woke up this morning? Jesus.

She's staring at me with her eyebrows lifted, her mouth forming a little O. Her eyes travel down from my face to my chest. Down. Further. They reach about crotch level and snap back up to my face, wider now. I glance down at myself. I suppose I should have put on some clothes. But I'm barely fucking awake and I do not understand why the roommate is sitting in the kitchen having coffee with my random from last night. What the hell?

"Oh, I'm sorry," she says. "I didn't realize you had someone over. I mean, it's fine, of course. I just wasn't expecting..."

What does that mean, she didn't realize I had someone over? Who does she think she's sitting with? There isn't a third person living here, as far as I'm aware.

And if there is, and it happens to be the girl I hooked up with last night, I'm moving out. Now.

Kendra and I both start to talk at the same time, but before we figure out who's going to go first, her phone rings.

"Sorry, let me just check." She picks up her phone and looks at the screen. "It's my brother. Excuse me for a minute."

I lean against the wall at the entrance to the kitchen and wait.

"Hey. Yeah, I'm home. Sorry, I was chatting with... What? No,

I met her already. Yes, her." Her eyes narrow and she looks at me again, then gets up and walks a short distance into the living room. Not like it matters; I can still hear her. "Wait, what? Weston? I thought... Caleb, why didn't you—Oh." She laughs and glances back at me again. "Oh my god, that is so funny. No, his girlfriend is here and I totally thought she was... Yeah, exactly."

My back clenches at the word *girlfriend*. Lady, do not be giving this chick any ideas.

"Of course he has a girlfriend, she's right here. Yes, he does. I just spent the last few minutes chatting with her. Lana. Yes, his girlfriend. Geez, Caleb, are you listening? Look, it's fine, it's just funny. But it's cool I get to meet them both right away, because I bet she'll be here a lot."

I cough, my throat suddenly feeling dry and closed off. This is fucking ridiculous. Be here a lot? Oh, hell no. Lola is smiling at me, flicking her tongue across her lips. She is getting some very wrong ideas in that pretty little head of hers. I don't care how hot she is, *girlfriend* is not a word in my vocabulary. Nor are words like *dating* or *I'll text you later*. Fuck that.

Kendra's still talking—does she ever shut up?—and what's-her-name stands and walks over to me.

"I should probably get going," she says, twirling a strand of platinum blond hair around a finger. "Text me later, and we can hang out again."

I shoot a quick glare at the roommate. She's finally hanging up her phone. "Whatever, Lisa. You have a cab coming or something?"

"It's Lana," she says, crossing her arms.

I shrug and walk past her into the kitchen. This scene is giving me a headache. I need some coffee.

"Are you for real right now?" Lana says.

I open three cupboards before I find a mug, then pour some

coffee and glance over my shoulder. "Well, yeah. We're kinda done here. If you were expecting me to cook you breakfast, you went home with the wrong guy last night." Where the hell does Kendra keep the sugar? I check another cupboard and find a small white sugar dish.

Lana lets out an angry huff and stomps across the creaky floor.

"Wait, do you have a ride?" Kendra asks. "I can call you a cab if you want."

"No, I'll just Uber," Lana says. She pauses at the front door. "Asshole."

"It was nice to—" The door slams. "Meet you?"

I find cream in the fridge and pour in a splash.

"Wow, that was... interesting," Kendra says.

I take a sip of my coffee and turn around. "What?"

"You basically just threw her out," she says. "Do you always treat your girlfriend like that?"

"No, because I don't have a girlfriend."

"Oh," Kendra says, her eyes full of judgment.

For fuck's sake. I do not need lectures from this messy-haired skinny chick. "Look, it's a three-day weekend, so it's my day off. I didn't exactly get a lot of sleep last night, and your little friend-fest out here woke me up."

"Somebody's grumpy in the morning," she says.

I pinch the bridge of my nose and shake my head. "I am when I should be sleeping in, and rude fucking roommates start giving me shit."

"Maybe rude *fucking* roommates wouldn't give you shit if you quit acting like a dick."

The fuck did she just say to me? She's got her arms crossed over her flat chest; she probably never filled out a training bra. She's this lean little ball of sass, her head cocked to the side, one eyebrow arched.

"A dick, huh? Classy."

She sighs and drops her arms. "Look, maybe we got off on the wrong foot. Can we start over?" She walks over to me and holds out her hand. "Hi, I'm Kendra."

I switch my coffee cup and shake her hand. "Weston."

"There," she says with a smile. "That's more like it."

"Whatever makes you feel better, honey." I head down the hallway toward my room. "Don't worry, I won't be here long. I'll stay out of your way if you stay out of mine."

She doesn't reply—thank god—and I close my bedroom door behind me.

What was I thinking? This is not going to work. Moving in with a roommate was clearly a fucking mistake.

3

KENDRA

The trickle of water through the coffee maker and the rain beating against the window are the only things breaking the silence. I'm getting sleepy, but I still have work to do. Hence the coffee, even though it's getting late and I know it's going to keep me up.

Although, that's the point.

It's been a week since Weston moved in and I haven't seen much of him. Which is just as well. What an ass that guy is. He hasn't had any more girls over, thank god. When the weekend hit, I was wondering if I'd be treated to another bleached-out blonde at my kitchen table in the morning. He wasn't around much, but I know he slept here—alone.

I have no idea what he does when he's not here. It's not like he chats about his day—or about anything, for that matter. He leaves early, often before I'm up. He doesn't seem to have a set time he comes home—it's been anywhere from four in the afternoon to ten at night. When he's here, he mostly retreats to his bedroom. One evening, when he'd come back earlier in the afternoon, he actually sat on the couch for a while with his tablet. He had earbuds in his ears, and hardly said a word to me.

I guess in one sense, he's not a terrible roommate. He doesn't make a lot of noise. He leaves his dishes in the sink sometimes, but he doesn't eat here often enough that I've felt the need to say anything about it.

But it sure would be nice to share my space with someone who is at least a little bit friendly. And *friendly* is something Weston Reid is not.

I blow out a breath and make my eyes focus on my screen. This edit is so much more work than I expected. My client is a new author, and the bones of this story are good, but the mechanics are a disaster. I underestimated the number of hours this would take—by a lot.

The front door opens and Weston comes in. He tosses his keys on the little table by the door and walks past without so much as a glance in my direction.

I shake my head and tighten my messy bun. I didn't leave the house today, so I never did anything with my hair. Or change out of my pajama pants. But oh well. It's not like I have anyone around here to impress.

Weston comes back out a few minutes later dressed only in his underwear. Again. This guy walks around in nothing but boxer briefs all the time. I'm torn between asking him to stop —because awkward—and not asking him to stop—because holy shit. Asshole or not, he's fabulous eye candy. His early mornings have to be due to trips to the gym because he's in fantastic shape. Well-defined shoulders, chest, and back. Muscular arms. And abs. God, he has abs for days. He's lean and strong, and maybe I'll just keep my mouth shut about the underwear thing. After all, he has to live here for a few months. I'd hate for him to feel like he can't make himself comfortable.

His eyes meet mine and I quickly look back at my screen. Damn it, he caught me staring at him. Again. I need to quit doing that. The last thing he needs is me feeding his already overinflated ego.

He opens the fridge, then comes into the living room with his tablet and a bottled water. After a quick glance at me—I'm sideways on the couch with my legs stretched out—he sits at the other end. I have to move my legs out of the way to give him room; he was about to sit on my feet.

Does he ask if I'd mind moving? Does he say thank you when I do? No, of course not. He says nothing, just starts tapping on his tablet screen, his earbuds draped around his neck.

Maybe he'd be friendlier if we got to know each other a little bit. "So, hey. How was your day?"

His gaze turns to me for half a second. "It was a day."

"It was bad, then?"

"I didn't say that."

"Okay..." Maybe I'll try a different angle. "So, we never did a very good job introducing ourselves. How do you know my brother?"

"College," he says.

I feel like I now know twice as much about Weston Reid as I did two minutes ago. "Are you a surgeon, like him?"

He still doesn't take his eyes off his tablet, nor does he stop tapping on the screen. "I'm a surgeon, yes."

"Do you work at Swedish?"

"No. Private practice."

"That's interesting." Okay, so he's not really looking at me, but this is the most conversation we've had since the Lana incident. This is good. "What kind of surgery do you do? You guys have specialties, right?"

"Plastic and reconstructive."

"Oh, really? Like, you fix people when they've had a disfiguring injury or something?"

"No, mostly breast augmentations."

My mouth hangs open for a few seconds before I realize I'm gaping at him. "Wait, you do boob jobs?"

His eyes flick over to me again. "Yep."

"What made you decide to go in that direction?" I ask.

"Not heroic enough for you?" he asks, sounding bored.

"I'm just curious," I say. "I like hearing people's stories."

"It's profitable," he says.

I'm not really sure what to say to that. Weston looks at boobs all day? Why does this not surprise me in the least?

"Do you like your job?" I ask.

He shrugs. "I suppose."

"Are you good at it?" I ask, then cringe. Nice question, Kendra.

"I'm the best," he says, without a hint of sarcasm.

Well, then. I pause for a moment, trying to think of something else to say. "Have you seen Lana again?"

"What are you doing?" he asks, finally turning to look at me.

"What do you mean?" I ask. "I'm sitting on the couch trying to have a conversation with you. It isn't easy, you know."

"Why?"

"Why isn't it easy? Because you—"

"No, why are you trying to have a conversation?" he asks.

His brow is furrowed—no, it is not the *least* bit sexy—and I think he's genuinely confused.

"I just figured, you know, we're roommates," I say. "Maybe we'd be more comfortable if we knew each other a little better."

"I'd say you're a little too comfortable," he says, gesturing to my pajama pants.

I glance down at my pants—dark blue flannel with little cartoon pigs. "They're cute."

He arches an eyebrow at me. "They have pigs on them."

"At least I don't walk around in my underwear all the time."

He snorts out a short laugh. "Thank god for that."

My mouth drops open and I stare at him. "Excuse me?"

"And what's up with the hair? Is that intentional, or are you just lazy about it?"

I keep gaping at him. What the fuck did he just say to me? He shrugs. "I'm just saying, it's not doing anything for you. If this is your usual thing, I'm not surprised you didn't have plans over the weekend."

"Oh my god." I swing my legs over the side of the couch and stand up, trying not to drop my laptop in the process. "What the hell is your problem?"

"I don't have a problem," he says, his voice still nonchalant. He puts in his earbuds.

"You are so obnoxious," I say, but I don't think he can hear me. I stomp to my room and slam the door behind me. Only it doesn't really slam, and it takes me three tries to get it to stay closed. Stupid door. The latch is loose, so it pops open all the time. So much for my dramatic exit.

I set my laptop on the bed and put my hands on my hips. I just let him chase me out of my own living room. Son of a bitch. The last thing I want to do is go back out there. He'll probably gloat. In fact, he was probably trying to run me off the whole time so he could have the living room to himself.

Asshole.

I do have more work to do, but I'm so annoyed. I need to get out of here.

After sending Mia a quick text to see if she's free, I change into a pair of distressed jeans and a gray sweater. I'm tempted to go out in my pajama pants, just to make a point, but I know I'll regret it as soon as the front door closes behind me. I tug on a pair of brown ankle boots, grab my phone, and head out.

Weston doesn't look up as I stomp past, grab my coat and purse, and leave.

"Asshole," I mutter under my breath.

Mia answers my text while I'm on the way to the coffee shop, saying she'll meet me there. I order a latte and find us a table next to the front window.

She comes in a few minutes later and her toe catches on something only Mia could trip over. She manages to keep her feet and rolls her eyes. "Coffee," she says, pointing to the counter.

When her coffee is ready, she comes back, latte in hand. She walks carefully, her face tense with concentration, her eyes locked on the hot liquid in her mug. When she gets to the table, she gently sets it down and lets out a long breath.

"Phew," she says. "Sup, K-law."

"Did you just say *sup*?"

She pushes her dark-rimmed glasses up her nose. "I can't really get away with saying that out loud, can I?"

"Not quite," I say with a laugh.

"Okay, *what's up*, then?" she asks. "Why the emergency coffee session? Everything all right?"

I sit back in my seat. "Yeah, I'm just frustrated. This room-mate thing..."

"What's going on?"

"Weston is such an asshole," I say. "He barely acknowledges I exist. When he does, he always gets in some jerkoff comment."

"Like what?"

"Like making fun of my clothes or my hair," I say. "Tonight he said he wasn't surprised I didn't have weekend plans if this is what I look like."

Mia's eyes widen. "He said... I mean... What the... How could..." She pauses and takes a breath. "He did not."

"He did," I say. "My hair is fine. Messy buns are a thing. How can he not know they're a thing?"

She shrugs. "I don't know. He's a guy?"

I touch my hair. "Anyway, my point is, he's such a jerk. I had to get out of the house for a little bit."

"Are you sure *Caleb* suggested he move in?" she asks. "Why would he even be friends with a guy like that?"

"I don't get it either," I say. "Maybe Weston isn't such a dick to everyone. Maybe he hates me for some reason."

"No one in their right mind could hate you. You're basically the least hate-able person ever." She picks up her mug and drips some coffee on her pants. "Ow."

"I don't know, maybe he's angry or something," I say. "He's not like, stomping around mad. But I feel like he's holding onto a lot of anger."

"Hmm," Mia says, tapping her chin. Her eyes widen. "Oh my god."

"What?"

"I know what's happening."

"What are you talking about?"

A smile creeps across her face. "This is a hate-to-lovers thing."

"What?" I ask, my voice sharp.

Mia puts up a hand. "No, I know. But hear me out. You know all the romance tropes as well as I do. Second chance, secret baby, jilted bride, forbidden love. I think they're a lot more real than people give them credit for. It happened to me. Alex and I were totally a friends-to-lovers story. With a twist, maybe, but still. Maybe you and Weston are going to be a hate-to-lovers."

I glare at her. "No. That's a hard no, Mia. Not even a chance."

She gasps. "And you're roommates! Kendra, this is totally a thing."

"Not a real thing, Mi. This isn't a book."

"Doesn't matter," she says, adjusting her glasses. "I predict that's where this is going. You hate him now, but just wait."

I lean back in my chair. "I don't *hate* him. That's pretty harsh. I mean, sure, he's an asshole. But I don't hate him."

Mia nods sagely, like she's suddenly possessed of great wisdom. "You know what? I bet there's an answer to that question."

"What question?"

"Why he's an asshole."

"What are you talking about now?"

"There are basically three kinds of asshole men." She holds up one finger. "The first are dicks for no good reason. They're just assholes who were made that way. Those ones are hopeless and your best bet is to stay far, far away."

"Okay..."

"Second are asshole men who use being a dick as a tool," she says. "They're not really jerks deep down, but they act like it a lot. They use being cocky and kinda selfish to get what they want in life, but they're big softies on the inside."

My mouth opens, but I don't even know what to say.

"Third," she says, ticking off a third finger, "are men who are assholes for a really good reason. They have some deep-seated pain that they're masking with their assholedom—like a suit of armor. It's a defense mechanism. And they keep it up because, like the second type, it probably works for them. They get what they want a lot. But there's a deeper reason they are the way they are. Those kind... they're the most compelling, if you ask me."

"God, Mia, Weston isn't some romance hero," I say.

"Are you sure?" she asks. "Oh my god, Kendra. You have to find out his reason."

"What?"

"His reason," she says, rolling her eyes like of course I should know what she means. "Weston is absolutely the third type. I bet he has a reason for being the way he is. Maybe he had his heart broken when he was younger, or he had a really dark childhood. Was he in foster care, by any chance?"

"Um, I have no idea."

"Okay, so maybe, but we're not sure," she says, putting a finger to her lips. She pauses, staring at the table. "I don't know, it could be a lot of things. But you have to find out."

"How do you know he's the third kind? Maybe he's the first —maybe he was made that way."

Mia purses her lips for a few seconds, then shakes her head. "No, I think he's the third. I think he has a reason. If he was the first type, you'd hate him for real. Like, legit hate him. But you already told me you don't."

I roll my eyes at Mia, but it does make me wonder. At least a little. "Look, whatever kind of asshole he is, he's the kind who's going to move out in a few months, and that will be that. I'm not going to start digging into his life, trying to figure him out. I don't think that would end well."

Mia leans forward. "Oh come on. Now I really want to know."

"No," I say with a laugh. "I'm just going to do what he said and stay out of his way. He'll stay out of mine, and in a few months, things will go back to normal. I'll have my house back and he'll forget this little blip in his perfect life ever happened."

She looks at me through narrowed eyes. "If you say so. But I'm going on record right now. If this turns into something, I called it."

I shake my head. Mia reads *way* too many romance novels. "Whatever makes you happy, Mi. If you're right, you can rub it in all you want. Your life might be straight out of a novel, but mine is definitely not."

"Okay," she says. "We'll see."

4

WESTON

"Dr. Reid, your patient is ready for you in exam room three."

I glance up at Tanya, my nurse, and nod. She disappears from my office doorway.

I pull up the patient's chart on my tablet. New consultation. Mid-forties. Two children. Clean health history. I put in the order for blood work—standard procedure. Notes indicate significant weight loss over the last two years. Yep, this one definitely needs me.

She's sitting on the exam table wringing her hands together, her upper body draped in a paper gown.

"Afternoon," I say, offering a hand. "Dr. Reid."

"Hi." She shakes my hand, her grip light. "Thanks for seeing me."

I go through a few standard questions. More about her health history. Her reasons for seeking breast augmentation. I walk her through the basics of the surgery and recovery process, although Tanya will give her more details. She nods along, her eyes wide, her face eager.

"Okay, let's take a look," I say.

She nods and I move her paper gown aside. Significant loss of skin elasticity. Nipple height too low. I take measurements and enter them into her chart.

"So, um, can you make them look better?" she asks.

I glance up from my tablet. "Absolutely. This is very standard for a woman your age after having children. I recommend a three-hundred cc implant." I take one of the samples and hand it to her. It's soft and pliable, filled with saline solution. "This will put you at about a C cup, but more importantly, you'll have lift." I point to her nipple with my stylus. "Instead of the nipple sitting here, it will be up here. You'll be pleased with the results."

"Wow, that would be amazing," she says, closing the gown so she's covered.

"Do you have any more questions?" I ask.

"No, I don't think so. Seems like you've gone over everything." She meets my eyes and chews on her lower lip. "I'm just nervous."

I clear my throat. "I'll send Tanya back in to get you on the schedule."

"Oh, okay," she says. "Thanks, Dr. Reid."

"Have a good afternoon."

I'm out the door and send Tanya in to see her. I don't have time for hand holding. That's Tanya's job. I don't deal in hugs and warm feelings. There are surgeons that do. They'll sit with their patients and listen to their sob stories about why they hate their bodies. Reassure them that they're beautiful.

My job is to *make* them beautiful. And no one is better at it than I am.

When people hear I do breast augmentations, they usually imagine me surrounded by hot twenty-somethings with tiny waists and triple-D boobs that defy gravity. I've had patients who fit that mold, but most of the women I see are like my last patient. Thirties, forties, fifties. They pop out a bunch of kids and aren't happy with what it did to their breasts. They come to me for a solution.

That's what I do. I take their soft, sagging skin and drooping tissue and give them a set of tits they love. I restore their contours and curves to the best versions of their bodies I can manage. I make them look better than they did when they had perky little teenage boobs. No one cares that my bedside manner is shit. I take them from drab and frumpy to fucking spectacular, and that's what matters in the end.

I check my schedule when I get back to my office. That was my last patient. Thank god. I pinch the bridge of my nose. I haven't been sleeping well since I moved in with Kendra. That fucking house makes so much noise. The floors creak. The windows rattle. It's drafty. And it smells like... well, it smells like the dried lavender and eucalyptus she keeps everywhere, and I have to concede, that part is nice.

And she does more or less leave me alone. I guess it's marginally better than living out of a hotel room.

It's a little after four, and I text Caleb to see if we're still on for basketball. He replies with a *yes*, so I head out to meet him at the gym.

Caleb is already here when I come out of the locker room. He takes a shot and makes it. I've known Caleb a long time, and I guess we're unlikely friends. He was a pretty good wingman while we were undergrads, but that didn't last long. We both went off to med school, in different states, and then he got married. For whatever reason, we've kept in touch over the years.

Since he moved back to Seattle, we've made a habit of getting together to play basketball once every week or so. He has to cancel pretty often if he doesn't have someone to watch his daughter, but it's not a big deal. I'm not a high maintenance friend.

In fact, other than Caleb, I don't really have friends. I hang out with my business partner, Ian, sometimes. But I don't know that I'd call him a friend.

"Hey," Caleb says as I approach. He passes me the ball.

I dribble a few times. "Hey. Save a bunch of lives lately?"

"Yeah, actually," he says. "Been a busy week."

Caleb and I always had different ideas in mind for our careers. My dad was adamant about me pursuing a specialty that would pay off. He's a surgeon, so the pressure was on for me to live up to his expectations. Caleb was an idealistic young pre-med guy, intent on saving people. I guess he's doing what he always said he wanted to do, working as an ER surgeon. His hours suck, though. Private practice was definitely the right call for me.

"So I haven't talked to my sister in a while," Caleb says. "I guess that means everything is fine over there?"

I shrug. "I'll make it work."

"What does that mean?" Caleb asks. "Is there a problem with the house or something?"

I take a shot and watch the ball swish through the net. "It's not the greatest. But it's better than living in hotels."

"I would have thought you'd love hotel living," Caleb says, grabbing the ball. He takes a shot. Swish. "Room service. Someone to turn down your bed."

"Yeah, it's great until some chick who works there gets a bug up her ass," I say.

"What?" Caleb asks.

"I was staying at the Hyatt for a little while. Hooked up with one of the front desk chicks. She worked mornings. A couple nights later, I scored with one of the girls on the evening shift. I don't know why either of them gave a shit, but apparently they weren't happy. They kept deactivating my key card so I couldn't get into my room."

Caleb takes another shot. Misses. "Okay..."

"So I moved to the Paramount Hotel. It's not bad. The bartender was hot as fuck. Took her back to my room every night for a week," I say. "But then she wanted me to take her out and date her or something, and when I blew her off, she got weird."

I take another pass and shoot. Bounces off the rim and goes in.

"Then there was the Mayflower Park. This fine piece of ass worked in housekeeping, and she came in and surprised me a few times," I say. "But then she walked in when I was with some random I met at a bar, and she flipped her shit. I don't know what her problem was. It wasn't like we were in a relationship; she knew that as well as I did. When I was at work the next day, she let herself into my room and cut up all my underwear. I didn't even realize it until the next morning when I was trying to get dressed. All my underwear had fucking holes in them."

Caleb laughs, hard. "Dude, are you serious?"

I pass the ball back to him, a little harder than necessary. "Yeah, I'm glad that's amusing to you."

He tucks the ball under his arm. "Are you really telling me that you had to move hotels because you kept shagging women who worked there, and then they'd run you out of the place?"

"Yeah, basically."

"Do you actually have that much trouble keeping it in your pants?" he asks.

I shrug. "Beautiful women love me."

He takes another step forward, his face suddenly serious. "You watch yourself with my sister."

Now it's my turn to laugh. "Kendra? Bro, you have nothing to worry about there."

"I'm not sure if I should be relieved, or pissed that you just insulted her," he says.

I take a shot. Miss. "I'm not insulting your sister. She's fine. Just not my type." I get the ball and pass it to Caleb.

"Oh, so beautiful, smart, driven, and funny aren't your type?" he asks.

"You just told me to watch myself and now you're trying to convince me to go for it with her?" I ask, my mouth half turned up in a smirk.

"Fuck you, no." He shoots. Scores. "It's just... you're still chasing hookups? I thought maybe you'd outgrown that by now."

"Outgrown what? Enjoying beautiful women? I don't think men outgrow that."

"Sure, but some men decide to have something with one beautiful woman," he says. "A relationship, maybe?"

"Some men are wired that way," I say. "You are, and if that works for you, great. But I'm not made for relationships."

"That sounds like a cop-out. When was the last time you dated someone?" He passes me the ball. "Seriously dated."

I shoot again and the ball goes in. "I don't know. Never."

Caleb retrieves the ball and tucks it under his arm again. "Never? You've never actually dated a woman before?"

"Not really." I'm getting tired of this conversation. "You gonna babysit that ball, or are we going to play?"

"Why?" Caleb asks.

"I don't know, you want to analyze me?" I ask, my voice sarcastic. "I don't want to deal with the drama of a maintaining a girlfriend. I don't get why anyone does, but do you see me making a big deal out of it? If it's your thing, have fun. It's not my thing. At least I recognize it. I know what I want."

"But you'll just sleep with women wherever you go, and that's better?" Caleb asks.

"Since when did you get so fucking judgmental?"

"I'm not being judgmental, and when did you get so defensive?" he asks. "Fine, you do your thing. You're happy with your life, so I don't know why I'm questioning you. Just remember, my sister isn't a hookup girl."

He passes the ball and I take another shot. Swish. I wince at the thought of seeing Kendra like that. "No. No, she is definitely *not* a hookup girl."

5

KENDRA

I finish up the dishes in my dad's kitchen while he takes his glass of whiskey to the other room. It's been a while since we were all over here for dinner—Alex and Mia, Caleb with Charlotte, and me. I got here early to cook dinner for everyone, and the meal turned out great. It was one of my staples—chicken fettuccine alfredo—and they all made appropriate yummy noises. Even my niece Charlotte, who rarely talks much, giggled when she slurped her pasta and told the whole table about the book her teacher read at school. Caleb positively beamed the entire time, he was so excited to see her opening up to us like that.

Caleb comes back into the kitchen and grabs a towel. "Charlotte's reading books with Dad. Need help?"

"Sure."

He starts drying pots and pans, and putting them away. Alex and Mia wander back into the kitchen and take a seat at the table. We all usually end up back in here after Dad retires to his recliner with his nightly drink. Alex grabs four beers and sets them out on the table while Caleb and I take care of the last few dishes.

"So how's the roommate?" Mia asks with a very obvious wink.

I sit down and take one of the beer bottles. Alex reaches across the table and opens it for me. "He's fine, I guess. He's not around much."

Alex frowns at Caleb. "What's that look for?"

"What look?" Caleb asks.

"You look guilty," Alex says.

"I don't... fine," Caleb says. "I feel like I owe Kendra an explanation about Weston. And maybe an apology."

I tilt my head and give Caleb a cherubic smile. "Oh really? Like maybe you'll explain to me how on earth you even know a guy like that? And what could have possessed you to suggest he live with your sister?"

Mia snorts.

Caleb winces. "Something like that."

"I'm all ears, o brother of mine."

"Look, I've known Weston for a long time," Caleb says. "He's always had his own thing going on. He's not really the kind of guy who gets close to people. Ever. I didn't realize he was such a—"

"Dick?" I fill in.

"No, I know how he comes across," Caleb says. "He's kind of a dick to most people. But believe it or not, he's not always like that."

"Yeah, right," I say.

"I'm serious," Caleb says. "He's just... he's the kind of guy who has your back, even when you don't expect it. When Melanie died, he was really there for me."

Weston being less dickish to some people? Fine, I can buy that. But being a support system when his friend's wife died? I can't see it.

"He was there for you? I'm not saying you're making that up, but... honestly, are you making that up?"

"Not at all," Caleb says. "He flew out to Houston the next day. It wasn't like he sat around and listened to me talk about my feelings. But he stepped in and took care of things when I couldn't. He made sure the rent on my apartment got paid and had food delivered so I didn't have to worry about it. He even made sure I had diapers and formula for Charlotte. I didn't ask him for any of it, he just showed up and did it."

I pause for a second, unsure of what to say. That seems so out of character for Weston. "He did all that? Seriously?"

"Yeah," Caleb says. "He didn't act any different. It's not like he was offering emotional support or something. That's not him. But he didn't hesitate to drop everything to make sure I had what I needed. I guess that was his way of helping. He heard what happened, flew out for about a week, and went home again. He was there when you guys came out, but I guess you never saw him. He sort of did his thing and disappeared."

"I'm having such a hard time picturing that," I say.

"I know, I do too in a way," Caleb says. "And we never talked about it later. I felt like he didn't want me to mention it. But even after he went back home, he'd text me about once a week to make sure I had what I needed. He's really not a terrible guy. He just acts like it sometimes."

I arch an eyebrow at him.

"Okay, a lot of the time," he says.

Mia catches my eye and gives me her wise nod again.

I roll my eyes at her and turn back to Caleb. "What were you going to say before? You didn't realize he was such a what?"

"Player?" he says, making it into a question.

"Oh, he's a man-whore," I say. "Yeah, I know."

Mia laughs, but Alex looks alarmed.

"He's what?" Alex says. "And you put him in Kendra's house?"

"I didn't realize he was still like that," Caleb says. "He hooked up with a lot of girls back in college, but I figured he would have settled down by now. I knew he didn't have a serious girlfriend or anything. But he doesn't talk about women that much. Although, he doesn't really talk about anything that much. He's not a talker."

"You're telling me," I say. "He gets all grumpy when I try to make conversation."

"He just keeps people at a distance," Caleb says. "A big distance."

"Why?" Mia asks.

Caleb shrugs. "I honestly don't know. Like I said, he doesn't let people get close to him. Even when we used to hang out a lot, I didn't know that much about him. I think his mom died when he was little, but other than that, I don't know."

Mia points at me. "See? I bet that has something to do with it."

"To do with what?" Alex asks.

"Nothing," Mia says, waving the question away with her hand and almost poking Alex in the eye in the process. "Kendra, I told you."

I ignore Mia and look at Caleb. "So why did you stay friends with him?"

"I don't know," Caleb says. "Sometimes I didn't. He'd be a prick and I'd decide I didn't need that bullshit, so I'd walk away for a while. But eventually, I'd get curious and wonder what he was up to, so I'd text him or something. After he helped me out when Melanie died, I felt like he'd been a better friend than I'd given him credit for. So I kept in touch. And when Charlotte and I moved back here, we started hanging out."

"Please tell me you mean something other than *trolling for women at skanky bars* when you say *hanging out*."

Caleb laughs. "Yeah, that's not my scene. Although somehow I don't think a guy like Weston Reid needs to hang out at skanky bars to get women."

"The girl he had at my house the first time we met would indicate otherwise," I say.

"Whatever. I don't know what's up with him," Caleb says. "I meet him once a week or so to shoot hoops. We play some one on one, and that's about it. Alex comes too, sometimes; he's met him. That weekend you were gone, he was complaining about being tired of living in a hotel while his house is being remodeled. And I thought hey, my sister is looking for a roommate and keeps getting calls from crazies. Weston's a decent guy for the most part. It seemed like a win-win for both of you. He gets a place to crash that isn't a hotel. You get a not-crazy roommate for a few months until you can find someone else."

"He might be not-crazy, but also not-very-nice," I say.

"Can we go back to the part where he's a man-whore?" Alex says. "Because I know how that works."

I roll my eyes again. "Not a novel, Alex. Not all man-whores are so irresistible that every woman they spend time with is powerless against their charms. I won't accidentally fall into bed with him just because he sleeps one room away."

Alex half-glares at Caleb again and I can tell he's not convinced.

"Honestly, I'm in zero danger here," I say. "Weston doesn't even *like* me. The last thing he's going to do is try to get in my pants. And if he did, there's no way. Not a chance. I don't care if some women go for that cocky asshole thing. Not me."

"I don't know, the cocky roommate..." Mia says.

"Too cocky," I say. "Don't worry about it, Caleb. He's gone a lot. And who knows, maybe he'll relax a little and show me that not-asshole side you claim he has. But until then, I don't think it exists."

Caleb takes a deep breath. "Sorry, sis. I didn't mean to saddle you with a pain-in-the-ass roommate."

"It's fine," I say. "I've got him under control."

6

WESTON

*T*he redhead to my right. She's the one tonight.

She's dressed nice—short black dress. Heels. Wavy hair. Red lips. The blonde she's sitting with is trying way too hard. Fake boobs—not nice enough that they're a set of mine. Tight clothes. Lots of makeup. There's a line between sexy and trashy, and she's well on the wrong side of it. Granted, my hookup a couple of weeks ago was firmly in the trashy realm. She was a bar top dancer at a cheesy bar, for fuck's sake. What can I say, once in a while I'm into that kind of thing. But tonight, I already have my sights set on the smart-looking one of the pair.

Which means I made eye contact once, and now I'm ignoring her.

But she's not ignoring me. Not at all.

Ian walks up and takes a seat next to me. My business partner has the top button of his shirt undone, his sleeves cuffed. His salt-and-pepper hair and the fine lines around his eyes show his age, but women—even young women—are rarely turned off by it. Apparently they think he looks distinguished.

I glance at his left hand. No ring tonight.

He might enjoy appearing distinguished, but he doesn't want to appear married.

"Brianna out of town?" I ask, using his wife's name on purpose. It digs at him when I do.

I see the slight twitch of his eyes, but otherwise he doesn't react. "Yeah, for the weekend. Again."

He acts put out, but I know he doesn't give a shit when his wife leaves. He welcomes it. His eyes land on the girls at the table to my left and I don't bother disguising my eye roll. He's such a douche. I don't care how many women I send packing after a few hours of fucking. I don't have a *wife*.

"So you're here for what?" I ask. "Someone else to stick your dick in tonight? Brianna not giving it up these days?"

"Fuck you," he says.

Ian's been cheating on his wife for years and I've never hidden my disdain. Not that he gives the slightest shit about that either. He couldn't care less that I think he's an ass. And it's not like there's anything I can do about it. He's going to pick up women whether he does it when I'm watching or not. His extramarital debauchery doesn't have anything to do with me.

Although sometimes I regret going into business with him.

"That one?" he asks, with a slight gesture toward the redhead. "She's watching you."

I lift one shoulder, like I don't care.

"You are the master of that," Ian says.

"Master of what?"

"Playing it cool," he says. "I watch you do this all the time, and it always works. You act like you don't need her in the least. She's going to be throwing herself at you before the night is over."

"I'm not *playing* anything," I say. "Yeah, I noticed her. If she wants to talk to me, she will. If I want to talk to her, I will. It's pretty simple, Ian. Guys who think otherwise are making things way too complicated for themselves."

"You don't give yourself enough credit," he says. "You're a closer. I've always liked that about you."

I lift one shoulder again. What Ian thinks of me is completely uninteresting. I wish he'd just shut up and get on with whatever the fuck he's going to do tonight. I don't want to sit here and have a chat.

"I'll take the blonde then," he says. "Subtlety works for you, but I like the direct approach. I'm going in."

This *is* a game to Ian, and one he's good at playing. He'll saunter over to their table and start right in with the charm. From the corner of my eye, I can see him. He's ignoring the redhead, his focus on the blonde, almost to the point that it's rude. But he's going to make the blonde feel like she's something special to have attracted his attention. And probably send the redhead straight over to me without so much as a word.

It works, as I figured it would. The redhead stands, shouldering her little purse, clutching a cosmo in her other hand. She makes a gesture toward my table, letting her friend know she'll be right over here.

I stand as she approaches my table and suddenly I'm no longer ignoring her. I give her unflinching eye contact, a subtle smile.

"Hi," she says, her voice a little breathy. My rapid change in demeanor has her off balance, but she offers me her hand. "I'm Autumn."

"Weston," I say, taking her hand. My shake is firm, but not domineering.

I sit, but don't invite her to do so.

She glances around. "Um, mind if I join you? I think my friend and your friend might want to talk alone."

I nod to the other chair. "Sure."

She smiles again and sets her drink down. "Thanks."

I lean back in my seat and rest my hand on my glass while she sits. I don't take my eyes off her and her cheeks get a little pink.

"So, do you come to this place a lot?" she asks.

"Some," I say.

"I think I've been here twice," she says. "Once was on a date, although I guess you don't want to hear about that."

I raise a shoulder. Like I give a shit about one of her past dates. She's not here with him now, so what does it matter?

"It's nice though," she says, glancing around. "I like the ambiance."

"Me too," I say.

"So what do you do?" she asks.

"I'm a surgeon."

Her eyebrows lift. "Really? That must be very stressful."

"It can be," I say. "What about you?"

"My job isn't very interesting," she says. "I work for an insurance company."

Her drink is only half empty, and I'm not finished with mine. But I'm sensing it's time to move her. It's faster than I usually work, but my gut rarely steers me wrong. "How about we go over to the bar and I'll buy you a fresh drink."

Without waiting for an answer, I stand and she follows with a smile. "Sure."

It's also time to touch her. I put my hand on the small of her back and guide her to the bar, moving her as far from Ian and her friend as possible. I can almost feel the anticipation coming off her, like little zaps of electricity. I have this in the bag already.

I buy us both a drink and stay near the end of the bar, leaning casually against it while she talks. I don't add much—generally I don't need to. Women like to talk and they really like it when they have a willing audience. She's not hammering me with inane babble that makes me want to stab my eyes out. She's mildly interesting and I ask leading questions to keep her talking. I hold eye contact and gradually shift closer so I can touch her occasionally.

She responds perfectly to everything I do. Her attention is entirely focused on me. Her body language is open, she smiles easily and often. She touches me back, and blushes a little when I touch her.

"Anyway, that weekend was a little crazy," she says, finishing up a story. She brushes her hair back from her face. "So, do you live nearby?"

The question catches me slightly off guard, because I wasn't expecting her to escalate so quickly. But her tone leaves no doubt in my mind as to why she's asking where I live. Most guys miss this moment; it's often the first opportunity a woman gives you. She's testing me, feeling out whether I'm interested in taking this all the way, and letting me know she's open to it. Or at least, open to me convincing her that she is.

And I'm about to do just that, when an unwelcome and very annoying thought goes through my mind. The roommate. Kendra.

I'm sure she's home. I swear, she's always there.

She's so fucking friendly. I have a sudden vision of walking this Autumn chick in the front door and Kendra jumping up to make us all a goddamn snack. Or suggesting we watch a movie. And even if I do successfully navigate Autumn back to my bedroom before Kendra can interfere, I bet she'll be out there when the chick leaves. She'll strike up a conversation. Offer to make her coffee or some shit. Next thing I know, a girl who I do not want hanging around will be all buddy-buddy with my roommate.

Oh my god, Kendra would probably get her number and

then invite her over for fucking girls' nights. She'd do it just to piss me off. I'm sure of it.

The little cockblocker.

I falter a little, but answer, hoping to plant the notion of going back to her place instead of mine. "No, I don't live close. I'm up north a bit. What about you?"

"I live just off Denny, but my roommate is home," she says. "Like, share a bedroom roommate."

Damn. That's a harder sell, although it wouldn't be the first time I've fucked a girl under the covers with a roommate sleeping nearby. But I can tell by Autumn's tone that the idea's a non-starter.

I'm being way too hesitant and I can see my window of opportunity closing. Autumn's gaze is wandering, her body language changing. She's turning away from me, her attention elsewhere.

Should I risk bringing her back to my place? Walk her in and out so Kendra can't get in the way? Maybe I should tell her my roommate's crazy. But then she'll have the idea of a crazy female roommate in her mind, and that could bother her for too many different reasons. God, what the fuck is wrong with me? I never overthink things like this.

Autumn glances around. "I should see where Lindsey went."

Damn it. I was right there and now she's losing interest. Fucking Kendra.

I follow Autumn across the bar to where Ian is helping Lindsey put on a coat.

"We're taking the party to Foundation," Ian says. "You two coming?"

"Yeah, sounds great," Autumn says.

She doesn't look up at me. I could probably still salvage this if I go with them. I'll have another shot at closing the deal with Autumn. She's hot enough, it might be worth the extra effort.

But I'm going to run into the same problem. Where do I take her? Her place isn't an option. My roommate situation makes my place less than ideal. I'm not usually a *rent a hotel room for a hookup* kind of guy, but the Marriott isn't far from here. Although, if what's-her-name is working the front desk tonight, she could give me trouble. Car sex can be great, but that's only fun when it's spontaneous—not when I don't have a decent place to bring a girl.

The whole thing pisses me off, ruining my mood. Fuck this noise. "I'm calling it a night. You guys have a good one."

Autumn looks at her friend and shrugs, as if to say, *I don't know what his problem is.* I start to walk away and hear Ian smoothing things over—something about my high-pressure job, and she can still come along, it will be fun with just the three of them.

Ian will probably end up banging both of them before the night's over.

I turn and point to Ian, pitching my voice so the girls can hear me. "He's married, by the way."

Both girls' mouths drop open and Ian tries to murder me with his eyes. I keep walking. Fuck him.

I'm not in the mood to go anywhere else, so I drive home. Sure enough, Kendra's car is in the driveway and the windows glow with light. She's here, and she's awake.

I come inside and toss my keys on the table by the door. Kendra's on the couch, her legs stretched out, her laptop on her lap. She glances up at me and starts to smile.

"Don't," I say and head to the kitchen.

"Don't what?"

I pull the bourbon out of the cupboard. "Don't ask me about my day or where I've been tonight."

"Geez, touchy much?" she asks. "I didn't even say anything."

"You were going to."

"So you're a mind reader now?" she asks. "That's a talent I didn't realize you had."

My temper flares, sending a jolt of anger through me. "What the fuck are you doing home tonight, anyway? Can't find a guy who likes ugly pajama pants? There's a shocker."

"Oh, so now you're going to criticize my clothing choices *and* my social life," she says. "Awesome."

"Social life? What social life? Every time I walk in that door, you're right there, on that fucking couch."

"And this is a problem for you because...?"

I ignore her comment and pour my drink, then put the bottle away.

"No, seriously," she says and her laptop clicks closed. "Why do you have such a problem with me? I don't ask for an exorbitant amount of rent money. I didn't make you sign a lease, so you aren't locked into living here. I try to be nice to you when I see you. And half the time you act like a jackass."

God, what a pain in my ass this whole thing has turned out to be. "Look, this was obviously a bad idea. I'll find somewhere else to stay until my house is done. I'll be out of your way in a couple days at most."

"Weston, wait," she says as I stalk past her. "You don't have to move out."

"Yeah, I do." I shut my bedroom door behind me.

I down the bourbon in one swallow. I fucking hate people. They make things complicated. Frustrating. I don't need this bullshit in my life.

I'll go back to a damn hotel. And I'm calling the fucking contractor in the morning to tell him to get my goddamn house finished. I need my space back. Now.

7

KENDRA

*W*eston is gone by the time I get up in the morning. Good. I don't want to deal with his shit today.

I shower, get dressed, dry my hair. I wonder if he's coming back tonight. For all I know, he won't sleep here again. He'll come back for his bedroom furniture at some point, I suppose. But it wouldn't surprise me if he's already found somewhere else to stay.

It's just as well, so I don't know why I'm kind of disappointed. Probably because I usually get along with people. I've never met someone who dislikes me so intensely. And for no good reason, I might add. I was nice to him. He didn't need to be such a jerk.

I work for a few hours, then head to the gym. I run a few miles on the treadmill, then swim laps for about half an hour. By the time I'm done and dressed, it's time to go to Caleb's to watch Charlotte for a few hours. I take care of her sometimes when Caleb has to work, and today I'm relieving Mia who had her for the morning. We hang out for a while; I read her a few books and we watch a cartoon.

Caleb texts a little while later, saying he's running late, and offers to bring dinner. I tell him not to, and Charlotte and I head into the kitchen to make dinner for her daddy. She's a little chatterbox today, telling me all about her pretend games and stories she makes up in her head. She's quiet around most people, but I've managed to break through, and now she talks to me like crazy. It feels good, like I'm in on a secret she keeps hidden from most people.

After Caleb gets home, the three of us have spaghetti. He thanks me profusely, and I tell him not to worry about it. I don't bother telling him about Weston moving out. He'll find out eventually, but I don't want him to feel bad about it. He has enough on his plate.

After saying my goodbyes and getting big hugs from Charlotte, I head out. I could go home, but I don't want to. If he's there, it will be so tense. If he's not there, it will be so still. So silent.

Lonely.

I take my laptop to a coffee shop. There's a table near the back, so I get coffee and settle in to do some work.

It's quiet, just a low hum of noise filling the air. I should come work here more often. It's nice. I make progress on my latest edit—which is good because I'm losing so many afternoons to watching Charlotte.

My phone buzzes with a call. It's Caleb.

"Hey, what's up?" I ask. "Did I leave something at your place?"

"Kendra, listen to me," Caleb says. The tone of his voice sets me on edge before he gets the next words out. "Weston was in a car accident."

"Oh my god." My heart leaps and I sit straight up. "Is he okay?"

"No," Caleb says. "He's not okay. He's alive, but he's in surgery and honestly, that's all I know."

"Holy shit." I cover my mouth and try to take a deep breath.

"I wish I had more news, but I wasn't there," he says. "He's at Swedish, but I was already off. I know the guy who's working on him, and he's in great hands. We don't have anything to worry about there."

"Okay, that's good," I say. "I just... I don't even know what to think right now."

"Yeah, it's crazy," he says. "I see this stuff all the time, but when it happens to someone you know it's pretty surreal."

"Oh god, Caleb, are you okay?" I ask. His wife died in a car accident, and I bet this is bringing up all sorts of sad memories.

"Yeah, I'm fine," he says. "Don't worry about me. I just figured you should know what's going on."

"Thanks," I say.

"I'll call you as soon as I hear something," he says.

"Okay, thanks again."

I hang up and stare at my phone for a long moment. Weston was in an accident. He's alive, but he's not okay. He's in surgery.

I'm sick with worry and I don't really understand why. He's a jerk. He was about to move out, and I was happy about it. No more dealing with his bad moods and dickhead comments.

But now I'm imagining him with one of those tubes down his throat, his eyes closed. Is he bloody? Does he have broken bones? Internal bleeding? How serious are we talking? How bad is this?

Is he alone?

There's no way I can sit here and work. I grab my stuff and head to my car. Maybe I shouldn't—I'm nobody to him, just a roommate he doesn't like—but I'm going anyway.

I get to the hospital and ask about him at the front desk. They won't tell me anything, just ask me to wait. I sit in the lobby for a while, feeling increasingly jittery. And impatient. And frustrated. I watch the clock tick by, one second dragging into the next.

An hour passes, and still no one tells me anything. I haven't even been brought back to where he'll be. I'm sitting out by the stupid front doors.

I text Caleb and tell him I'm here, but no one is helping me. He doesn't answer.

Finally, I go back to the front desk. "Hi, excuse me. I'm here for my, um, friend, Weston Reid. He was in a car accident. I think he was in surgery. My brother is Caleb Lawson, he's a surgeon here." I'm going to fucking name-drop like a boss until someone takes me back there. "I've been waiting forever and I'm really worried about Weston. Can someone take me... somewhere? I feel like I could at least be in the surgical waiting room."

A nurse in blue scrubs seems to have overheard. She comes up to the desk. "What's your name?"

"Kendra Lawson."

She nods. "I'll take you."

She opens a side door for me and I follow her through a maze of hallways to an elevator.

"Do you know if he's okay?" I ask.

"I'm sorry, I don't," she says. "I just overheard you and I know your brother. What's the patient's name again?"

"Weston Reid."

"Dr. Weston Reid?" she asks.

"Yeah, that's him. Do you know him?"

"I know who he is," she says. "He has surgical privileges here."

It's weird, but I'm a little bit relieved she doesn't say she knows him personally. I'd have to wonder if he'd slept with her. Not that it matters—or is any of my business. But still.

We get out of the elevator and she leads me to a nurses' station. She types a few things into the computer.

"He's out of surgery," she says. "I can take you to his room."

Relief washes over me. If he's out of surgery and in a room, that means... well, it means he's alive and probably not in danger of dying. That's a start.

My phone buzzes with a text and I check while I follow the nurse down another hallway.

Caleb: Sorry. Are you still waiting? He's out of surgery.

Me: Yeah, I know. I'm on my way to his room.

Caleb: Wow, you really are there.

Me: Of course I am. What else would I do? Does he have family or anyone else we should call?

Caleb: I called his partner, Ian and left a voicemail. His dad is local. I called, but he didn't pick up. Left a message. I don't know of anyone else.

Me: Okay.

Caleb: Do you need me to come down?

Me: Isn't Charlotte in bed?

Caleb: Yeah.

Me: No, it's fine. Get some sleep. You probably haven't slept in a while.

Caleb: I haven't.

Me: Then definitely sleep. I've got this.

Caleb: Thanks sis.

The nurse stops outside a room and peeks through the curtain. "He's in here, but he's sleeping. The nurse taking care of him this shift is Joel. He'll be able to give you more information."

"Thank you so much," I say. "I really appreciate this."

She smiles. "No problem. Good luck."

With a deep breath, I duck through the curtain.

I take a few halting steps into the room, clutching my phone. I don't even recognize the man in the bed. A nasal cannula rests below his nose and he's hooked up to an IV. His eyes are closed, his skin sallow. One arm is in a cast, from his wrist to his shoulder. His face is bruised, parts of it swollen. Both lips are split. He has a bandage that winds across his forehead. I can't even tell what's going on with the rest of his body. He's covered in blankets, his torso and legs a shapeless lump beneath them.

"Oh god, Weston," I say, my voice nothing but a whisper.

I reach out and tentatively touch his hand. His skin is cold. The monitors beep and I watch his heart rate go up and down across the screen. I know he's alive and breathing, but his hand is like ice. It's disconcerting.

There's a chair nearby, so I pull it close to the bed and sit. I wonder if his dad is on his way. That might be a little awkward. He's going to walk in and see some woman sitting here with his son. I suppose I'll tell him I'm a friend. Or his roommate. I don't know. Are we friends? Are we still roommates?

I guess it doesn't matter now. I'm here, and I'll stay until someone else comes. I don't want him to be alone.

The curtain pulls back and a tall, dark-skinned guy wearing scrubs comes in. "Hi, I'm Joel. I'm Dr. Reid's nurse tonight."

"Kendra," I say. "I'm Weston's friend."

"It's good of you to come," Joel says. "He's doing well, considering. I take it the accident was pretty bad."

"What can you tell me?" I ask. "I literally know nothing, except he was in an accident, and now..." I gesture toward him.

Joel goes to the computer near the curtain. "Dr. Reid came in via ambulance, unresponsive but breathing. He had acute external injuries including bruising and lacerations, possible broken bones. Once he was here, it was determined he had internal bleeding. Lacerations of both the spleen and liver. He underwent surgery to repair the internal damage." He looks over at me. "Surgery was successful, but he's in bad shape. He's going to be in a lot of pain when he wakes up. We'll do our best to keep him comfortable while he's here."

"How long do you think he'll be here?" I ask.

"Hard to say right now," he says. "I'd guess five days, depending on how he does."

I nod. "Okay."

"You can expect him to be tired and groggy for a while. Or he might sleep through the night at this point." He brings out what looks like a remote control, but it's connected by a thick wire. "This has a nurse call button. If he wakes up when you're here, feel free to alert me. But I'll be back regularly to check on him."

"Thanks," I say.

Joel leaves through the curtain and I'm left alone with the beeping monitor. Weston's so still; he hasn't so much as flinched. I take his hand, sliding mine below his so our palms touch. I place my other hand over the top of his. He's so cold.

"Hey," I say quietly. "I doubt you can hear me, but you're going to be fine. I'm just going to hang out here until your dad comes, okay?"

My only answer is the incessant beeping and a low buzz as the blood pressure cuff starts to inflate.

"You just rest now," I say. "Rest and get better. I'll stay."

I squeeze his hand and move one of the blankets so his hand is covered, careful not to mess with his IV. I lean back in my chair and try to get comfortable. Weston doesn't move and after a while, my eyes get heavy. I scoot the chair closer and lean forward, laying my head on my arms on the edge of the bed. I'll just close my eyes for a few minutes. I'm sure he'll either wake up soon, or someone else will come. Until then, I'll rest.

8

WESTON

Beep. Beep. Beep.

My eyes don't want to open, but that fucking beeping is pissing me off. Is it my alarm? It doesn't sound right. What day is it? Why won't my eyes open?

I pry my eyelids apart and wince. Everything hurts. Literally every part of my body registers pain. The flood of agony makes it hard to breathe. Something tickles my nose and I try to swat it away, but my right arm won't move. I blink a few times, but nothing makes sense.

Where the fuck am I?

The beeping comes into focus; it's a cardiac monitor. And it's hooked up to me.

I try to take a deep breath, but I wince. It hurts like a motherfucker. Things are coming back now. I was driving. My car. Was I alone? Yeah, I was alone. I don't know how it happened, but I must have been in an accident. It's so hazy, I can't remember much. One second I was driving down the freeway, and the next all hell broke loose. It was that fast—absolute chaos. There was crunching and spinning. Did my car roll over? I'm not sure.

I remember being slammed around, harder than you can

imagine. Blood in my mouth. In my eyes. And pain. So much fucking pain. I couldn't breathe. Couldn't speak. Couldn't think. I knew I needed help, but I couldn't move to get to my phone. I didn't know if anyone was around. Did anyone stop? Was someone calling for help?

A moment of terror that I was going to die before they could get to me, then everything started to fade.

That's it. That's all I remember. Everything else is muddled and hazy.

I don't know how long I've been out. It feels like minutes. I've lost time, my brain not comprehending the passage of hours—days?—since the accident. It's an awful feeling, almost as bad as the agony that presses on my chest.

My eyes are closed again, so I force them open. I need to wake up and assess the damage. My right arm won't move and I look down at it. There's a cast from my shoulder down to my wrist. Bent elbow. Fuck, that's not a good sign. I try to wiggle my fingers, but they're slow—swollen and thick.

A thread of panic tries to uncurl itself in my chest. I'm a surgeon. My entire life depends on my hands. I wiggle my fingers again. They're moving. At least they're moving. I'll have to hold on to that for now, until I can talk to whoever put me back together.

Another breath tells me there's something wrong with my torso. Ribs, maybe. But I think it's more than rib damage. My left hand is free, except for the IV. I gingerly touch my chest and move down, probing for what might be wrong. Left side, just below my ribs. It's very tender. Maybe an incision. Was I in surgery? I don't know.

I test my feet, moving my toes, then rolling my ankles. Sore, but I don't think I have serious injuries there. Bend my knees. Same thing. My legs ache, but neither of them are immobilized. They move.

Come to think of it, I'm lying at a slight incline, so chances are my spine is okay.

It's hard to keep my eyes open. I'm so tired. The room is dim, and a clock on the wall reads seven sixteen. Is that morning? I think back to what I can remember. It was after eight when I was driving. Maybe I've only lost one night. Maybe it's the next day.

I wonder if anyone's been here, but I dismiss the idea quickly. Who the fuck would come? I guess it's possible Caleb knows I'm here. If I'm at Swedish, it's his hospital. If I had surgery, he could have been the one to do it. That's a weird thought. I think Caleb knows my dad's name, but even if someone did get in touch with him, he won't come. He'll find a way to make this about me being weak or inept. He won't give a shit—won't have time to deal with it.

I don't want it to, but that thought tightens my chest and I grind my teeth. Fuck him.

Someone walks by rolling a cart, the wheels rattling against the hard floor. When the noise disappears down the hallway, I'm suddenly aware of another sound in my room. It's softer than the beeping of the cardiac monitor. So soft I wonder if I'm imagining things.

I turn my head. How the hell didn't I realize it before? Someone else is in here.

She's sitting in a chair, leaning forward with her head on the edge of the bed. Her dark hair is loose, spilling around her shoulders, a tendril lying across her forehead. Her eyes are closed and her back moves up and down with the movement of her breath.

Is that Kendra?

My brow furrows and I stare at her. Am I hallucinating? I blink again, trying to make my eyes focus.

It *is* Kendra. What the hell is she doing here?

A tall guy in scrubs comes in. His eyes flick to Kendra and

when he speaks, his voice is quiet, so he won't wake her. "Dr. Reid, good, you're awake. I'm Joel, your nurse, although I'm about to hand you over to the next shift. Do you know where you are?"

"Yeah," I say, my voice hoarse. "Swedish Hospital."

"Do you know what day it is?" he asks.

"Monday. Morning, I think."

"That's right," he says. "You arrived last night. You were in a car accident. Do you remember that?"

"Barely."

He nods. "That's okay, very normal. You sustained multiple injuries, including fractures to your right arm, and a ruptured liver and spleen. You had surgery last night. You're going to be okay, but you have a lot of healing to do. How's your pain level?"

Fucking awful, but I don't want more drugs. "Fine." My eyes flick down to Kendra, still sound asleep.

"She got here just after they brought you out of surgery," he says.

"Really?"

He nods. "Yeah."

I can't stop staring at Kendra. "She was here all night?"

"Yes," he says. "She said she's your friend?"

I nod. My friend? Is she? Last time I saw her, I was kind of a dick. I blamed her because I didn't hook up with some girl whose name I've already forgotten, and I told her I was moving out.

Why would she come here? After all that stuff I said to her.

I shouldn't ask, but I find myself doing it anyway. "Has anyone else been here?"

Joel shakes his head. "No. Just her." He pauses and looks at her again. "She wouldn't leave."

I don't have a reply to that. I just keep staring at her.

"I'll let you rest for now. The doctor will be in to see you later." He leaves, the curtain dropping down behind him.

Kendra's lips part and she takes a deep breath. Her brow creases and she shifts a little, her eyes still closed. That chair has to be uncomfortable as hell.

There's a wispy memory, tugging at the corner of my consciousness. Kendra's hands, warm against mine. Her voice soft, telling me I'm going to be okay. That she's here, and she'll stay.

She'll stay.

I tear my eyes away from her. Obviously it was a dream. Even if she did talk to me when I was asleep, I wouldn't have been able to hear her. I don't remember anything else. How could I have been aware of something like that?

But her voice seems so clear.

I have too many drugs in my system. I can't think straight.

She moves again and draws in a quick breath, sitting up and rubbing her eyes. "Oh, hey. You're awake."

"Yeah."

She stands and stretches her arms above her head. Wincing, she rubs her lower back. "Let me go get you some water. Your throat must be so dry."

Before I can tell her not to, she disappears behind the curtain.

I let my eyes close again. I'm having trouble processing everything.

I'm not sure how much time passes—probably minutes—but I think I fell asleep. Kendra comes back with a small cup of water and a straw.

"Here," she says, holding it up to my lips. "The nurse said you can sip water for now. Maybe eat something later."

I press my lips around the straw and suck in a mouthful. The cool water feels so good in my dry mouth. It slides down my raw throat, soothing as it goes. I take another sip and nod. Kendra sets it on the counter.

Fuck, I hate being so helpless. I can't even get myself a damn drink of water. I want to get up and get the hell out of here, but I move and a sharp pain stabs through me. I clutch my stomach, wincing, trying not to groan.

"Hey, don't," she says, putting a gentle hand on my chest. "I don't think you're supposed to get up yet."

I'm about to tell her to go home, but I meet her gaze and the words die on my lips. She keeps her hand on my chest, like she can hold me down. As fucked up as I am, she can.

"I know." I want her to take her hand off me, but I hope she doesn't. What does that even mean? I'm not making sense.

She draws her hand away. "How's your pain level? The nurse told me last night that you might be in a lot of pain and they can help with that."

I'm sure they can, but I'm fuzzy enough as it is. I'd rather deal with the agony than not be able to think. "It's fine. I don't need anything."

"You don't really look fine."

"I was in a fucking accident," I snap at her. "How am I supposed to look?"

She sighs and moves the chair back, then sits. "Oh good, the surgery improved your personality."

I scowl at her, but I think the expression is pretty useless. I wonder what my face looks like.

She pulls out her phone and types.

"What are you doing?" I ask.

"Checking in with people."

"What people?"

Her eyes lift. "Nosy. Would you like to read my texts?"

I look away.

"I'm telling Caleb that you're awake," she says. *Type, type,*

type. "And that you're grouchy, which means you're halfway back to normal already." *Type, type, type.* "Now I'm texting Mia. She's engaged to my other brother."

"I know who she is."

"Do you?"

"I've met Alex. And you talk a lot."

"Hmm," she says.

"You're not telling them to come here, are you?"

"I'm just letting them know how you're doing. If you don't want visitors, it's fine. You need to rest anyway."

I almost snap at her, but again, I stop myself. My head is so fucking fuzzy. "Why are you here?"

Her eyes meet mine again. Wait, did I ask that out loud?

It takes her a second to answer. She looks at me, then around the room, like she's not sure what to say. "You're hurt."

"So?"

"What do you expect me to do?" she asks. "Just leave you here alone?"

Yes, that's exactly what I expect her to do. I don't understand why she came at all. It's not like I deserve it. "You didn't have to stay all night."

"I know," she says. "But, we're friends. I guess. This is what friends do."

I have to look away from her again. There's a weird sensation thrumming through my chest. I don't like it.

She puts her phone down and stretches her arms up again, then presses her hands into her lower back. "I'm not gonna lie, though, I think this chair broke my ass."

I glance at her and can't help but laugh a little. My face hurts when I try to smile, so I wind up half laughing, half grimacing.

She stands, laughter on her own lips. "I'm sorry, I shouldn't laugh at you." She runs her fingertips carefully down the side of my face, her touch light. "This must hurt." Her thumb touches my lower lip. "But that was kind of cute."

Her eyes are so brown. Rich, coffee brown with a hint of green circling her pupil. I've never noticed that before.

"I guess I can't complain about how much my butt hurts when you look like you got in a fight with a semi-truck and lost," she says.

I laugh again, but I'm careful not to move my mouth too much. "Yeah, no shit."

"Uh-oh," she says. "He smiled twice and it's not even eight in the morning. Watch out, Weston, you'll go over your quota."

"I wouldn't want you thinking I have a sense of humor."

"Don't worry, I would never think that," she says, totally deadpan.

I shake my head. "Fuck off and go home."

She smiles and squeezes my shoulder. "Nah. But I am going to go find coffee and maybe food. I'd bring you something, but I don't know if they're letting you eat yet. Don't go anywhere."

"Yeah, not likely."

Kendra squeezes my arm, then leaves, the blue curtain swishing shut behind her. The room suddenly feels stark, barren. Sterile. The cardiac monitor beeps, the sound itching inside my skull. My chest hurts, my incision burns, my head aches.

I hope she comes back soon.

Squeezing my eyes shut, I wonder what the fuck I'm thinking. I hope Kendra comes back? Why? It must be the drugs. I'm in pain and high on meds. I'm not thinking clearly.

But when she returns ten minutes later, coffee in hand and a smile on her face, I can't deny how fucking relieved I am.

9

WESTON

The pain meds make it hard to stay alert. I've spent the last several days drifting in and out of consciousness half the time. Everyone tells me to just sleep, it's better for me. It will help me heal. The doctor in me knows they're right.

The rest of me wants to rip the IV out of my arm and get the fuck out of here.

I was up and walking the first day, but holy shit it hurt like hell. Still does, although the time I spend on my feet increases each day. Breathing hurts, thanks to my bruised ribs and internal injuries, and it's worse when I'm standing. But the longer I'm able to stay on my feet, the sooner they'll let me out of this hell hole.

I've never been so helpless. I couldn't even take a piss by myself until this morning.

Forcing my eyes open, I blink against the light. I fell asleep again, damn it. I want to wake up. Be alert. Get off these drugs. Go home.

Although I'm not sure where home is, exactly.

I glance over at the empty chair, then at the clock. Kendra's been gone a couple of hours. She said she wanted to go home and shower. Get some clean clothes.

She's been here the entire time, visiting hours be damned, apparently. But no one has told her to leave. In fact, the nurses brought in a recliner that folds down into a narrow bed for her to sleep on. She's spent every night sleeping there next to me, waking up every time the nurses come in to check my vitals.

I didn't ask her to stay. She didn't ask me if I wanted her to. She just... did. She spends her days sitting sideways in that chair, her legs draped over one armrest, laptop in her lap. Spends her nights curled up under one of the beige hospital blankets.

I need to make her go home and stay there. It's stupid of her to sit around my hospital room. Why would she do that? She can sit on the couch at her place and do whatever it is she does on that laptop all damn day. I've had the words in my mouth a dozen times—*Kendra, fucking go home, I don't need you here.* And every time I try to say them, they wither away, turning to ash in my mouth.

Because I don't want her to go.

But it hurts, looking at her there. Especially at night. I watch her sleep. Watch her brow furrow as she shifts and tries to get comfortable, pulling the blanket higher, her toes sticking out the bottom. I don't like the way it makes me feel. It's a sharp mix of guilt and gratitude, and it does shitty things to my insides. I've had enough internal trauma for one week, for fuck's sake. I don't need her ripping me open again.

The curtain moves aside and Kendra walks in. Her damp hair is in a thick braid that hangs over one shoulder and her clothes look fresh—an open gray sweater with a white t-shirt underneath, and a pair of jeans. She grins at me and holds up a brown paper bag.

"What is that?" I ask, trying to keep my face expressionless. I don't want her to see how glad I am that she came back.

She puts a finger to her lips and looks around, then pulls the curtain all the way closed. "Shh. I doubt you're allowed to have this, but I won't tell if you don't tell."

I wince as I sit up, but I'm determined to deal with the pain. She pretends not to notice—I've snapped at her enough that she seems to realize I don't want to talk about it—and opens the bag.

The smell hits my nose and my mouth waters. "Holy shit, did you bring French fries?"

Her smile widens. "Not just fries." She pulls out another bag, this one white and stained with grease, the orange Dick's Drive-In logo on the front. "I brought you a big bag of Dick's."

The laugh rolls through me before I can stop. I clutch my side and wince, still laughing. "Damn it, don't do that." I take a few wheezy breaths. "It hurts when I laugh."

"Sorry," she says. "I couldn't resist. When was the last time you had burgers from Dick's, though?"

"I have no idea, but you better quit teasing me with that shit and give it up."

She tucks the bag against her chest. "Demanding, aren't we? You sure you want my greasy bag of Dick's? I might have to keep the greasy Dick's to myself."

I shake my head, trying not to laugh again. "You love tormenting me."

"So much," she says. "But we better eat this before they smell it out there."

She takes out the burgers and two orders of fries, then flattens the paper bag to make a tray. I wait while she unwraps my burger. I only have one hand, so I have to let her do it for me. My stomach rumbles the more I smell the food. The shit they've been feeding me in here is not cutting it.

I grab a fry and pop it in my mouth while she finishes setting everything out. God, it's good. I almost never eat stuff like this, but right now, it's perfect.

"Okay, dinner is served," she says.

She sits cross-legged on the end of the bed, our illicit feast laid out between us. It's one of the most satisfying meals I've had in a long time. Obviously it's because I've been so deprived. Anything would taste better than the bland hospital food I've had to live with.

We both eat fast and she cleans up the remains. There's a little grease spot on one of the blankets, but she just laughs and shrugs it off. I sit back and adjust the pillow behind my head while she takes up her usual spot on the chair.

"What are you always doing on there?" I ask, nodding toward her laptop.

"Working," she says.

My brow furrows. She's working? "Really? I figured you were really into Pinterest or something."

She looks at me. "First of all, seriously? You think I sit here fucking around on the Internet all day long?"

"I don't know."

She rolls her eyes. "Second, I'm questioning your manhood a little bit because you know Pinterest."

"Shut up. I've just heard of it."

"Right," she says. "What kind of things do you enjoy pinning, Weston? Do you have a *fashion* pinboard? What about *recipes to try?*"

"Fuck off, Lawson."

She laughs. "Yes, I'm working. I take breaks to check Facebook or email or whatever. But most of the time, that's what I'm doing. I can't believe you didn't know that."

"What do you do?"

"You are literally the least observant person in the universe," she says. "I'm a freelance editor."

"You edit what, books?" I ask.

She regards me with a slightly confused expression for a few seconds before she answers. "Yeah, I edit books. I used to work for a small press, but I quit a couple weeks before you moved in and decided to try to make it as a freelancer. That's why I need a roommate. I went from a steady income to, well, freelancing. It's scary, so I figured renting out the extra room would help me make ends meet."

Before I can reply, she sets her laptop on the counter next to her and gets up.

"I almost forgot." She grabs her messenger bag and pulls out my tablet, then fishes my earbuds out of a side pocket. "Here, I thought you might want these."

I take them from her, feeling more unsettled than ever. Maybe it's all that greasy food I just ate, but I get a strange feeling in the pit of my stomach.

"Thanks."

"Sure," she says, then goes back to the chair.

I stare at my tablet for a long moment, then press the button to turn it on. The battery is full. I'm almost positive it wasn't the last time I used it, and I don't think I plugged it in. Did she charge it?

Why is she so fucking nice to me?

"You should go home," I say.

Silence hangs between us, broken only by the steady beeping of the cardiac monitor.

"It's fine," she says.

"No, Kendra," I say, putting more heat into my voice. "There's no reason for you to be here."

"I told you, it's fine."

"It's not fine," I snap. "I don't fucking need you here."

"Weston—"

"Goddammit, Kendra, go the fuck home."

She doesn't reply, and I keep my eyes on the ceiling. My head is getting fuzzy again, my eyes trying to close. After a moment, I hear her get up. The zipper on her bag. Shuffling.

"I was just trying to help," she says.

I look up, but she's already gone, the curtain swaying in her wake.

THEY KEEP me here for two more fucking days.

I'm going out of my mind with boredom. Caleb checks in on me, but he's headed home from a long shift, so he doesn't stay. Other than that, it's just me and the incessant-vitals-checking nurses.

Not a word from Kendra. Although I don't expect to hear from her.

Doesn't stop me from checking my phone constantly.

Today's nurse comes in, but to my surprise, she doesn't check my vitals. She goes straight to the computer and sets a stack of paperwork on the counter next to her.

"Well, Dr. Reid, you're going home today."

What? Home? "I didn't think I was being released until tomorrow at the earliest."

"You're recovering faster than anticipated," she says. "Doc says you're ready today."

As much as I want to get the hell out of here, I don't know where I'm going. Or how I'll get there. My car is totaled. Kendra probably threw all my stuff out onto the street by now.

The nurse is giving me my discharge and home care instructions, but I'm not hearing any of it. I'll have to call Caleb and see if he can give me a ride to a hotel. Or maybe I can crash at his place for a few nights, because I'm pretty sure the nurse just said I shouldn't be alone for a while. The only other alternative is my father, and that isn't an option.

She hands me my discharge papers.

"Thanks."

"No problem." She goes around to my other side and unhooks my IV. "This will hurt a little." It pinches as she pulls it out, but it's nothing compared to the ache in my ribs.

She unhooks me from the rest of the monitors, talking the entire time about how to care for my incision, what to look for, signs that I need to come to the ER, pain management. I wish she'd get on with it so I can call Caleb and figure out where I'm going.

"I'll help you get changed."

She grabs the duffel bag Kendra left for me and pulls out a pair of underwear, socks, a t-shirt, sweats, and a pair of shoes. Gingerly, I stand and shrug off the hospital gown, although it's hard to get my broken arm out of it. The nurse threads the t-shirt over my casted arm first, then pulls it down over my head.

"You want to get the rest, or do you need help?"

"I got it," I say. I'm going to have to dress myself, so I might as well start now.

She nods and leaves me alone. I pull off my underwear and manage to get the clean pair on with one hand. The sweats are harder, but I get it done. It hurts too much when I try to pull on the socks, so I jam my feet into the shoes without them. I can't tie the shoes either, but fuck it.

I don't know what happened to the clothes I was wearing in the accident. They probably had to cut them off me. I'm lucky they found my wallet and phone.

It feels good to be in real clothes again, even without socks, but now I'm exhausted. My side aches something fierce. I lean against the bed, wondering if I should lie down.

The nurse returns with a wheelchair. "Hospital policy. I have to wheel you down."

I'm so tired, I don't even argue. I gather up the rest of my things and sit, the duffel bag on my lap. Without another word, the nurse wheels me out, turning toward the elevator.

"I still need to call a ride," I say as we head down to the first floor.

"Are you sure? They told me to bring you downstairs, which means your ride is here." Paperwork shuffles. "It says Lawson on your paperwork, but there's no first name."

Must be Caleb. He probably logged in and checked my chart so he knew I was being discharged. "Oh, okay."

The elevator dings and opens. She wheels me out through the front lobby, toward a set of wide automatic doors. A breeze blows in as they open, filling my nose with fresh air. It feels good after a week in a stuffy hospital room.

I look around for Caleb's car, but I don't see it. Instead, the nurse wheels me toward a black Honda Civic pulled up next to the curb. Wait, is that...?

Kendra gets out and opens the passenger side door.

I stare at her. Is she serious? What is she doing here?

She sighs, impatient, and grabs the duffel bag from my lap. I stand and take a couple of slow steps toward the car.

"Take care, Dr. Reid," the nurse says behind me.

Kendra's standing next to me, as if she's waiting to see if I need help getting in. I don't meet her eyes, just focus on getting my ass in her car.

I sit, and without saying anything, she leans across me and fastens my seat belt. I want to tell her to knock it off, but I know I can't do it myself. My right arm is useless, and I can't twist far enough to reach it with my left.

She goes around and gets in, then turns on the car. She pulls away from the curb and heads toward the street.

I'm so confused. Why is she here? How did she know to come get me? Where are we going? My mind is still hazy and I'm having trouble putting the right words together. "Where did you know for us to be going?"

"What?" she asks, casting me a sidelong glance.

Fuck. What did I just say? I lean my head against the backrest. "Fucking pain meds."

"Caleb knew they were discharging you," she says. "He called me a little bit ago. That was part of your question, right? How did I know to come get you?"

"Yeah."

She keeps driving in silence.

"Where are we going?" I ask.

"Home?" she says, almost like it's a question.

"What do you mean, home?"

"Did you forget what words mean too?" she asks. "Home. You know, the place where we live."

We? "Your house?"

"Yeah, where else would we go?" she asks. "It's a little early to hit the bars."

My eyes don't want to stay open. "Figured you must have thrown my stuff out by now."

"Oh, I did," she says. "I gave your bed to a nice guy with a white van who says it will fit perfectly in the back. He offered me some candy, but he looked kinda sketch, so I said no. I put the rest of your stuff by the curb, in the rain. You can sleep on the couch, though."

I open my eyes and shift my head so I can see her. She gives me a quick glance, her lips turned up in a little smile. She has a tiny dimple right at the corner of her mouth.

"Why are you..." I trail off, not sure what I was going to ask.

She takes a deep breath. "Let's just get you home so you can rest. You've had a rough week."

I nod and let my eyes close. I don't think I've ever been so grateful to have a woman taking me back to her place in my life.

10

KENDRA

"He is the absolute worst patient in the history of patients," I say. "And doctors. And injuries."

"Doctors always make terrible patients," Caleb says.

I shift the phone to my shoulder so I can turn over the chicken as it sizzles in the pan. "He keeps trying to do things he's not supposed to do."

"Let him bust open his incision," Caleb says. "That'll slow him down."

"I'm afraid he's going to," I say. "Although he seems to be healing really well. I did have to fight with him for twenty minutes the other day before he'd let me help change his bandage. And he does not like being told he can't do something."

"That doesn't surprise me," he says. "Do you need me to talk to him?"

"Nah, I just wanted to complain," I say. "I have it covered. He's just a handful."

Caleb laughs. "You're a saint, I hope you realize that. I don't know how you're putting up with his shit."

"There better be something amazing in it for me when this is all over," I say.

"No doubt there will be," he says. "Listen, I have to go to work, but if you need anything, let me know."

"Yeah, I will," I say. "Thanks."

"Sure. Talk to you later."

I hang up and put the phone on the counter. I'm whipping up a quick dinner for me and Weston. When I first brought him home last week, I relied on takeout a lot, but I'm getting sick of restaurant food. I think he is too, so I'm cooking.

I glance over at my laptop, sitting open on the coffee table. I've been behind on work since his accident. I did my best to keep up, working while I was hanging out in his hospital room. But it was hard to stay focused, and I wasn't getting a lot of sleep.

I probably should have just left him there and checked up on him once or twice, instead of staying at the hospital for days on end. But after the first full twenty-four hours, I realized something.

No one else was coming.

Caleb contacted Weston's dad, but as far as I know, the man didn't so much as call to see how his son was doing. Neither did his business partner. No one else came by to see if he was all right. No get-well cards or silly balloons. Caleb came by, but that was it.

Does this guy really have no one else in his life? No family or friends to help him out in a crisis?

After I woke up in his room that first morning, I kept expecting someone else would show up. It was like I was waiting for someone to come relieve me. Take over. When no one did— literally no one, not even a single phone call—I stayed. I didn't bother to ask him if he wanted me to; he would have said no. But I could sense he needed me there, even if he wasn't going to admit it.

The week went on, and still nothing. Knowing that made it a lot easier to go back to pick him up from the hospital when Caleb told me he was being discharged. It hurt my feelings when he yelled at me to go home, and I was livid when I left. But the ensuing couple of days gave me time to cool off. And where else was he going to go if I didn't come bring him home?

We haven't talked about what happened at the hospital—not how I stayed with him, nor how he ran me off by being a dick. I guess that's just part of being friends with Weston. Sometimes he lashes out and pisses you off.

I have a feeling he's not used to having people around who stick.

The chicken is done, so I pull it off the heat and check the potatoes. They're fork tender, so I take them out of the oven and dish up two plates. I set his on a tray with a glass of ice water and pick it up to take to his room.

I turn to find Weston coming down the hall.

"Hey, you didn't have to get up," I say. "I'll bring dinner to you."

"I don't want to eat in bed again." He comes into the kitchen and gingerly sits down at the table.

I don't ask how he's feeling. He hurts, and he keeps the dosage on his pain meds low, but he doesn't want to talk about it. I've gotten a crash course in Weston-ology since he came home from the hospital, and I've realized his standoffish demeanor isn't always because he's being a jerk. He simply doesn't like to talk a lot.

That, and he keeps himself completely walled off from other people. I've never met anyone so guarded. I hate to admit it, but I think Mia was right. Weston wears his assholedom like armor. What he's protecting himself from, I don't know, and I doubt he'll ever tell me. He's locked up so tight, I can't imagine anyone getting in. But now that I understand him a little better, he's easier to get along with.

Actually, I have to admit, I like him. He's very smart, and has a sharp sense of humor. What seemed like cockiness is mostly confidence, and when he's not arguing with me about changing his bandages or lying down so he doesn't hurt himself, his self-assurance is pretty appealing. And god, he's easy on the eyes. Is it bad to like having him around just so I can look at him?

"Okay, we can eat here." I put down the plates and waters, then sit across from him. "There's rosemary, garlic, and some salt and pepper on the potatoes." I reach across and start cutting up his chicken so he can eat one-handed. "I cooked the chicken in butter, so it's extra delicious."

"Smells good."

"Thanks." I finish cutting his food and start eating. It could use a little more salt, but other than that the flavor is good.

"Your face looks better." I put down my fork and reach across the table to touch his chin. He lets me turn his face so I can look. There are still discolored bruises, but the split in his lip is just a scab and the swelling is gone.

"Yeah, feels better," he says.

"Good," I say. "Just think, soon you'll be back in business, picking up hot girls."

He pauses with his fork halfway to his mouth and looks at me, his brow furrowed. But he doesn't say anything, just goes back to his dinner.

We eat in silence for a while. I've gotten used to that too. He's not a talker, so it's easy to mistake his silence for anger or disdain. But sometimes he's just quiet. I don't mind. It's comfortable.

He puts his fork down, his plate clean. "This was really good. Thank you."

I smile and my cheeks warm a little. Coming from him, that's a nice compliment. "You're welcome."

He gets up and takes both our plates to the counter, then walks into the living room and lowers himself onto the couch. "Want to watch a movie?" He picks up the remote and turns on the TV.

I pause for a second, considering. That's the first time he's ever suggested we do something together. We've spent a lot of time together since he got home, but it's mostly just the two of us existing in the same space. He can't work, and I work from home, so we're both just... here. But he wants to actually hang out with me? Huh.

"Yeah, sure." I walk into the living room and sit down on the other side of the couch. "What do you have in mind?"

He flips through the choices. "How about *Die Hard*?"

"Nah, I'm not in the mood for a Christmas movie."

"Christmas movie? *Die Hard* isn't a Christmas movie."

I raise my eyebrows. "Are you kidding? Of course it is. Everyone knows that."

"It's a Bruce Willis action flick," he says. "How is that a Christmas movie?"

I shift so I'm facing him, and tuck my legs beneath me. "For one, it takes place on Christmas eve."

"That doesn't make it a Christmas movie."

"No, not by itself," I say. "But that isn't the only reason."

"Enlighten me."

"The entire theme is Christmassy."

"What theme? Kicking ass and witty one liners?"

"No, kicking ass is not the central theme of *Die Hard*," I say. "Although I concede, John McClane does his fair share of ass-kicking. But what is he really doing? He's trying to reconcile with his wife and save his family before Christmas morning. That's why he's in L.A. in the first place."

"That doesn't prove anything," he says. "Christmas is just part of the setting. It provides a ticking clock—a reason that McClane, and hence the audience, feels a sense of urgency for him to achieve his quest."

"Okay, points to you for knowing about literary devices like ticking clocks," I say. "But, what is his real quest? He's not there to save hostages from a fake terrorist-slash-criminal mastermind. That's just what gets in his way. He's there to save Christmas."

Weston furrows his brow. "Can I see your phone?"

I grab it off the coffee table and hand it to him.

His fingers tap the screen for a few seconds, then he holds it up for me to see. "Nope. It was released in July. If it was a Christmas movie, they would have released it in December."

"Doesn't matter," I say.

"Of course it matters."

"*Die Hard* is a classic that has transcended the intent of its creators," I say.

"How many times have you seen it?" he asks.

"I grew up with two brothers. More times than I can count." My mouth turns up in a little smirk. "And we always watched it at Christmas."

He smiles and shakes his head. "Fine, maybe *Die Hard* is a Christmas movie." He clicks the remote a few times. "What about *Casino Royale*? Or can you only watch James Bond at Halloween?"

"No, that's perfect," I say. "Daniel Craig is suitable for all seasons."

"I'm glad he meets your expectations," he says, his tone wry.

"Are you kidding? That man blows every woman's expectations straight out of the water."

He smiles at me again, then brings up the movie and hits play. There's something about that smile. He usually swings between stoic and cocky, but this is somewhere in between. It's like I'm getting a tiny glimpse into the real Weston. The guy under the asshole armor.

My feet are cold, so I pull a throw blanket off the back of the couch and drape it across my lap. He glances at me and I lift the edge, offering to let him share it with me. He props his feet up on the coffee table and pulls part of the blanket over his legs.

I settle into the cushions to watch the movie, but my eyes keep flicking back to Weston. He looks relaxed, his good arm slung over the back of the couch. After a while, his eyes start to drift closed. His pain meds make him sleepy. By the time the movie ends, he's fast asleep. I consider waking him so he can go to bed, but he looks so peaceful.

Instead, I move the blanket over him, pulling it up to his chest.

"Night, Weston."

11

WESTON

*M*y phone rings and I grab it off the nightstand, wincing a little when I twist. My incision site is healing well, but I'm still sore as fuck.

I see the name on the screen and consider ignoring the call. Do I want to talk to him right now? Not really, but if I don't answer, I'll have to call him back eventually. Might as well get it over with.

"Yeah."

"Weston," my dad says. "What's going on? Did you wreck your car?"

Of course he asks about the car first. "I was in an accident."

"You weren't drunk, were you?"

I grit my teeth for a second before answering. "No, Dad. I was sober. The accident wasn't my fault."

"That's good. Something like that could ruin your career."

"I'm well aware."

"Are you back to work yet?" he asks.

"No," I say.

"Why not? Who's seeing your patients?"

I let out a slow breath. "Dad, I spent a week in the hospital. I needed emergency surgery, not to mention I have a broken arm."

"What about your patients?" he asks.

"Ian is taking the ones who can't wait, and Tanya rescheduled the rest," I say. "And since when do you give a fuck about my patients?"

"I give a fuck about the practice," he says. "So, how are you?"

"Don't," I say.

"Don't what?" he asks.

"Pretend like you care," I say. "It happened two weeks ago, Dad. I haven't heard a word from you."

"I've been out of town," he says.

"I suppose you were on a tropical island with no cell service," I say. "For two weeks."

"I took Jenny on vacation," he says.

"Who the fuck is Jenny?"

"You've met Jenny," he says. "Well, maybe not."

I pinch the bridge of my nose. My dad has had an endless string of girlfriends since my mom died. "Is there any other reason you called, or did you just want to find out what happened to my car?"

"Speaking of cars, I just bought a new one," he says. "Borrow my old one until you get yourself a replacement. I'll send it over so you'll have a way to get to work."

"Fine, whatever." I just want to get off the phone at this point. "I'm not at the house, though."

"Where are you?"

"I'm staying with... a friend."

"Get me the address," he says. "Listen, I have to go. Jenny and I have brunch reservations."

There's a muffled woman's voice in the background. I hang up without waiting to see if he was going to say more.

I shouldn't expect anything else from my father. He didn't give a shit about me when I was a kid. Why would he start now?

I get up out of bed, breathing through the burning ache in my ribs. My arm itches beneath my cast, but there's nothing I can do about it. Another couple of weeks and the cast comes off. Then I'm going to need physical therapy to get my strength and dexterity back. I move my fingers as much as possible, hoping to keep them limber.

Living with the use of only one arm—my non-dominant arm, at that—is shitty. And with the pain in my midsection when I bend, twist, reach—basically when I do anything—I'm fucking useless. I do need to go back to work. Get a new car. Start putting things back together. But for now, I'm stuck here until I can be on my feet for more than an hour without wanting to die.

I give my armpit a quick sniff before I open my bedroom door. I haven't showered in a couple of days—it's a pain with the cast—but I smell okay. God knows Kendra will tell me if I don't.

It's weird, depending on her so much. She helps me with almost everything. But she never makes me feel like a burden. She just goes about her business, taking care of me like it's something she's always done.

Her voice carries down the hallway. She must be on the phone.

I don't know how she does it, but just hearing her voice soothes my shitty mood. Despite how bored I am being stuck here, I'd hate it a lot more if Kendra wasn't around. She's not annoying to talk to. She doesn't pry or ask me a lot of stupid questions. She's... pleasant.

I find her at the kitchen table, her laptop open; looks like she's on a Skype call with someone. Her hair is up, bits of it sticking out in all directions. I don't know what I thought was wrong with her hair when I first met her. It's cute. She's wearing a black t-shirt and another pair of pajama pants—striped ones today. But hell, I hang out at home in my underwear all the time. I guess she just likes to be comfortable.

It does occur to me that maybe her messy hair and clothes struck me as odd when I first moved in because I'm not used to seeing women like this—at home, relaxing, being themselves. I'm used to meeting them in public, when they're out looking for men, just like I'm out looking for them. Full makeup. Careful attention to their hair. Sexy clothes. But now I wonder how many of the women I've shagged once or twice sit around their own houses just like Kendra—hair up, makeup off, in a t-shirt and striped pajama pants. I'm just never around to see it.

I only see the show they put on. I don't see them being real. Natural.

Kendra is all natural.

She glances at me over her shoulder, giving me a smile. I catch sight of that little dimple by her lips and my mouth twitches in a grin.

Client, she mouths at me.

I nod and head for the fridge, but she puts up a hand to stop me, then turns back to her screen.

"Sorry, Shannon, just give me a second. Roommate." She turns back to me and whispers, "Don't get in front of the webcam."

"Why?" I whisper back.

Her eyebrows lift. "You're not wearing pants."

I glance down. I have on a gray t-shirt and boxer briefs.

Her client—Shannon, I guess—covers her mouth, but we can both hear her laugh. Kendra's eyes close and she shakes her head.

"Hot roommate?" Shannon asks.

Kendra snorts. "Don't encourage him. Sorry, apparently

Weston is allergic to pants, so I'm trying to keep him out of view."

Shannon laughs. "Don't worry about it. Maybe he'll inspire me."

"Yeah, well, he's definitely..." Kendra glances at me again, her cheeks flushing. "Anyway, where were we?"

I wonder what she was about to say; he's definitely what? I walk around the other side of the table and get a bottled water out of the fridge. Without stopping her conversation, Kendra holds out her hand. I give her the bottle and she opens it for me, not breaking stride for a second.

"I think you're good up until they get to the bedroom," Kendra says, handing the water bottle back to me. "It's once they start taking their clothes off that we run into problems."

That gets my attention. I lean against the counter and take a drink. What kind of book is her client working on?

"I agree," Shannon says. "I'm just not good at sex scenes. I needed a ton of help with them in my last book, and even then, I know they could have been better."

I take my water to the table and sit across from Kendra. She meets my eyes and for a second, it looks like she's going to say something to me. But she gives her head a little shake and turns her attention back to her screen.

"You just need to get out of your own way. Let it flow," Kendra says. "I think your biggest problem is you're too mechanical. There's a lot of tab A into slot B stuff. Including a little of that is good; it grounds the scene and helps the reader picture what's happening. But you also need to include the sensations— the feelings."

"That makes sense," Shannon says. "I'm just not sure how to do it."

"Think about things like skin touching skin," Kendra says. "Her nipples, erect against his chest. His stubbly chin, dragging against her cheek. Think about the juxtaposition of hard and soft."

My eyes are locked on Kendra's mouth, and my cock twitches at the word *hard*. I probably should have put on pants.

"Let's walk through this scene and maybe I can give you some specific ideas," Kendra says.

"Sounds good," Shannon says.

"Okay, so Cherry and Max get to the hotel room. I think Max needs to be more aggressive with her. Instead of gently laying her on the bed, he should be more frantic. The reader needs to feel like he has to have her, now."

"What do you mean, like he pushes her down?" Shannon asks.

"Why not?" Kendra asks. "Have him shove her onto the bed. Women love that."

I take sip of my water. Damn straight, women love that. I wonder if Kendra does.

"That's not too intense?" Shannon asks.

"No, you want intense," Kendra says. "He's not trying to hurt her. He's just being kinda rough. Dominant. Trust me, that's sexy as hell."

There's more keyboard clicking. "All right, I'm taking notes."

"Good," Kendra says. "Now, for this particular scene, I think you have them taking too long before they get to the good stuff. Sometimes that works. But here, they've had an entire day of thinking about how much they want to bang the shit out of each other."

"What was happening before this?" I ask.

"What?" Kendra asks.

"You said they've been hot for each other all day," I say. "What was going on?"

Kendra pauses, looking at me like she's confused. "Well, they were at work, and then at a company party, like after hours. But

Max is Cherry's boss, and they can't be together in the open. So they spent the party flirting and kind of sneaking around. Now they're alone and they can finally unleash all their pent-up sexual tension."

I nod. "Then he'd be aggressive at first, but he doesn't want to blow his load too fast. So he won't just toss her on her back and pound her into oblivion. I'm assuming this guy is good at sex?"

"Yeah, she's writing a romance. That's pretty much expected."

"And I need to turn up the heat," Shannon says. "Way up."

"Turn up the heat, huh. Well, if he knows what he's doing, he's going to drag it out for a while to drive her crazy," I say, an image forming in my mind. "Throw her down, but tease her and make her wait. He'd get his mouth on her pussy and make her come like that first."

"This is great," Shannon says. "What else?"

I shift in my seat and take another sip. "So he really goes to town on her, right? Licking and sucking that clit like it's fucking candy. He loves it and she comes hard. Now he can't take not being inside her anymore, and she's begging for his dick. He gets on top of her because he wants to be the one in control. He's taking her for a ride and she doesn't need to do anything, just let him fuck her senseless."

Kendra is staring at me, her lips parted. I can hear Shannon's keyboard clicking.

"He pushes her legs open and thrusts inside her," I continue. "Hard, you know? Now he's not playing around."

"And she's relieved she can finally let loose," Kendra says. "So she makes a lot of noise. Moaning, exclamations of how good it feels, repeating his name."

"That'll get his blood pumping—hearing her." Shit, this is getting *my* blood pumping. I should definitely be wearing pants.

"Exactly," Kendra says. "And don't forget the other senses. He hears her, but he also smells her, tastes her on his lips."

"Everything will make him want to fuck her harder," I say.

Kendra's nodding along. "Absolutely. Ramp up the intensity here, and don't forget to focus on what it feels like. Her body is responding to him. She gets hotter, wetter. He's overwhelmed with how good it feels."

"Should they stay in one position the whole time?" Shannon asks.

Kendra meets my eyes and we nod to each other. "Yeah, I think so," she says. "The purpose of this scene is to show them giving in to all that pent-up lust. Sex gymnastics can come later."

Sex gymnastics. That sounds fun. Although thinking about it kind of makes my ribs hurt.

"This is so helpful, Kendra," Shannon says. "Thank you. And thanks to the hot roommate."

I wink at Kendra and her eyes linger on me for a long moment, a mystified expression on her face. "It's no problem." Her eyes move back to her screen. "Let me know if you have more questions or want to go over any other sections in detail."

Taking advantage of Kendra's attention being elsewhere, I stand, nonchalantly tugging on the edge of my t-shirt so it covers my erection in case she does look up. She's still talking; I leave the kitchen and head down the hall.

I had no idea Kendra had such a dirty imagination—or such a dirty mouth. I don't know what's wrong with me, but the entire time I was talking, I was picturing myself with Kendra. My mouth on her pussy. Tasting her. Making her come so hard she can't breathe. Driving my cock into her. Giving in to our pent-up lust.

I slip through the bathroom door and run a hand through my hair. Fuck, where did all that come from? What pent-up lust? What the hell, Weston?

But god, Kendra is fucking sexy. I have no idea how I missed it before.

She's beautiful, and not in a fake, done-up way. She's gorgeous stumbling out of her bedroom in the morning, making a beeline for her coffee maker. Her smile does weird things to me. And her body. I could destroy that body in a hundred different ways.

There's one of her tank tops and a pair of panties on the floor. She must have left them there when she took a shower. Careful of my ribs, I lean down and pick up her panties, then bring them to my nose and inhale. My eyes roll back in my head. Oh fucking hell, she smells good.

I can imagine that smell all over me. In my bed, on my sheets. Tasting it on my fingers. Licking it off my lips. I need to stop. I drop the panties back where I found them.

But I can't get the image of fucking the shit out of Kendra out of my mind.

12

KENDRA

*T*here's a car I don't recognize in the driveway when I pull into my spot. Looks expensive—a silver Audi this time. Did Weston get a new car? I don't know how he could have. I've been gone for hours watching Charlotte and he doesn't have a way to get around.

I head inside and put down my purse. Weston's in his room, and I'm worn out from being on kid duty for half the day. This calls for comfies.

After changing into a tank top and pajama pants, I head down the hall and knock a few times on Weston's half-open door.

"Come in."

He's sitting up in bed, a mess of file folders and paperwork spread out all over. Two more boxes are stacked on the chair in the corner.

"Hey, sorry to bug you, but there's a car in the driveway," I say. "Did you get a new one?"

"No, it's my father's."

Holy shit, his dad? He's hardly said a word about his father. I only know he exists because Caleb mentioned calling him after the accident. I glance around, like I could have missed another grown man in the room. "Is he around? Or did he just drop it off and leave?"

"Neither," he says. "He had it sent over."

"Oh. That was nice of him."

"Mm."

Okay, I guess we aren't talking about his father. I take a few steps into the room. "What is all this stuff?"

"Work," he says. "I had it couriered over this morning."

"Are they patient records?"

"No, financial records." He blows out a breath and drops the file. "There have been some discrepancies in the accounts that I've needed to check into. Since I can't see patients yet, I figured I'd go through these. But I'm not even sure what I'm looking for."

I sink down onto the edge of the bed. "Can I help?"

He looks up at me for the first time since I walked in and holds my gaze. His gray eyes are intense and suddenly I'm very aware that I'm sitting with him in his bedroom. I haven't been in here a lot, other than to bring him food or a glass of water when he first got home from the hospital. Lately he's been able to do more things for himself, so he hasn't needed me as much.

"No," he says. "But thanks."

"Sure." I'm feeling a little weird, and he's obviously busy, but I find myself casting around for an excuse to stay. God, Kendra, what's that about? You don't need to hang out in Weston's bedroom.

He starts shuffling the papers and files into a stack. "I've been at this for hours. I need a break."

His cast makes it awkward, so I crawl across the bed and help. He doesn't react—at first he complained a lot when I helped him with things, but after a while, he quit resisting. Now I just try not to make a big deal out of it. I get them in a neat pile and he moves them onto the floor on the other side of the bed. I notice he doesn't wince.

Thinking about his injuries, my eyes travel to his midsection. He's wearing a shirt today, but of course no pants. I glance down at his muscular thighs. He has the perfect amount of leg hair—enough to be manly, but not so much that he looks like an animal. His body is basically amazing.

I swallow hard and tear my eyes away. Fortunately, he's busy plugging in his tablet and setting it on his nightstand. He lays his earbuds on top.

"What are you always listening to with those?" I ask. "Music?"

His eyes meet mine again and his mouth quirks in a smile. "You're curious tonight."

Normally when he says something like that, there's a sharpness in his tone. He's annoyed, or being sarcastic. But this voice is completely different. There's a hint of humor in it, like he's teasing.

That's when I realize I'm sitting in the middle of his bed. Not near the edge, or the foot. Center.

My heart is a little jumpy, but I smile back at him. "Sorry, I'm just wondering. You wear them a lot."

"Once in a while it's music," he says. "But I listen to audiobooks."

"Do you?" That's an interesting surprise.

He shifts so he's partially facing me. "Yeah. I'm..." He pauses. "I'm dyslexic, so listening is easier."

I freeze for a second, afraid to even breathe. He just shared something personal with me. He almost never does that.

"I'm impressed."

"By what?"

"You," I say. "That must have made med school even more difficult."

He shrugs. "It's not a big deal. I *can* read. It just takes me longer."

I think it *is* a big deal, but I'm not going to press him about it. "Well, I read a lot, so let me know if you need any recommendations."

He smirks. "The sexual adventures of Max and Cherry might not be quite what I'm looking for."

I laugh. "Stop. That was for a client. Although yeah, I read books like that. But I read a lot of stuff. I just finished a really good one about a serial killer."

"Sex and serial killers," he says. "Kendra is not the woman I thought she was."

God, what is he doing? Is he flirting with me? If he is, I'm totally responding to it; my *body* is responding to it. My tummy is fluttery and my core tingles.

"I guess I'm full of surprises."

"Yes, you are."

I'm going to positively melt under that gaze of his. My heart is beating so fast, and I don't know if it's butterflies or a flock of birds that just took up residence in my stomach. I need to defuse this. Fast.

"So are you sure you're feeling okay?" I reach out and touch my hand to his forehead, like I'm checking for a fever. "You're in such a good mood tonight."

He smiles again and I snatch my hand away. Bad move. Touching him is not going to defuse anything.

"Very funny," he says. "Since when are you such a comedian?"

"Have you met me?" I ask. "I'm hilarious."

"Your pants are what's hilarious," he says.

I glance down at my pajama pants. "Hey man, this is what it's like to live with a woman. You have to deal with me in my natural state."

"Your natural state involves fuzzy polka dot pants?"

"Yes," I say, giving him a smug smile. "Yes, it does."

He shifts and winces, rubbing the back of his neck.

"You okay?" I ask.

"Yeah, fine," he says. "Neck hurts from sitting here reading all those damn files."

Don't do it, Kendra. Don't offer to rub his back. "Here, let me rub it for you." *Oh god, you did it.*

He scoots forward so I can get behind him. He's a lot taller than me, even sitting, so I have to get on my knees. I start kneading my thumbs into the taut muscles at the base of his neck. This close, I can smell him—clean and masculine. I work my hands across his upper back and he relaxes against me. I lean my thighs against him, which puts my hips—and certain other areas—in contact with his warm body.

His back moves up and down as he takes a deep breath. I keep rubbing, keenly aware of the heat building in my core. I've never been this close to him before. Half my body is touching his. His head droops forward a little and he makes a low noise in his throat. I pinch my lower lip between my teeth, biting back an answering moan.

I feel him turning to liquid at my touch. I stare at the back of his neck, imagining my lips there. What would he do if I leaned in quietly and kissed him? Slid my tongue across his skin. Nipped at his ear.

Oh my god, what am I doing? He'd turn around and ask me what the fuck is going on, that's what he'd do. It would be humiliating.

My hands start to ache from the effort of rubbing his muscular back, but it's hard to make myself stop. After all, he is one of the sexiest men I've ever laid eyes on. I thought that the first time I saw him. Sure, he can be an asshole sometimes, but when you get to know him, he's not half bad.

In fact, he's a lot less than *half* bad. And the part that *is* bad...
I bet it's the right *kind* of bad. The kind that would make *me*
be bad.

Fuck, there I go again. I need to get out of here.

I stop, hesitating for a moment with my palms splayed out
across his back.

He straightens and glances at me over his shoulder. "Thanks.
That felt really good."

I can think of more ways to make you feel good.

No, Kendra. Stop it.

Please let my voice sound normal. "Good. I hope it helps."

He moves his head around, stretching his neck and I take the
opportunity to get out from behind him. Since I'm already
moving, I do the smart thing and get off his bed. Although, god,
his sheets smell like him. I could bury myself in them and roll
around.

Out, Kendra. Get out while you still can.

"Okay, well, I'm kinda tired, so I think I'll go to bed. Maybe
read or something."

He nods. "Good night, then."

"Good night."

I leave his room, shutting the door behind me before I lose
all sense and do something incredibly stupid. Like kiss him.

What is my problem? Kiss Weston? That would be a ridiculous thing to do. There's nothing wrong with admitting he's
attractive. Okay, he's more than attractive; he's spectacular. But
he's not the type of guy I need in my life. I want something with
a future—maybe even a *forever*. I'm not looking for a hookup or
a few nights of sexual adventure. Granted, with him, I'm sure it
would be incredible. And if I thought he might want me, it
would be very tempting.

But that's not me. I've never been able to separate sex from
my emotions. If I slept with him, I'd only get attached. And

Weston Reid is not the kind of man to get attached to. I know enough about him to realize that.

It's nice to be friends with him, and I can appreciate him for the hot piece of man candy that he is. But that's where it has to end. If I let it go further than that, I'll only end up hurt.

But after all those little smiles and flirty laughs, sitting on sheets that smell like man heaven, and having my hands all over his back, I am a throbbing ball of need. I slip into my bedroom, strip off my clothes, and get into bed.

I can take care of this myself, and maybe I won't be so crazy around him tomorrow.

My eyes drift closed as my hand slides down. I don't even try to stop the fantasy from forming. It isn't the first time.

Weston's mouth on my skin. His body braced above me. His cock, sliding in and out of my wetness, hot and throbbing. His muscles flexing as his hips drive into me, over and over.

I definitely shouldn't let anything happen with Weston. But I can imagine it, and even that is mind-blowing.

13

WESTON

*L*eaning back against the pillow, I let out a long breath. Shit, what just happened? Yeah, back rubs feel good and all, but that's not what has me slow blinking like my brain just broke.

Kendra, sitting on my bed. Flashing me those cute little smiles. Teasing me, like she's so good at doing. And then touching me, her hands all over my sore back, her body pressed against mine. Holy shit, that felt good. I was putty in her hands, and that is *not* normal for me. No matter what I'm doing, I like to stay in control. Be in charge. But thirty seconds of Kendra's fingers kneading my back, feeling her warmth against me, and I was done.

It's probably good that she got up when she did. I don't know what would have happened if she'd stayed. I don't know what I want when it comes to her.

No, I know what I *want*. That's not a question. But I don't know if I *should*.

I always steer clear of women I know well or spend a lot of time around. I'm never looking for more than casual sex, so it's easier with strangers. Less complicated.

So why am I thinking about Kendra this way? *Complicated* doesn't even begin to describe it.

I turn out the light and try to go to sleep. It's late, and I'm tired, but I stare at the ceiling for a while. My ribs ache, probably from the way I was sitting. I haven't been taking my pain pills—I hate the way they make me feel. But maybe I should tonight. It will just put me to sleep anyway. I'll probably feel better in the morning if I do.

I need water, so I shuffle out into the hallway, quiet so I don't disturb Kendra. When I walk past her room, a noise catches my attention. Her door isn't quite latched—she really needs to fix that—and it hangs open an inch or two.

I pause, hearing the sound of her sheets sliding across each other, like she moved in bed. That makes me think of Kendra in *my* bed, which makes me think of her naked, which makes my cock spring to life. Great, just when the last Kendra-induced hard-on had gone away, here we go again.

Another noise. A breath. But it isn't the deep breath of someone falling asleep. It's a quick gasp, followed by more bed noise.

Fully aware that I'm being an enormous fucking creeper, standing outside her bedroom door, I shift so I'm closer to the crack without her being able to see me if she looks up.

The bed moves again—a little squeak. Sheets rustling. She's either having a hard time getting comfortable or she's—

A tiny moan, stifled, like she's trying to be quiet.

Oh my fucking god.

I'm stuck now, my feet rooted to the floor. I'm only going to listen for a minute. Or maybe two. Just until I remember how to move my legs again, because somehow I've forgotten.

The rest of the house is completely silent, shrouded in darkness. All I can hear is the quickening of her breath. My eye is glued to the crack between the door and the threshold. Without meaning to, I push it open a little more. I wince, sure it's going to squeak. Everything in this damn house squeaks. But somehow, it doesn't—just drifts open a couple more inches.

It's too dark to see much, but there's movement under her sheets. Maybe one of her legs, bent at the knee. I hear another stifled moan and I imagine her fingers between her legs, rubbing her clit. Her breathing is rhythmic now, little catches in her breath revealing the pleasure she's giving herself.

My hand slips into my underwear. It's my left, so not as useful for jacking off. But I'm not going to whack it while Kendra gets her rocks off anyway. I just need a little pressure. Just until I can tear myself away.

Her breathing quickens and her attempts at silence loosen. Either that or I'm so focused on her, I can hear every tiny sound she makes. God this is one of the hottest things I've ever experienced. My eyes adjust to the darkness and I can make out her form beneath the sheets. She reaches one hand behind her and grabs one of the wrought iron bars of her bed frame.

My cock throbs and I squeeze. Kendra shudders. I can practically see her fingers, gliding along the outside of her pussy, rubbing up and down, the tips dipping inside.

I wonder what's going through her mind right now. Do women fantasize when they're singing solo? I know what I'm thinking about. That it's me making her moan like that. My fingers, or my tongue, or my cock, sliding in and out of her. Our bodies, skin to skin. Me, on top of her, her legs wrapped around my waist. Thrusting, grinding, grabbing, licking, sucking.

Fuck, I'm so hard. I rub my dick a few times, wetting it with pre-cum. She whimpers and I can barely stand it. I want to bust through her door, climb on top of her, and show her how it's done. Give her the biggest, hardest orgasm of her entire life.

She's close. I can hear it in her breathing—see it in the way she moves beneath the sheets. God, I'm an asshole for creeping on this, but I'm captivated. I couldn't rip myself away if the kitchen was on fire.

A shaking breath. Another whimper. Quiet creaks from her bed in a steady rhythm, the pace increasing. She starts to say something, her voice a whisper. Holy shit, she's going to—

"Oh god, Weston."

My body stiffens, my fist jerks once, and I come unglued. Hot pulses roll through me, my cock throbbing. My brain is drenched in endorphins, erasing my ability to think. For those few euphoric seconds, I'm coming inside her and she's moaning in my ear instead of across the room, alone in her bed.

I move away from her door and lean my shoulder against the wall. I'm breathing hard, my eyes are fuzzy, and my legs feel like they're going to buckle beneath me. What the fuck just happened? I came in my underwear like a horny teenager.

A few more breaths and my mind comes back to me. I listen for any sound that indicates she knows I'm here. She takes a deep breath and the sheets rustle again.

Forget my pain meds. I walk back to my room, as fast as I can without making a sound. She'll murder me if she knows I was listening to her. How the fuck would I explain that? Or the mess in my underwear?

Oh hey, Kendra. Listening to you come made me jizz all over myself. No big deal.

Careful so my bedroom door doesn't make noise, I shut it behind me and take a deep breath. I clean up and put on fresh underwear, still reeling from what she did to me. I've never felt so out of control. To have her undo me like that...

I lie down and close my eyes. Kendra's voice echoes in my mind. She breathed my name when she came. She was imagining *me*.

Still floating on the waves of the craziest orgasm I've ever had, I drift off to sleep, my thoughts full of the woman lying one room away.

14

WESTON

This thing with Kendra is turning me into an idiot.

I feel stupid when I'm around her. Tongue-tied, like a kid with a crush. I don't like what she does to me. And the fact that she's so fucking sweet is not helping. I try to push her away, but she just rolls her eyes and smiles. Pats me on the back. Teases me about being surly.

Nights, though. Nights are the worst. I know she's right there, on the other side of the wall. Is she touching herself again? Imagining me? Is she making herself come, breathing my name?

Sleep isn't easy to come by, but the memory of her making me blow my load in the hallway helps me get off every time. But I still don't know what to do about her.

My solution? Stay away from her as much as possible.

Going back to work helps. My arm is still in a cast, so I can't perform surgeries. But I'm healed enough that I can see patients. Ian is a fucking dick about it, complaining about how hard his schedule has been since I've been out. I ignore him; I don't need to dignify his bullshit with a response.

Although I'm able to work, that doesn't mean it's easy. I shrug off Tanya's concerns when she asks me if I'm doing all right. But the truth is, by the end of each day, I'm exhausted and sore.

Still, I go back to the gym in the mornings and work around my injury. I buy a new car so I won't be beholden to my father any more than necessary. I start getting back to my life—my routine. I find excuses to be out of the house so I won't be around Kendra too much.

Saturday rolls around, and I stay in bed late, letting my body rest after a long week. I hear Kendra moving around the house and the rich aroma of her coffee wafts beneath my door. After a while, the front door closes, and the house goes silent.

I get up, shower, throw on some clothes. I keep pants on more often than not lately; I don't trust my dick to behave around her.

Several hours go by, and she doesn't come home. My body needs rest, so I lie around and listen to a book that barely holds my attention. I wonder where she is. Obsessing over her is the dumbest thing. I want to kick my own ass. But my brain won't cooperate; thoughts of her roll through my mind no matter how hard I try to ignore them. I pick up my phone to text her and put it down again at least a dozen times.

She comes home and I stay in my room, feeling like a dumbass for avoiding her. Finally, I get up and go out to the living room, planting myself on the couch. This is not a big deal. She's sexy, and I'm attracted to her. She must be attracted to me. Why not just go for it and fuck her already?

Because I actually *like* her.

And I don't like anyone.

It's not just how she took care of me after my accident, although for fuck's sake, she's some kind of angel for that. But she's fun and easy to be around. Most people piss me off— they're annoying and stupid, or they get in my space. Kendra doesn't. She's the first person to exist in my world in a way that doesn't chafe. I enjoy being near her. I've missed her this week—missed the incessant clicking of her fingers on the keyboard. Her late-night coffee to keep her up so she can work. Her warm smile.

I couldn't just fuck Kendra a few times and be done with her. There are too many feelings involved. And I don't do feelings. Ever. I don't get close to people.

She comes out into the living room, breaking me from my thoughts. It's all I can do to keep my eyeballs in my skull. She's wearing a dress—sort of. It's strapless with a black top, the neckline dipping down like a heart. The skirt starts just below her boobs—thin layers of fluttery cream fabric. But it ends way too soon. This thing is short, making her legs look a mile long. Hot pink heels take it to another level. They scream *I'm here to party*.

"What the fuck are you wearing?" I say before I can stop myself.

She glances down at herself. "A dress?"

"Barely."

She laughs and I notice the rest of her. Hair done in waves that fall around her shoulders. Makeup, including pink lipstick that matches those shoes. She's sex on a stick and it's a good thing I put pants on because just the sight of her in this getup is making me hard.

"What are you all dressed up for?" I ask.

"I'm going out with some friends." She grabs her phone off the coffee table and puts it in a little purse. "I thought I mentioned I had plans tonight."

She's leaving the house in that thing? I glance away, trying to act like I don't care what she's doing. "I don't know. Maybe you did." *Don't ask questions. You don't care where she's going.* "Where are you going?" *God, what is wrong with me?*

"Dinner at the Pike Brewery, and then Monkey Loft." She

raises her arms and gives her hips a little shimmy. "We're going dancing."

My brow furrows and my back knots with tension. She's going to a club, in *that* dress, to go *dancing*? "Since when is clubbing your thing?"

She shrugs. "It's fun to go out and let loose once in a while. Besides, I think I'm allowed to celebrate."

"Celebrate what?"

She laughs again, rolling her eyes. "My birthday, Mr. Observant."

Oh shit. It's her birthday? Why didn't I know that? I would have... What would I have done? I have no idea, but... something. "What the fuck, Kendra? It's your birthday?"

"Well, it's not for another week. But I'm celebrating tonight with friends." She quirks her lips at me. "Why, you wanna come?"

"No."

She laughs again. "I know. It's a girl thing anyway. Mia should be here any minute."

"She's driving?" I ask.

"No, we're using Uber so we can drink, but our ride is picking her up first, then me," she says.

She's not driving so she can drink? In that outfit? In a club? I fucking hate this so much I want to murder someone. She can't go out looking like that. Especially if she's planning on drinking. This is bullshit. I'm about to say so, but I snap my mouth shut again. What the hell can I say? *I don't want you to go out in that dress?* That won't make me sound like a lunatic at all.

She goes into the kitchen, her dress swaying with the movement of her hips.

I try to get myself together. I'm being stupid. People go out, they party. So what? I do. Or I did, before I turned into a fucking invalid. I could, now. I can move around without a lot of pain. I could probably even have sex, as long as I was careful.

God, I miss sex.

Kendra comes back out, sliding a chunky black bracelet onto her wrist. She pauses, looking at me. "You okay? You look angry. More than usual, I mean."

"I'm fine," I say and cringe at my voice. I sound really defensive.

"You sure?"

Deep breath, Weston. Calm your ass down. "Why wouldn't I be?"

"Aw," she says, sticking out her lower lip. She comes over and taps me on the nose. "Poor baby. Are you going to be lonely without me?"

Yes. No. Fuck you, Kendra. I laugh it off, but it sounds fake. "Yeah, you wish."

She ruffles my hair, then pulls her phone out of her purse. "She's almost here. I'm going to meet her outside. I'll probably be late, so don't wait up." She winks at me.

I clench my fists and swallow hard. Don't wait up? What the fuck does that mean? Does she think she's going to hook up with some guy tonight?

Well, fuck you, whoever you are; she whispers *my* name when she comes.

She opens the front door, and with a glance over her shoulder and a little wave, she's gone.

I get up and try to distract myself by getting dinner. Leftover spaghetti. Packaged neatly by Kendra with a little post-it note on the top that says *Weston*. She drew a little smiley face underneath.

God, what the fuck.

I reheat it and eat it at the kitchen table. What's Kendra eating? More importantly, what's she drinking? Does Pike

Brewery have a full bar? I imagine her doing some sort of gross birthday cake shot, the glass topped with whipped cream. I bet it would get on her lips. If I was there, I could lick it off.

Damn it, Weston.

Food doesn't help. I rinse off the dishes and put them in the dishwasher. Bourbon might. But if Kendra's out drinking, maybe I shouldn't.

What does Kendra going out drinking have to do with me having a glass of bourbon? That's ridiculous.

But I don't pour a glass.

I go back to the living room and cruise around Netflix for an hour or so. Kendra and I have been watching some show that's actually pretty good, but I don't want to watch the next episode without her. I grab my phone and check it to see if she texted me. I should keep it close in case she needs something. You never know.

Finally I pick a movie, but I keep checking my phone. It ends a couple of hours later, so I look for something else to watch. She said she'd be late. I'm obviously not waiting up for her. I'm just bored and not tired yet.

After the second movie I only half watch, I check the time. It's after one and she's still not home.

Fuck this. I'm going.

I change into a black short sleeved shirt—my cast gets in the way of long sleeves—and a pair of brown pants. I look up the address of Monkey Club—I've never been—and head downtown. The club is in an industrial area, and there's parking up the street. People loiter outside, but there's no line. Inside there's a narrow staircase leading up to the bar. I head up, pay the cover, and make my way inside.

The lighting is dark and the whole place has an underground vibe, even though it's on the second floor. It's busy, but not packed.

There's a cluster of people at the bar, and a crowd dances in front of the DJ. Speakers pump out electronic music; nothing that's familiar, but it has a good beat. I look around for any sign of Kendra. I've met Mia a couple of times when she stopped by the house, so I know what she looks like. But I don't know any of Kendra's other friends.

I wander the perimeter for a few minutes, wondering if she's here. She might be on her way home and I missed her. I get near the bar and that's when I spot her.

She's standing next to a table along the far wall, her arm slung over Mia's shoulder. Mia is dressed much more reasonably, in a pair of ripped jeans and a t-shirt. Three other women I don't know are with them. They're dressed more like Kendra—dresses and heels—and they're all laughing at something. One of the girls starts grabbing shots from the table and passing them out. Kendra stumbles when she takes hers, laughing again. They all hold up their drinks in a circle, yell something I can't hear over the music, and down them. Kendra raises her glass above her head and hollers, then one of her friends plucks it from her hand. Kendra grabs Mia's arm and drags her toward the dance floor, the other girls following.

I move so I don't lose sight of her, keeping to the outer edge of the room. Looking to my right, I do a doubletake. There's a guy standing near the wall, his hands in his pockets, watching the crowd of dancers. I think I recognize him. He turns and our eyes lock. Yep, it's him, and I have a feeling my face looks as guilty as his.

It's Kendra's brother, Alex. What the hell is he doing here?

He walks over to me and pitches his voice to be heard above the music. "What are you doing here?"

I think about making something up—telling him I was out and wound up here. But I have a feeling he's here doing the same thing I am, so he'll see right through me. Still, what do I say? It's one thing for Alex to be following his woman around—she's his fiancée. Kendra's not even my girlfriend.

"Just figured I'd make sure she's okay," I say. "You here with them?"

Alex shakes his head, looking a little sheepish. "No. Mia will kill me if she sees me here. Kendra too."

I just nod. I get it.

Alex and I hang back, watching the girls dance. Mia seems to be holding herself together, although I wouldn't call what she's doing dancing. She's moving, but it's obvious the only reason she's out there is the combination of alcohol and peer pressure. She keeps backing herself toward the edge of the dancers, like she's going to make a break for it. The good news is, that keeps Kendra and her little group out of the crowd, where I can see them.

Kendra, on the other hand, is dancing up a storm. And she's drunk as fuck.

She dances with her arms in the air, that fluttery cream skirt swirling around her ass. She tosses her hair. I have no idea how she's staying upright in those heels. She stumbles a little, but it only makes her laugh. The music shifts, the lights change color, and apparently that makes drunk Kendra very happy. She shrieks and hugs her friends. One of them gets behind her and Kendra arches her back, puts her hands on the tops of her thighs, and grinds her ass into her friend's crotch.

For fuck's sake.

Alex pinches the bridge of his nose and shakes his head.

We aren't the only ones noticing Kendra's stripper moves. A tall guy in a button-down shirt with the sleeves rolled up stops and watches her. He nudges the guy next to him and points, then they both head for the group of girls.

He worms his way into their circle, all smiles and slick moves. The other guy tries to break off one of Kendra's friends from the group, but she turns away from him. He gives up pretty quickly and disappears back into the crowd.

Button-down guy gets right up in Kendra's space, dancing behind her. She notices him and moves away a step, but she's laughing. He grabs her hand, puts his arm around her waist, and yanks her against him.

I ball my hands into fists. This guy needs to get his fucking hands off my girl.

What the hell am I thinking? She's not *my girl*.

He doesn't let go and for a few minutes, she dances with him. She's stumbling in her high heels, but he keeps her on her feet. Her friends watch, their concern obvious, but they don't intervene. Kendra seems to be having fun.

I'm about ready to lose my shit. Alex glances at me, his eyebrows raised. I think he's wondering if I'm going to do something.

The music shifts again and the guy stops Kendra, holding her tight against him. He leans his face near her ear and says something. Kendra shakes her head. He speaks again, his arms still around her, then he starts pulling her in the direction of the stairs.

I'm halfway to them before I realize what I'm doing. I stop in front of them and Kendra looks at me, blinking in surprise. Her eyes are glassy, her face flushed.

She's so drunk, she slurs my name. "Wesson?"

I level the guy with a stare. "Let go."

"Dude, chill," he says, pulling Kendra against him.

I step closer, but don't say a word.

"What, is this your girlfriend or something?" he says. "Because she's leaving with me, bro."

I hold this jackass's eyes for a long moment and lift one eyebrow, like I'm bored with him.

He makes a show of looking me up and down. "What are you going to do with one arm?"

Kendra pushes against him and mumbles something I can't hear.

The tension thickens. If this goes to blows, I'm pretty much screwed. I only have one arm. But I don't give a fuck.

"Come on, baby," I say to Kendra. I shouldn't call her that, but fuck it, at this point I might as well go all in. My eyes flick back to the guy. My voice is hard, my face still. "Get your hands off my girl. Now."

One eye twitches and he drops his arms. Kendra stumbles, but I'm there to catch her, drawing her against me with my good arm.

I'm vaguely aware of Kendra's friends around us, the douchebag backing away. A bouncer looks on. But I don't give a shit about any of them. I just want to get Kendra home.

She leans against me and giggles. "Weston? Am I your girl?"

"Yeah, baby," I say. "You are tonight. Let's get you out of here."

"But it's my birthday."

"Not yet," I say. "We'll celebrate later."

She laughs again and I glance up to find Alex standing with his arm around Mia.

"I've got her," I say. "I'll get her home safe."

"Thanks," Alex says, and Mia hands me Kendra's purse.

I keep my arm wrapped around Kendra and lead her to the stairs. She leans against me, and I help her down each step. Miraculously, we make it to the bottom and out to the street without falling. I'm glad my car isn't far away. I get Kendra into the passenger's seat. She leans her head back and giggles again.

She babbles about her night on the drive home, but she's not making much sense. I wonder if she's going to remember this tomorrow. She's pretty trashed; she might not.

We get to her house and I help her out of the car. She's barefoot—she must have slipped off her shoes in my car—but I leave them there. She stumbles to the bedroom and I leave her for a second to get a glass of water and some aspirin.

When I come back, she's twisting and contorting, trying to reach behind her back.

"Can you get my zipper?" she asks. "Can't reach."

Oh shit. Okay. This is fine. "Sure."

I set the water and aspirin on her nightstand and step in behind her, putting my good hand on her arm to steady her. She leans against the bed, tilting forward slightly. Her hair is in the way, so I brush it to the side and over one shoulder. Then I pinch the zipper between my thumb and forefinger and lower it. Slowly.

My heart pounds in my chest. I'm hyper aware of how close we are. Of the skin I'm exposing as I open her dress. Her back is bare—she's not wearing a bra. I swallow hard. The dress falls and I quickly back up to her doorway.

She turns around, her pink nipples erect. Her tits are small, but they're perfectly shaped. And her body. Holy fuck. She's tight and toned with the hint of a line running down her abs. She's lean, but not boyish, with a narrow waist and a gorgeous curve to her hips.

I know I'm staring, but I can't tear my eyes away.

"Oh my god, feels good to get out of that dress." She lifts her arms and shakes out her hair. "I gotta pee."

She walks past me, pulling her white lace panties down as she goes. She steps out of them in the hallway and goes into the bathroom, leaving them lying on the floor.

I'm so stunned, I don't move. The toilet flushes, making me jump, and she comes out, completely naked.

She waxes. Kendra fucking waxes her pussy.

I'm literally going to die right now.

She stumbles a little and puts her hand against the wall for balance. "Holy shit. So drunk."

I shake my head so I break out of this trance and quit watching my naked roommate. "Come on, get some pajamas on or something."

She laughs and walks past me into her room. "You hate my pajamas."

"Baby, you need to get dressed." God, Weston, stop calling her *baby*.

"I'm good." She falls face down on her bed.

She's on top of the covers, her ass right there. Fuck me. Did she pass out? Should I leave her like that? She's going to get cold.

I groan and go over to the bed. It's impossible to move her with one arm and not be all over her hot as fuck body. I have to lean over her and slide my arm beneath her hips to roll her over. Then I pick up her legs and swivel her so she's facing the right direction. She's still half awake and she sighs as I pull the covers up.

"Do you hate me?" she asks.

I pause, still leaning over her, my hand on her comforter. "No, I don't hate you."

She slow blinks, but when her eyes open, they focus on me. Before I can move out of the way, she reaches up and touches my face.

"Do you like me?"

I take a breath. "Yeah, Kendra, I like you. I like you a lot."

Her hand slides down my neck and she grasps my shirt. "Come here." She tugs, trying to pull me closer.

Oh god. I would love to kiss her. Get my mouth all over her. She's naked, biting her lip, making my cock ache.

But she's also sloppy drunk, and that is not how this is going to go down.

I resist, leaning away and unlatching her hand from my shirt. "Not tonight."

"But tonight I'm your girl." Her eyes drift closed.

"Yeah, baby, you are," I say, backing up toward the door. "But you won't be tomorrow."

15

KENDRA

My pounding head wakes me up. At first I can't remember what's real and what was a dream. Was someone really knocking on my forehead with a tiny hammer? No, that's just the headache. And my stomach feels like it's been ripped to shreds. I cover my eyes with my hand and groan.

God, what did I do to myself last night? I was totally fine at dinner. I had a couple of drinks, so I felt a little buzz—just enough to make me smiley. But at Monkey Club, my friend Lori started buying shots. After that, everything gets pretty blurry.

I roll over onto my side and squeeze my eyes shut. I don't even want to know what time it is. But something feels weird. I crack an eye open and lift the sheets.

I'm naked.

Oh, no. Oh, no, no, no. Why am I naked? I can't remember. I freeze, my back muscles clenching. Is there someone in bed with me? I didn't have sex last night, did I? Please let me be alone. Please let me be alone.

I glance over my shoulder, but there's no one there. The

covers aren't messed up like someone slept next to me. I breathe out a sigh of relief.

But why am I naked?

I search my memory, hating myself for getting so drunk. I remember the club. The music. Dancing. Some guy buying me a shot. More dancing with my friends. Mia trying to get us to leave. Me doing another shot at the bar. Lori buying our whole group a round. I have a feeling I drank twice as much as my friends. God, once you cross the line of no inhibitions, decision-making goes right out the window.

After that, everything is too booze soaked and hazy to make sense. Music and lights. My head swimming. How did I even get home?

I guess Mia must have made sure I got here, but I don't remember her coming in with me. Which is weird, because if I was that smashed, it seems like she would have brought me in and made sure I got to bed. That's something Mia would do.

But I only remember being in my room, trying to get my dress off.

Oh.

Oh, no.

Weston.

He was in my room. He took off my dress. And I was definitely not wearing a bra. Oh fuck me running, I got naked in front of him.

That's just great. I stood in front of Seattle's hottest boob job doctor, showing off my tiny ta-tas. He'll probably ask me if I want him to give me an upgrade.

Fuck.

I'm so embarrassed. I cover my face with my hands and groan again. I'll just stay here forever. I'll never leave the room again. At least not until he moves out.

And I'm never, ever, ever drinking again. Ever.

When I uncover my face, I notice something on my night-stand. A glass of water and a bottle of aspirin.

Well, shit. That was a nice thing for him to do.

I sit up and take two aspirin, washing them down with the lukewarm water. My bladder isn't going to cooperate with my plan to live in my bedroom for the next couple of months, so I get up and put on some clothes.

With a deep breath, I open my bedroom door.

The first thing I notice is my panties from last night on the floor in the middle of the hallway, and I want to die of humiliation all over again. The second thing I notice is the smell of bacon coming from the kitchen.

What the hell?

I make a quick stop to use the bathroom. Glancing in the mirror, I cringe. I look like a hungover panda after a one night stand. I wash my face—no makeup is much better than smudged going-out makeup—and grab a hair tie. While I walk down the hall, I put my hair up and listen to the sounds of crackling and popping. The smell of food beckons me on, calling to my raw stomach.

Is Weston cooking? He doesn't cook. I've never seen him do anything in that kitchen except pour a glass of bourbon.

I come in and he's standing at the stove with a spatula, dressed in just a t-shirt and boxer briefs. He doesn't seem to notice me, so I sit down at the little kitchen table.

There is something about a man cooking in his underwear. Even when it's Weston Reid.

Especially when it's Weston Reid.

He glances over his shoulder, but keeps doing what he's doing. I give up trying to be even a tiny bit dignified and lay my head down on the table. I feel like I got run over.

A few minutes later, and without saying a word, he sets a plate in front of me. I sit up and my mouth hangs open. It's a breakfast sandwich with an egg, cheese, and bacon, all on a toasted English muffin. He puts a cup of coffee next to the plate.

"Might wanna close your mouth," he says, pushing the plate closer. "I'm not going to feed it to you."

"What is this?"

He looks at me like I'm an idiot. "What the fuck does it look like? It's hangover food."

"You cooked me breakfast?" I ask, staring at the sandwich.

He just shrugs and goes back to the stove.

I didn't think I'd be able to eat, but this smells amazing. I take a bite and my eyes close. It's salty and bacony and buttery and the cheese is all melty.

"This is delicious," I say. "I didn't think you knew how to cook."

He puts his breakfast on the table—his is just some eggs and a couple of slices of bacon—and slides into the chair across from me. "Of course I can cook."

"I don't think you have since you've lived here."

He shrugs again. "You always do. But if you want me to, I can."

I stare at him for a second, but his brow furrows and he focuses on his meal.

After I eat about half of it, my stomach decides it's done. I sip my coffee in silence while he finishes his breakfast. I'm not sure what to say. Do I mention that I remember he saw me naked last night? Do I pretend it didn't happen? I guess *he's* going to pretend it didn't happen. If he was going to tease me about it, he probably would have done so already.

He's so quiet. Even for him. He finishes eating and takes our plates to the sink, still without saying a word. I'm getting a weird vibe from him. Did I do something to make him angry? I doubt he'd cook me breakfast if he was mad at me. Did I do something horribly embarrassing—other than taking my clothes off? That's likely. He seems so tense, standing at the sink, rinsing off the dishes.

"I'm sorry about last night," I say. "I'm sure I was acting really stupid."

He doesn't turn around. "Don't worry about it."

"Well, I am worried about it," I say. "I was so drunk, I probably did a hundred embarrassing things. I'm just glad I got home okay."

He glances over his shoulder. "Do you remember coming home?"

"Not really," I say. "I remember being at the club. And I remember being home later. In between is pretty hazy. I, um..." My cheeks heat up. "I guess you got me into bed?"

"Yeah."

"Thanks," I say. "And for the water. And the aspirin."

"Sure."

I take a deep breath and lean back in my chair, holding my coffee. The food is helping and the aspirin is taking the edge off my headache. "Did Mia bring me home? It's weird that she didn't come in, although maybe I just don't remember."

He doesn't answer.

My head clears a little and more of the night comes back to me. Someone's hands on me, holding me too tight. His voice in my ear. I wince. I think I was dancing with some guy. But then he tried to get me to leave with him. Something about going out to his car. I remember him dragging me off the dance floor.

Holy shit. Weston.

I gasp and look up. "You were there last night."

"What?"

"You were there, at the club." It all floods back to me in a rush. "That guy was trying to make me leave with him and all of a sudden, you were standing there. You stared him down until he backed off and then you took me home."

Weston grunts and starts down the hallway.

"Wait a second, don't leave." I stand up and follow. "Why were you there?"

He stops outside his bedroom door, his back still to me.

"I'm just... well... thank you for that," I say, my tongue tripping over the words. I'm so confused. "But I don't get what you were doing there. Did you follow me?"

He puts his hand on the door frame, like he needs to brace himself. "Yeah, I did."

"Why?"

"I don't know," he snaps. He turns around. "But it's a fucking good thing I did. You were so drunk you almost let some jackass take you outside."

"Yeah, I know, that was bad," I say. "I'm sure my friends weren't going to let that go down, though."

"Your friends weren't doing jack shit," he says. "Just letting him fucking manhandle you."

"Well, I'm glad you—"

"Don't," he says. "I shouldn't have even been there. You want to be some asshole's quick fuck next to a dumpster? Knock yourself out next time. I don't give a shit."

He walks into his room and shuts the door behind him.

I stand in the hallway, blinking at his door. What the hell? Asshole Weston rears his head again. Fabulous. I was just trying to figure out what happened.

"Asshole."

I go back to my room and step over my dress, then crawl under the covers. Closing my eyes, I take a deep breath. Why is he so hot and cold? He takes such good care of me, but then he's angry about it? What did I do? I wish last night wasn't so fuzzy.

I think back, trying to remember more details. I was in bed, Weston tucking me in. What did I say to him? *Tonight I'm your girl*? Why would I say that? I think I tried to kiss him and he had to push me away. That brings a renewed flood of embarrassment. Maybe that's why he's mad.

And there's something else. How did he answer? *Yeah, baby, you are.* He was calling me *baby*. He said it at the club. And again when he was getting me to bed. Why was he calling me that? It's kind of sweet, but Weston isn't a nickname guy. I'm not his baby, or his girl. But I remember him saying both.

I don't think I've ever met a more confusing, infuriating, aggravating... yet intriguing and captivating man. Just when I think I have him figured out, he cooks me breakfast. And then stomps away, angry for reasons I don't understand.

With another deep breath, I roll over. He can be a dick all he wants. I'm taking a nap.

16

WESTON

*T*he club thing seems to blow over. Kendra doesn't ask about it again, which is good, because I don't fucking want to talk about it. I don't want to explain to her why I went down there. What it did to me when I saw some guy with his hands on her.

All these goddamn feelings are screwing with my head.

Monday at work I get a call from my contractor, updating me on the progress on my house. It's like I'd forgotten I even have a home—that I really live somewhere else. Things are finally moving forward and he gives me a projected finish date. I thank him and put it on my calendar. I'll have to arrange to have everything brought out of storage, and move what I have at Kendra's.

It's good that I'll move out soon. Maybe when we're not living under the same roof, I'll be able to get over whatever it is that's messing me up lately.

Kendra's distant all week. Doesn't talk to me much when I'm home. Probably because I snapped at her on Sunday. I shouldn't have been such a dick to her. She didn't do anything wrong. She got drunk. So what? And what did I expect her to do when she figured out I followed her? *Not* ask me about it? I should have just said I was worried about her and left it at that. Accepted her thank-you like a decent person, instead of throwing a tantrum like a fucking two-year-old.

Friday I don't have any patients after noon, so I head home early. I keep flexing my right arm, trying to keep it from getting stiff again. I've had my cast off for a few days, which is such a relief. But the time it was immobilized took its toll. It feels weak.

Kendra isn't home when I get there, but she gets back about ten minutes later while I'm staring into the fridge, trying to decide what to eat.

She has a big garment bag slung over her shoulder. She gives me a weak smile and shuffles to her room without saying anything.

"Hey," I say, following her out of the kitchen. She's been quiet lately, but this is different. Something is off; she looks upset. "You okay?"

"Eh," she says and goes into her room.

I stop in her doorway while she hangs the bag over her closet door. "What's going on?"

"Oh, nothing. Just picked up my bridesmaid dress for Alex and Mia's wedding." She sighs. "It's... no, it's nice. It's fine."

"Fine?" I arch an eyebrow at her. "What's wrong with it?"

She laughs. "There's nothing wrong with it." She unzips the bag, revealing pale lavender fabric. "I think Mia's sister probably picked them, but they're pretty. I'm just kind of over bridesmaid dresses in general."

"Why?"

She opens her closet and points to a line of garment bags shoved to one side. "This lavender thing makes nine. One more bridesmaid gig and I'll be in the double digits."

Holy shit. Nine weddings? I don't think I have nine numbers in my contacts; at least not nine numbers I recognize.

"God, number ten will probably be Caleb again," she continues. "He'll get remarried before I ever—" She stops, pressing her lips together. "Never mind. I sound like I'm whining. I'm really excited for Alex and Mia. They're amazing together. I've never seen my brother so happy."

"Alex is a good guy."

"Yeah, he is."

She closes the closet door with a sigh.

"You sure you're okay?" I ask.

She sinks onto the edge of her bed. "I had lunch with my mother. She's... I don't know."

That's strange. I always thought the Lawsons had a nice little white-picket-fence thing going on. "You don't get along or something?"

She shrugs. "I don't see her very often."

I lean against her doorframe. "Why not?"

"She walked out on us when we were kids."

I pause for a second, not sure what to say. I'm not usually the guy people confide in. "Really?"

"Yeah," she says. "She left and we didn't see her for months. Then she and my dad came to some sort of arrangement, but we still didn't spend a lot of time with her. I don't think she wanted a family."

"That must have been hard."

She nods. "Now I see her a few times a year. She took me to lunch for my birthday, but mostly she just criticized my life choices. Sometimes I wonder why she bothers with us at all. I guess she's not as hard on my brothers, but still. If she didn't want us, it would have been better if she'd just stayed away. Her half-hearted attempts at being a mother make her abandonment sting all over again."

It's weird how much I want to hug Kendra right now, but I stay where I am. "Shit, that's brutal. I'm sorry."

"It's okay," she says. "It doesn't usually bother me that much.

But there have been times I could have used a mother, you know?"

"Yeah, I do know. My mom died when I was eleven." Oh my god, why did I just say that?

"Oh... Weston, I'm sorry. I didn't know."

I look away. I never talk about my mother. Why am I doing it now? But I find myself continuing. "She had breast cancer. No one even told me she was sick until it was really bad."

"That must have been awful," she says. "I guess I should be grateful my mom is alive, at least."

"No, that's not why..." Fuck, I'm terrible at this. "I don't mean I had it worse than you. I just mean, I get it. I understand what it's like to not have a mother. At least mine isn't just too shitty to be there for me. It's not her fault she's gone."

"Still sucks, though."

"Yeah. It does. You know, I always figured you guys had a perfect family."

"No, not really," she says. "My dad's a good guy, though. He did his best."

"You have me beat there," I say, my tone wry. "My father's a prick."

"Is he?"

I nod. "Always was. He was cheating on my mom, even when she got sick. He never treated her very well, but once she got cancer, she pretty much stopped existing. He hired nurses to take care of her, but he was never around. He ignored me until I got to high school. And then he just wanted to make sure I kept my shit together so I could go to med school."

"Oh my god," she says. "I guess now I know why you never talk about your family."

"Yeah."

She's quiet for a minute, then meets my eyes. "Thanks."

"For what?"

She just smiles and gets up, squeezing my arm as she walks by. "I need to go to the store. Wanna come?"

"Sure."

I WALK beside Kendra down the aisle of a grocery store while she pushes a cart. We don't talk much. I love that about her. She likes to talk sometimes, but she doesn't have to fill every silence with a bunch of inane bullshit. We both grab things off the shelves, placing them in the cart, moving slowly through the store.

She glances at me and smiles. It's nice feeling like we're back to normal. Things were so strained between us all week. I don't want to admit how much that bothered me.

Maybe it wasn't such a bad thing to bring up my mother when she was talking about hers. I can't remember the last time I told anyone about her. Usually I avoid the subject; I don't want people's pity. But Kendra didn't react with pity; she simply understood. Sometimes life deals you a shitty hand, and we've both been there.

It felt like we connected. Is that what it's like to bond with another person?

I don't know what the fuck is wrong with Kendra's mother, though. Kendra is... well, she's kind of amazing. It pisses me off that her mom blows her off like that. And she criticizes her? Sounds like my father. What could she have to criticize? Kendra's independent and smart. She's one of the most selfless people I've ever met. She drops everything to help Caleb with his daughter. She took care of me for weeks when I certainly hadn't done anything to deserve it. It's her mom's loss. But the fact that it hurts Kendra bothers me.

"Oh, coffee," she says. "Don't let me forget."

"That would be an emergency situation for you," I say, nudging her with my elbow.

"It would," she says. "Do you need anything else?"

"I don't think so."

"How's your arm doing?" she asks.

I extend it and twist my wrist around. "Not bad. Stiff, but it's great to be out of that cast."

She reaches over and squeezes my left bicep. "Are your arms lopsided now?"

I glare at her. "Fuck off."

She laughs and pauses in front of the pasta sauce before choosing a jar. "You like this one, right?"

"I have no idea."

"Yeah, it's this kind." She puts it in the cart.

How does she even know that?

We double back to the coffee aisle and she grabs what she needs.

"Oh, you know what? I should get the ingredients to make lasagna again. You loved it last time."

She starts down the aisle, but I stop and stare at her. I did love her lasagna.

She remembers.

But that's the thing, she remembers everything about me. A hundred details that most people wouldn't think are important. How I take my coffee. Foods I like. Movies I've never seen that she wants to watch together. The last book I read and whether or not there's a sequel.

No one has ever given a shit about me the way she does. Maybe my mom did before she got sick, but no one since then. Certainly not my father. I don't have any other close family. I've never had a lot of friends. I'm too much of a dick to people. They don't stick around. The women I'm with are always temporary. The ones I've seen more than once are only interested because

I'm good-looking and have money. They don't care about me beyond what I can do for them.

Kendra does. She *cares*.

My chest squeezes and it has nothing to do with my ribs. Lasagna? Fucking *lasagna* is what breaks me?

She stops and turns around, her eyebrows lifted. "You okay?"

I cross the distance to her and slide my hand to the back of her neck. Her eyes widen as I lean in close, but she doesn't pull away.

My lips press against hers. At first it's *me* kissing *her*, but then her mouth softens, her face tilts. She melts into my kiss, wrapping her arms around my waist.

Nothing could have prepared me for what it would feel like to kiss her; she's overwhelming. I'm immersed in her—in her taste, her scent. In the way her soft lips feel silky against mine. My mouth moves against hers, slow and tender. I get a taste of her tongue and take the kiss deeper. Wind my fingers through her hair.

Our tongues dance in a slow caress. I can't get enough. She feels so good and I don't give a fuck that we're standing in the aisle at a grocery store. I could kiss her forever.

Eventually, I have to stop. I slowly pull back. Our lips part, and my eyes open.

Her arms drop, and she gasps. "Oh."

17

KENDRA

*D*azed, I step back, staring at Weston. He just kissed me. Right here, in the grocery store. And it wasn't a little kiss. Not a hello kiss, or a thank-you kiss, or a silly little we're-just-roommates-and-I'm-messing-around kiss.

That was a real kiss. And oh my god, it was good.

His eyes are glued to mine and there's something in his expression I've never seen before. He's vulnerable.

I should say something else, but my mind is blank. All that's there is the feel of his mouth on mine, my lips still tingling, my heart racing.

"Wow." It comes out breathy, barely a word at all.

His mouth moves in the hint of a smile and his piercing gray eyes sparkle. "We should probably go."

I nod and he takes the cart, pushing it toward the front of the store. We stand in line and I'm like a zombie, staring at nothing. It's good one of us is still functional, but it certainly isn't me. He unloads the cart, nods to the cashier, pulls out his wallet.

What just happened? Why did he do that? I was talking about what, lasagna? I didn't think Italian food would get a guy hot for me, though they do say the way to a guy's heart is through his stomach. But this isn't just *a guy*. This is *Weston*. Angry, cocky, asshole Weston. Fun, sexy, captivating Weston.

He just kissed me. And I kissed him back. Holy shit, did I ever kiss him back.

We load the groceries into his car and drive home in silence. I'm buzzing with anticipation, wondering what happens now. Is he going to say anything? Explain himself? Are we going to move on and pretend it didn't happen? There's no way that's going to work. Whatever that was, it broke something open between us and there's no going back now.

Is he going to do it again?

We get home and bring the bags inside. I set mine on the counter and feel Weston come up behind me. I freeze. He's so close—almost touching. His hand brushes down my arm, sending sparks dancing across my skin. I look over my shoulder and he touches my chin, the slight pressure of his fingers enough to turn me around. He watches me while my heart beats the seconds, his eyes intense.

Without a word, he leans down and takes my mouth in a hard kiss. Hauls me close, pressing me against him. He sucks on my lower lip, sliding his tongue across it, and my body comes alive. Desire surges through me, hot and so tempting.

His hand moves up my back and he fists it through my hair. I wrap my arms around his waist, my palms splaying across his back. His mouth demands more and I give it to him—let him in as deep as he wants to go. He answers with a low growl in the back of his throat, his hand tightening in my hair.

He is kissing the fuck out of me and I'm powerless to stop him.

The urgency between us heightens, like a rope being pulled tight. His hand cups my cheek and he alternates between deep and shallow. Kissing my lips, his so warm and soft and delicious.

Then delving in with his tongue, throwing me off balance, kissing away my breath.

His hands slide down to my jeans and he fumbles with the button. Reality comes crashing back and I pull away, breaking the kiss. I let go of him and try to move back, but I'm pressed up against the counter.

The shock of separating seems to leave us both reeling. We're breathing hard, still standing so close we're touching. Weston's jaw brushes against my temple, his chest rising and falling against me. After a long moment, he steps back.

This is insane. What are we doing? What am *I* doing? I can't let this happen.

"I'm sorry," I breathe.

He doesn't answer, just stares at me, his brow furrowed, his gray eyes like a storm cloud.

"I just..." I falter, trying to say something. Trying to keep this from going nuclear right here in my kitchen. "I don't think we should... This is... God, Weston, I don't know what to say."

"You don't want me to kiss you," he says, his voice strangely quiet.

"No, I..." I close my eyes for a second. Why is this so hard? This is a bad idea. *Weston* is a bad idea. I know this.

Then why do I have to fight to hold myself back from him?

"We're good, Weston," I say. "We're good the way we are. This would mess everything up."

"Looks like I already did that," he says.

"No, you didn't. I just... I didn't expect this," I say. "I don't really know how to feel about it."

"Because you don't know how you feel about me."

"No, because I don't know how *you* feel about *me*," I say. "You're not exactly good at communicating your feelings."

He looks away.

"Weston, I don't know what you want from me," I say. "I don't think *you* know what you want from me."

"Why can't we just let this happen?" he asks. "Maybe I *don't* know. Why can't we find out?"

Tears spring to my eyes and a lump in my throat threatens to choke off my words. "Because I like you too fucking much. And I don't want to get hurt."

The look on his face makes me ache. His eyes turn into deep pools of emotion and his lips part. He starts to say something, but I shake my head.

"Don't lie to me," I say. "Don't tell me you wouldn't hurt me. We both know you would. You could take me back to your bedroom right now and fuck me senseless, and maybe it would even mean something. But probably not. Because it never does, does it? Sex is just a thing you do for fun, because it feels good. That's not how I am. I've tried it, but casual sex never works for me."

"I never said this was casual," he says.

"No, but do you ever have anything else?" I ask. "Is any woman more than a diversion to you?"

His jaw tightens and his eyes turn flinty. I keep waiting for him to blow up at me, but he just keeps staring.

"I'm sorry, Weston," I say, my voice quiet. "If we let this happen, I'll only get attached to you in ways you don't want."

Leaving the groceries sitting out on the counter, I brush past him and walk quickly to my room. I need to get out from under those eyes. I know I'm doing the right thing, but the ache in my chest—and between my legs—is making it so hard. If he keeps staring at me like that I'm going to cave.

He doesn't say anything when I walk away. No angry reply. Part of me wants him to come after me. To lie to me and say I'm different. That I'd be more than a quick fuck, and he wouldn't bail when things got real.

But he doesn't.

I shut my door softly behind me, and for once it latches on the first try. I touch my lips, still sensitive and swollen from his kiss. I can't deny how good it felt. There was something there, like an unspoken word passing between us in the heat of our kiss.

Finally.

I flop down on the bed. I have to stop thinking like that. But I'm so confused. The swirl of emotions inside me is leaving me dizzy.

I think I should get out of the house for a little while, so I grab my phone to text Mia. But it buzzes as soon as I pull it out of my pocket. It's a text from Weston.

My hands tremble as I swipe the screen.

Weston: You're not a diversion.

Me: Then what am I?

Weston: I don't know.

Me: Exactly. You don't know.

Weston: If you were any other woman, I'd know exactly what I wanted. None of this makes any sense to me.

Me: You're in good company there. None of it makes sense to me either.

Weston: I'm sorry, Kendra. This is hard for me, I never know the right things to say. I don't want to hurt you.

Me: Okay, well, that's a start.

Weston: I don't know what else to say.

Me: Me neither.

There's a pause and I wonder if he's going to leave it at that.

Weston: Do you want me to go?

His question brings the sting of tears to my eyes.

Me: No. I just need space tonight.

Weston: OK

I put my phone down and take a deep breath. The floor

creaks a few times, but I'm not sure what he's doing. About five minutes later, my phone buzzes again.

Weston: I put away the groceries.

I burst out laughing—a testament to how ragged my emotions are.

Me: Thank you.

I lie back on my bed and stare at the ceiling, wondering what the hell is happening to me.

18

KENDRA

*T*he house is quiet when I get up in the morning. Weston comes out later, while I'm sitting on the couch with a cup of coffee. He doesn't ignore me, but he doesn't engage in conversation either. He meets my eyes, mutters *good morning*, then goes about his business.

We orbit around each other for most of the day. I try to be where he isn't, without making it look like I'm avoiding him. I know we can't go on like this forever, but I'm not sure what else to do.

Afternoon rolls around and I change my clothes. My birthday is tomorrow, but I'm having dinner with my dad and brothers tonight. At least that will get me out of the house and my mind off Weston.

I come out of my room to find Weston putting on a coat.

"Hey. I'm leaving too," I say. "I'm having dinner at my dad's tonight."

"I know," he says. "So am I."

"What?"

"I'm having dinner at your dad's."

I blink at him a few times. "You're having dinner at my dad's?"

"Yes," he says. "Alex invited me."

"Alex invited you?" I ask.

"Are you just going to keep repeating what I say in the form of a question?"

I put my hands on my hips. "Alex invited you to my birthday dinner with my family? You're kidding."

He pulls his phone out of his pocket and taps the screen a few times, then holds it up, showing me their text conversation. Alex did indeed invite Weston to come to dinner, and he accepted.

"Why didn't he tell me?" I ask.

Weston shrugs. "Maybe he figures we live together, so we actually speak to each other." He puts his phone back in his pocket and looks away. "I won't go if you don't want me to."

Weston having dinner with my family? This is obviously a terrible idea, but there's something in his tone. I think if I tell him I don't want him to come, I'll actually hurt his feelings. When we first met, I would have said Weston didn't have feelings to hurt. But I'm not so sure about that anymore.

"No, you should come," I say.

"You sure?"

"Yeah." I pick up my purse. "I'm sure."

He nods and opens the door, holding it for me. I grab my coat and head outside.

"Don't worry, I won't try to make out with you at the dinner table in front of your family," he says as I walk past.

I glance at him over my shoulder and laugh. "Oh, he's making jokes now?"

He just smiles and walks out to his car.

We pull up to my dad's house and park on the street. Caleb

and Alex's cars are already here. I take a deep breath as I get out of the car. This should be interesting.

I open the front door and Weston follows me inside. Caleb is sitting on the couch with Charlotte, reading her a book. She looks up and ducks behind her dad's arm.

"It's okay, Bug," he says and stands. "Hey, birthday girl."

I step in to give him a hug. "Hey. Thanks."

He shakes hands with Weston; he doesn't appear to be surprised to see him here. "Reid."

"Lawson."

I roll my eyes at their stoic bro-greeting. "Where's Dad?"

"Kitchen," Caleb says.

"Hi, Bug," I say to Charlotte. She waves at me and gives Weston a shy smile. I nudge Weston. "Hey, look at that, she likes you."

"Are you shocked?" he asks.

"No, she's just a little shy when she meets someone new," I say.

"Ah," he says. He smiles at Charlotte. "Hi, Bug."

"Hi," she whispers, then jumps up and runs to hide behind Caleb.

"Hey, baby sister," Alex says as he comes out of the kitchen. "Happy birthday."

I give Alex a hug. "Thanks."

"Hey man, thanks for coming," he says, and shakes hands with Weston.

I watch Alex, hoping for some hint as to why he invited Weston. But he's sporting his poker face.

"The bad news is, none of us cooked," Alex says. "The good news is, Mia and I brought Indian food."

"Sounds perfect." I glance up at Weston. "You like Indian food?"

"Yeah, Indian is great," he says.

We head into the kitchen and my dad is getting a stack of plates out of a cupboard. I love seeing him doing so well after his back surgery. He still walks with a cane, but he's much more mobile than he was before.

"Hey, Daddy," I say.

"Happy birthday," he says and gives me a kiss on the cheek. His eyes move past me and a look of confusion passes across his face.

"Oh, Dad, this is Weston." I realize I haven't told my dad about Weston moving in, and I'm hit with a wave of guilt. It didn't come up last time I was here, and I've been so busy lately. "He's my roommate."

"Excuse me?" Dad says. "What happened to the woman Caleb works with?"

I laugh. "Oh, no, Dad. There was a bit of a misunderstanding. Caleb said *colleague*, and I assumed he meant *female colleague*, but it was Weston."

Dad looks Weston up and down. "Is that so?"

I'm caught between laughing—because all my dad needs to complete the *protective father* motif is a shotgun in his hands—and wincing because Weston is standing stiff and straight, a bewildered expression on his face.

I wonder if Weston's ever met a girl's father before. Maybe not.

"Yes, Dad, that's so. He's renting the extra bedroom while his house is being remodeled. And he's..." I pause and glance up at him. He's what? My friend? An amazing kisser? So sexy I could die? "He's my friend, so it's cool."

Dad glares at Weston and grumbles something under his breath, then walks to the dining room, leaning on his cane.

"Sorry," I say to Weston. "He's, you know... a dad."

Weston shrugs. "It's okay." His eyes linger on my face and I'm momentarily transfixed by his gaze. He's hypnotic.

"Hey, Kendra..." Mia's voice trails off.

I blink, rousing myself from... whatever that was. "Hi."

Her eyes move between me and Weston a few times. "Oh-kay. Happy birthday."

"Thanks."

"Hey, Weston," she says. "It's really nice of you to bring Kendra to dinner."

I raise my eyebrows at Mia and her word choice. Bring me to dinner?

"Sure," he says.

I let out a heavy breath. This awkward-introductions thing is wearing me out. "So, are we going to eat, or what?"

"Yeah," Mia says, grabbing the plates my dad got out. "Everything's on the table."

We file into the dining room and find seats. Weston and I wind up sitting next to each other. Everyone dishes up and the spicy aromas fill the room. Conversation buzzes around the table. Caleb talks about work. Alex and Mia discuss their wedding plans. I let everyone know how freelancing is going. Caleb brings up sports and pretty soon my dad and brothers are deep in a discussion about football.

Weston doesn't talk much. I glance at him out of the corner of my eye, but he doesn't seem uncomfortable, despite the occasional glowering look my dad shoots at him. He's quiet, but it's normal-quiet. Weston-quiet.

His leg touches mine and he doesn't move away. But neither do I. My cheeks warm and I pretend I'm not hyper-aware of how close we are. He moves a little and his leg rubs against mine. My heart beats faster. *Calm down, Kendra.* He's oblivious to the world half the time. He probably doesn't even realize he's doing it.

Suddenly I feel his hand on my leg. Oh god, what is he doing?

His hand moves and I struggle to keep my expression calm.

Warmth pools between my legs. Just this small touch is enough to make my mind go to places it really shouldn't. Especially in front of my brothers—and my dad. Is he messing with me?

But then the strangest thing happens. Weston doesn't grab my leg or run his hand up my thigh. Instead, he shifts a little and crosses his wrist over my forearm. Then he slides his fingers through mine, our palms pressing together.

Did Weston Reid just reach under the table to secretly hold my hand?

Outwardly, there's no change in his demeanor. He seems relaxed, almost bored—the usual for him. But I sneak a peek at him and a hint of a smile plays on his lips. He squeezes my hand and after hesitating for a beat, I squeeze back.

I'm wondering who this is and what he did with Weston.

Eventually, everyone finishes eating and the conversation dies down. Mia and Alex bring in a chocolate cake. Weston squeezes my hand again before letting go. I flick my eyes to his face and he's watching me, his eyes smoldering.

After dessert, Mia gives me not-so-subtle nod toward the kitchen. Everyone else heads for the living room, but I follow Mia.

"Holy tension, Batman," Mia says. "Did something happen between you two? He was totally fucking you in his mind."

"Wow, straight to the point," I say.

She wrinkles her nose. "Sorry. You know I have no filter."

"No kidding," I say. "But you answer my question first. Why did Alex invite him to dinner tonight?"

"Oh, so you see... he was... I mean... I said..." She sighs. "Alex was impressed by what Weston did for you last weekend. And I might have told him about the whole *they're roommates who started out hating each other* thing, and we both got a little overexcited. I don't remember who had the idea to invite him first, so I guess you can blame both of us."

"You guys need to quit meddling," I say.

She grins a little. "Yeah, but it's nice having him here, isn't it?"

"Maybe."

"Okay, now you answer my question. Did something happen?"

"No. Yes. Oh my god, Mia, I don't know what's going on."

"I need specifics," she says.

Deep breath. "He kissed me yesterday."

Mia looks like she's going to explode. She scrunches up her shoulders and puts a hand to her mouth, like she needs to hold back a squeal. "Where? How? When? How was it? What happened then?"

"It was at the grocery store," I say. "Don't ask me why, I don't get it. So he kissed me and then we went home, and he did it again in the kitchen."

"Oh, in the kitchen," Mia says. "So hot."

"No, it wasn't." *Liar.* "Okay, yeah, it was. But I stopped it."

"Why?"

"Because it's *Weston*," I say.

"So?"

"You don't know him like I do."

"I know you thought he was an asshole," she says. "And then maybe not such an asshole?"

"He can be, but that's not the problem," I say.

"And the problem is?"

"I doubt the guy's ever had a serious relationship in his life. He's not the commitment type."

"People can change," Mia says.

"Can they?" I ask. "I mean, can they really, truly change? I don't know. Maybe they can uncover something that was already there. But what are the chances of a grown man letting go of

years of being an egotistical man-whore? I'm supposed to
believe that he's suddenly going to change for me?"

She shrugs. "What makes you think he *isn't* uncovering
something that was already there?"

I raise an eyebrow at her. "Mia, he's an ass. He's always been
an ass. Doing a few nice things once in a while doesn't change
who he is. Overall, he's out for number one. The man makes his
living giving women bigger boobs. He chose that specialty
specifically because of the money. He's not like Caleb, who really
cares about his patients."

Mia's mouth twitches in a smile. "He doesn't talk about his
other patients, does he?"

"What other patients?"

"He does post-mastectomy reconstructions," she says. "For
free."

"What? How do you know?"

"A few months ago I was assigned a patient who'd under-
gone a double mastectomy," she says. "She was in remission and
pursuing breast reconstruction. Ultimately, she couldn't afford
the portion her insurance didn't pay, so she dropped off my
patient list. But a week or so ago, her file came back to me, with a
certain Dr. Reid listed as her surgeon. So of course I looked up
the details. Kendra, not only is he doing the surgery for free, he's
paying for her hospital stay."

"He's what?"

She nods and adjusts her glasses. "Yep. And I did a little
digging; this isn't the first one. Just at my hospital, he does a
bunch of these every year. He doesn't always pay all the costs,
but he doesn't charge for the surgery, or the follow up treat-
ments. It's quite a process, and really expensive."

I'm so stunned, I can't even respond for a few seconds. Oh
my god, his mother. "Holy shit, Mia, his mom died of breast

cancer. I bet that's why he does them. I bet these women remind him of his mom."

"Ouch," Mia says, holding her hand to her chest. "That hits you right in the feels."

"Yeah, it does," I say. "But still. That doesn't change who he is. He's still been man-whoring his way through life. I don't need a guy who's a project. I'm too old for that shit."

"Okay, that's fair," she says. "I agree with you, most people won't change, at least not when someone else wants them to. But what if *Weston* wants to? It's not like *you've* been trying to change him. What if he wants something more in his life—specifically you?"

"But how do I know if that's what he wants? What if he's just hard up?" I ask, fully aware that after his little hand-holding stunt just now, I don't really believe my own argument. "He probably hasn't had sex since before his car accident. Maybe he's just horny and I'm an easy target because we live together."

She rolls her eyes. "Kendra, I saw what happened at the club the other night. I saw the way he was looking at you."

"How was he looking at me?"

"Like you're *his*."

Now it's my turn to roll my eyes. "He was not."

"Oh yes he was. Why was he even there? Were you expecting him to come out and join us?"

"No," I say. "But Alex was there too."

"Yeah, following me, like I didn't know," she says with a laugh. "I wasn't surprised Alex showed up. I know how he is, and he's my fiancé. But when I saw Weston walk in, I was pretty floored."

"Why didn't you tell me they were there?"

"Uh, you were drunk off your ass, for one," she says. "I was pretending I didn't know Alex was there—didn't want to blow his cover. And when Weston showed up... I had to see how that played out."

"Is that why none of you did anything about that guy grabbing me on the dance floor?"

Mia winces. "Yeah, I might have told your other friends to stay back. God, Kendra, you should have seen the look on Weston's face when that guy started dancing with you. Although, when the dude was dragging you toward the stairs, I was afraid I'd made a huge mistake. I thought Weston was going to murder him right there. He was scary as hell."

That is not making me tingle. Not a bit. "Was he?"

"Oh my god," Mia says. "You really don't remember? He walked right over and stared that guy down like a freaking lion defending his pride. *Get your hands off my girl.* Are you kidding me? He didn't say that for show. He wants you to be his."

"That's not the same as wanting a relationship with me," I say.

"No," Mia says, giving me a knowing look. "It's better. Trust me."

Before I can ask her what the hell that means, Alex comes into the kitchen. He levels Mia with a smoldering gaze and I quickly duck out of the kitchen before I have to be treated to an Alex-Mia makeout session. Wouldn't be the first time.

In the other room, I find my dad in his recliner, Caleb and Weston sitting on the couch next to him. Weston looks completely relaxed, sitting back with one ankle crossed over his knee. I pause before they see me, and watch. He's having a conversation with my father.

I shake my head a little, in case I'm seeing things, and come into the room.

"You ready?" Weston asks.

"Yeah, I think so," I say. "Thanks again for dinner, Dad."

He smiles at me. "Happy birthday, princess."

Weston is already standing, holding my coat out so I can slip my arms through. He smiles at me and brushes my hair back from my face.

I say my goodbyes to everyone. Weston puts his hand on my back as we walk out to his car. The fact that he's touching me like this is making me jumpy. It's so familiar. So sweet.

Truth is, I really like it. Same with holding his hand. I love the way it feels when he touches me, even innocently like this.

He opens the car door and gives me that seductive smile again, his lips turning up slightly, his eyes intense.

I'm in so much trouble.

19

WESTON

*K*endra smiles at me from the passenger seat of my car. I fixate on her lips. I want them again. Kissing has never been an objective in and of itself for me. It feels good, but it's usually a tool—a stepping stone to getting a woman naked so I can get what I really want. And I always back off on the kissing once I'm fucking her. It's too personal. I don't get personal.

But apparently now I'm doing a lot of things I didn't do before. Things I was sure I didn't need or care about.

When I kissed Kendra in the store yesterday, I thought that was it. I'd turned us down a new path, and it was going to end with her in my bed.

I was completely wrong.

She *did* kiss me back. Thoroughly, both in the store and back at home. The memory of our mouths crashing together is enough to get my dick twitching to life. It felt fucking amazing. I could have kissed her for hours, doing nothing but exploring her mouth with my tongue. But like a jackass, I went for her pants.

When she stopped me, I teetered on the edge of anger. A

part of me wanted to lash out at her. But I didn't. Hearing Kendra say she believes I'll hurt her was like getting punched in the gut. It hurt, but not in a way that made me mad at her. It sucked hearing the truth.

I'm not an idiot. My track record with women speaks for itself. She knows how I am. One thing I've learned—the hard way, more than once—is that you can count on people to be who they are. And that's who she thinks I am.

After Kendra walked away, I had a decision to make. Is that who I am? Am I going to chase random women for meaningless sex forever?

Caleb told me that Kendra isn't a hookup girl. He was absolutely right. She's not a quick fuck. And if I do want something with her, it has to be more than that. A lot more. It has to be something I've never tried before.

That's why I agreed to go to dinner with her family. Truth be told, it was eerie to get that text from Alex earlier today. Just when I was mulling over how I'm going to approach this, an opportunity fell into my lap. I'm not sure what prompted him to invite me, and I didn't ask. Whatever his motive, I was ready to take full advantage.

I have to show Kendra that I'm not in this to get laid. This is so far beyond wanting her body—although, hell yes, I do want it. But I want so much more. I want *her*.

This is uncharted territory. I could teach a class on how to pick up women and get them into bed. I'm a master at that. But dating? Making her my girlfriend? This is all new to me. It's something I've never considered with any woman I've ever been with. And yeah, the idea scares me a little. I'm man enough to admit to that.

But every time I look at her, I feel her pulling at me like gravity.

I don't have a plan. I'm running on pure instinct. Hold her

hand? I can't remember the last time I bothered with something so juvenile as hand holding. But in that moment, it felt like the right thing to do. And it was.

I'm not great with words. Talk is cheap and bullshit flies off the tongue too easily. I have to show her.

We park in her driveway and I walk her to the front door, my hand on the small of her back. I have my keys out, so she doesn't reach for hers—but I don't make a move to use them. I stand in front of her and step in close, then slip my hand around her waist. Before she can say a word, I lean down and place my lips against hers. She's hesitant, but I slant my mouth over hers, caressing her lips. She responds, kissing me back, brushing my lips with the tip of her tongue.

I pull away and look her in the eyes.

"You said you weren't going to kiss me," she says.

"No, I said I wasn't going to make out with you at the table in front of your family," I say. "We're not at the table anymore."

She laughs softly and bites her lower lip. "So, why did you now?"

I shrug. "I thought a goodnight kiss was appropriate at the end of a first date—especially if the date went well."

"Date?" she asks. "How was that our first date?"

"I took you to dinner."

"No, you *came with me* to dinner with my family," she says.

"I drove, so I took you."

She puts a hand on her hip. "You didn't even ask me out. My brother invited you."

"Okay, I guess it didn't start out as a date," I say. "But I think it turned into one."

"Hmm, I don't know," she says, and I smile at the hint of teasing in her voice. "I still don't think it was our first date."

"All right, tomorrow night will be," I say. "And I'll make sure you know it's a date."

"Do you always ask women out by *telling* them what they're doing?"

"Kendra, I don't ask women out on dates." I reach for her again, sliding my hand around her waist, and pull her close. "But I will ask you. Would you like to go to dinner with me tomorrow night?"

She blinks at me a few times, like she's surprised. I wait, giving her time to think it through, my eyes never leaving hers.

"Okay, yes."

"Good. How about eight?"

"Sure."

I'd love to kiss her again—press her up against the door and devour her. I will, soon. I'm going to ravage every inch of her when the time comes.

But not tonight.

So I just smile and unlock the door, then hold it open for her.

I head toward my room, but pause just outside the hallway and glance at her. "Goodnight, Kendra."

"Goodnight, Weston."

PICKING KENDRA UP for a date when we live in the same house isn't exactly *picking her up*. But she comes out of her room around seven-thirty, looking positively stunning in a sleeveless black dress and red heels. A touch of makeup gives her face a subtle shimmer and her dark hair is loose around her shoulders.

I stop and stare at her for a moment. The messy-haired skinny girl in pajama pants is nowhere to be seen. I love her that way—it's Kendra—but seeing her dressed up for me sends a ping of adrenaline rushing through my veins.

"Wow," I say. "You look beautiful."

She blushes and bites her lip. "Thanks. You look great too."

I'm dressed in a cream button down shirt and dark jacket, no tie.

"Ready?" I ask.

"Yeah."

I help her with her coat—that's a date thing, right?—and hold the front door open for her. We get in my car and as I head toward L'Oursin—the French restaurant I chose for tonight—there's a spark of tension between us that's never been there before. Anticipation. Whatever happens, everything is changing.

We get to the restaurant and the host seats us. The ambiance is perfect—soft light, a quiet hum of conversation. Each table feels secluded, like we're in our own space.

I open the menu and feel a spark of panic. It's all in French. I've been here before, and I'm positive it used to be in English. I don't know a word of French, and I have no idea what to order.

Kendra peruses her menu and it isn't long before the waitress arrives. We order wine—no French needed yet—and agree to the waitress's suggestion for an appetizer.

"Can I take your orders now?" the waitress asks. "Or do you need more time?"

"I'm ready if you are," Kendra says.

"Go ahead."

"I'll have the poulet chasseur," she says, the French words rolling right off her tongue.

"Excellent choice," the waitress says. "And for you?"

I pick something I partially recognize and point. "This will be fine."

"All right," she says. "Filet mignon a la bordelaise. Can I get you anything else?"

"No, thank you," I say.

The waitress leaves and Kendra looks at me with one eyebrow arched. "You like filet mignon a la bordelaise?"

"I'm not sure, actually," I say. "I've been here before, but I don't remember what I ordered."

"That has mushrooms," she says. "You hate mushrooms."

I stare at her for a moment. I don't even care that I just ordered a very expensive dinner that I'm probably going to hate. I'm mesmerized by her. How does she remember things like that? How does she know me so well?

"What?" she asks.

"Sorry," I say. "I have a feeling you know exactly what you ordered."

She laughs. "Yeah, well, I speak French. I took it all through high school and I spent a semester living in Nice when I was in college. I'm out of practice, though."

Kendra speaks French. Of course she does. Because there wasn't enough about her that was impressive.

"Wow. I guess I should have just admitted I couldn't read it."

"For a second, I thought maybe you could and you were about to flirt with me in French," she says.

I laugh. "I guess you'll have to flirt with me in French."

She regards me for a moment and smiles. *"J'ai peur de tomber amoureuse de toi."*

It's like music from her lips. "What does that mean?"

Her cheeks flush the slightest hint of pink and she glances away for a second. The waitress returns with our wine and pours.

"Thank you," I say.

"This is a nice choice," Kendra says after the waitress leaves. "I love French food."

I'm curious about what she said, but I let it drop. "I'm glad you like it. I figured it should be special, since it's your birthday."

"I've kind of overdone it on my birthday this year," she says. "I thought after last weekend, and dinner with the fam, I wouldn't have much going on today."

"I think this worked out well. Oh, I have something for you."
I pull an envelope from my inside pocket and hand it to her.

"What is this?"

"Open it."

She opens the envelope and pulls out a small card. "Elaia Spa, Wednesday at one o'clock?"

"I scheduled you a massage," I say.

Her lips part and she stares at me, the card still clutched in her hand. "You did?"

"Yeah, I figured you work so much, and you're always helping everyone else. You probably don't relax enough. I was going to just get you a gift card, but this way you don't even have to make the appointment. Just be there."

"Thank you," she says, her eyes glistening a little. "This is... I'm kind of speechless."

I shrug. "I just wanted to do something nice for your birthday."

"This is lovely," she says.

We chat for a few more minutes while we wait for our food. The appetizer arrives and it's delicious—mussels in a lemony cream sauce. A short time later, the waitress returns with our dinner and starts to put Kendra's plate in front of her.

"Actually, he's having this," she says. "The other one is mine."

"Are you sure?" the waitress asks.

"Yes, thank you," Kendra says.

The waitress puts the plate in front of me, and the other one in front of Kendra. "*Bon appetit.*"

"*Merci,*" Kendra says.

I glance between our dinners. "Didn't I order that one?"

"Well, yeah," she says. "But I don't think you'll like it, and I like both dishes, so this works out."

"Kendra, you don't have to do that," I say.

"I know." She cuts a piece of steak and takes a bite, sliding the fork between her lips, as if to emphasize her point. "Mm. I don't know what you have against mushrooms. This is delicious."

I just shake my head and smile. What else can I do? She's so much more than I deserve.

Dinner is excellent. We eat and talk and drink wine. We share a rich chocolate mousse and a pair of hazelnut truffles for dessert. Kendra tells me more about her semester in France. About college. She talks about her Dad's back injury—the surgeries, the worry, his recovery. I like hearing her talk, so I keep asking questions. There's so much I didn't know about her. I want to know it all.

Our meal ends, and I drive us home. Kendra pauses outside the door and I crack a little smile.

"So, was this a kiss-worthy first date?" I ask. Despite my question, I step in close and kiss her, not waiting for her answer. She doesn't hesitate this time, her lips soft and pliant against mine.

When we part, she takes a step back. "I know this is kind of unusual because we both live here. So there's no *do you want to come in for a drink* stuff. We're both going inside. And tonight was... it was so nice."

"But?"

She takes a breath. "But I don't think I'm ready for this to go further. I know this isn't the same as a first date with someone you just met. But I never sleep with someone until at least the third date, and even that's pushing it for me." She pauses and glances away. "I've been burned too many times. I just—"

I put a finger to her lips. "It's fine."

"Are you sure?"

"Look, I know why you think I'm standing here assuming I'm about to get laid," I say. "So all I can say is yes, it's really fine. You look absolutely beautiful and I enjoyed having dinner with you."

"Thanks," she says. "Me too."

I kiss her again. "Happy birthday."

We head inside and I pull off my jacket while Kendra goes to her room.

"Hey, Kendra," I call out.

Her voice carries through her half open door. "Yeah?"

"Change into those pajama pants and get your ass to the couch." I unbutton my shirt as I walk down the hallway. "We have episodes to catch up on."

I hear her laugh and a smile crosses my face. This is one of the top five weirdest days of my adult life. I took a beautiful woman out to an expensive dinner with no expectation of sex. Not that I don't want sex. I could fuck that woman in a hundred different ways tonight. But I had a feeling it wouldn't happen, and I wasn't lying when I said it was fine.

Now I'm about to sit on the couch with her and watch a show I'd have scoffed at someone else for watching. We'll probably cuddle.

Weston Reid does *not* cuddle.

Except the thought of Kendra curled up beneath a blanket with her head on my arm is about the best thing I can imagine.

20

KENDRA

*D*ating the man I'm living with is an interesting dynamic. In some ways, not much has changed. Weston goes to work. I work at home, help with Charlotte, get to the gym for some swimming.

In other ways, it's completely different. He comes home and smiles, greeting me with kisses instead of a passing hello on the way to his room. We spend our weeknights snuggled up on the couch watching Netflix, or sitting with our feet tangled together while I work and he listens to an audiobook.

He's respected my *at least three dates* rule. Not that it's really a *rule*; and it's not really about an exact number of dates. We aren't two strangers who have only been out a couple of times. But he seems to understand that I need something more before I'm ready to take that step with him. Even Wednesday night, when we spend an hour making out on the couch, he eventually pulls away and says goodnight.

He doesn't even try to cram in two more dates so he can get to the good stuff. We make plans to go out on Thursday after work, and technically that's only date number two.

I get the strong feeling that everything he's doing is thought-out and intentional. We don't sit and have lengthy discussions about where this is going. But that's not Weston. He isn't telling me he wants a relationship—he's showing me.

Thursday, he comes home after work and showers. I'm trying to finish up for the day, but I keep imagining him standing beneath the spray, water cascading down his naked body. He comes out of the bathroom with nothing but a towel around his waist, his dark hair tousled and wet, his muscles glistening. After giving me a little smirk, he walks to his room and shuts the door. I groan and lean my head back against the couch cushion.

I calm my raging hormones enough to get dressed for our date. He takes me to Toulouse Petit, a great little New Orleans-style creole restaurant. Neither of us have trouble finding something we love on the menu. By the time we finish, I'm a little buzzed from the wine and the thrill of Weston's eyes devouring me all through dinner.

We step out of the restaurant into a pleasantly cool evening.

"That shrimp was amazing, but I ate at least twice as much as I should have," I say.

"Should we walk it off?" Weston asks. "It's nice out."

"Sure."

We wander a few blocks toward Seattle Center, where the huge central fountain sprays high into the air, the bursts of water coordinated with music. Lights glow around the edges, illuminating the spray. We pause and watch for a few minutes, standing near other couples and small groups enjoying the show.

A man's voice comes from behind us. "Weston?"

Weston's expression hardens and he turns. A man in a sleek button-down shirt and slacks walks over to us. Weston tightens his grip on my hand. "Ian. What are you doing out here?"

Ian points his thumb at the building behind him. "My oldest has a school thing in the exhibition center." His gaze flicks to me, then down to Weston's hand holding mine. "Are you going to introduce me to your... friend, here?"

"Kendra, this is my business partner, Ian. Ian, this is my girlfriend, Kendra."

A zing of electricity races through me. Holy shit, did he just call me his *girlfriend*?

"Really?" Ian says and I don't like his tone. It's almost like he's trying not to laugh. "Huh. Okay, I'll let you two get back to your night, I suppose." He glances at me again, and it's hard to tell if the expression on his face is confusion or annoyance. "See you at work."

"Yeah," Weston says.

Ian walks away and Weston tugs gently on my arm, leading me in the opposite direction.

"So, that's Ian," I say. Weston has mentioned his business partner a few times, but he's never told me much about him.

"Yeah, Ian is..." He hesitates, like he's not sure what to say. "He's a good surgeon, but he's basically a douche."

"Must suck to have to work with him, then."

"It does. It sucks having my career tied to a guy like that," he says.

"How did you end up opening a practice with him in the first place?" I ask.

"It was his to begin with," Weston says. "Ian hired me straight out of med school. He knows my father. When the practice started having some financial trouble, my dad and I bailed him out. I bought in as a managing partner. My dad bought in as an investor."

"Wow," I say. "Have you thought about moving on?"

"Lately, yeah," he says. "He mostly stays out of my way, so I ignored what he's like for a long time. But, I don't know... it's getting harder to ignore."

"He's a good surgeon, though?" I ask. "It's not like he's putting his patients at risk or anything, right?"

"He's good, yeah," he says. "Although he'll take on any case, even when he shouldn't."

"You turn people away?"

"Sometimes we have to. The patient isn't healthy enough for surgery, for example. But sometimes I'll get a patient who won't benefit from the procedure. It will make her look worse, not better. I won't operate on someone like that, but Ian will."

There's something else I didn't know. That asshole armor Weston wears doesn't go nearly as deep as I thought it did. "It's good at least one of you has some integrity."

He glances at me with a little smile. "Yeah. I guess it is."

"So, are we going to talk about the other thing?" I ask.

"What other thing?"

I roll my eyes and nudge him with my arm. "What you said when you introduced me."

"What did I say?"

From the corner of my eye, I can see him trying not to smile. "Stop it."

"Was I wrong?" he asks.

I stop walking, and he turns to face me. "Is that what you want?" I ask.

He touches my chin with a gentle hand and rubs his thumb over my lips. "Yes. Honestly, I think you've been my girlfriend for a while now. It just took us both a little bit to realize it."

He looks down at me with those mesmerizing gray eyes and I want to melt into a puddle at his feet.

"I guess you're right," I say.

He brushes the hair back from my face and kisses me, his mouth warm and soft against mine. Desire pools, the heat of it spreading through me.

But before the kiss turns into something slightly obscene—

considering we're standing near the street with people walking by and I was about to jump up and wrap my legs around his waist—he pulls away and takes my hand again, leading me toward his car.

We drive home, and just like last time, he stops in front of the door. "How did I do?"

"You were perfect," I say.

He looks me up and down and bites his lower lip. "No, I think *perfect* is reserved for you."

I tilt my chin up to meet his kiss. My body is on fire for him before our lips even meet. He kisses me softly—a slow, measured kiss. A second date kiss. A the-kiss-is-where-tonight-ends kiss.

But I don't want tonight to end.

"So..." I tilt my head and trace a finger down the line of buttons on his shirt. "Do you want to come in? I know you live here, so you're coming inside, but... do you want to come in?"

He raises his eyebrows. "You mean, come in? With you?"

"Yeah," I say.

"I thought you said three dates."

"Well, I didn't mean it as a hard and fast rule," I say. "Besides, this is three."

"This is two. You said dinner at your dad's didn't count."

"Oh, I don't know," I say, running my finger back up his buttons. "Maybe it didn't start out as one, but it ended as a date, don't you think?"

In the space of a heartbeat, his whole demeanor changes. His eyes ignite and tension courses through his body. He grabs my wrists and backs me up against the door, pinning my arms over my head.

He leans his face close and brushes his lips down my neck. His voice is a low growl. "Does this mean I get to fuck you tonight, baby?"

"Oh my god, yes."

I gasp as he presses his body closer, nudging his thigh between my legs. He shifts, putting pressure on my clit, and my eyes roll back.

"Oh fuck, Weston, we're on the porch," I say. He moves his leg, just slightly, sending jolts of sensation through my entire body.

His laugh is soft in my ear and he trails kisses down my neck. "Should we go inside?"

"Yes. Now."

He kisses me again, and this time it's fierce and demanding. Without leaving my mouth, he lets go of my arms and pulls out his keys. I start unbuttoning his shirt as he fumbles with the lock and pushes the door open.

We stumble inside and he kicks the door closed. He pulls up on my shirt, ripping it over my head, and surges in again after he tosses it to the floor. Cupping my face, he kisses me hard, walking me backward toward the hallway.

"Where?" I manage to get out. The last of his buttons comes free and he yanks his shirt off.

"My bed."

Somehow, between the stumbling, kissing, and clothes ripping, we make it into Weston's room. My shirt and pants are already gone. He reaches around to unclasp my bra and I let the straps fall down my arms. His hands are everywhere, large and dexterous, sliding along my skin, like he wants to touch every inch of me.

I hook my thumbs under the waistband of his underwear— those damn boxer briefs he's been taunting me with since he moved in. He pauses, his face close, his eyes locked with mine. I pull his underwear down, freeing his solid erection. My eyes flick down to his cock. He has the magical combination of being thick *and* long—something I thought only existed in dirty fairy tales.

"Holy shit, Weston."

"You've been making me hard for you every fucking day."

He kicks his underwear off and pulls mine down slowly, kissing down my body as he goes. Leading with his mouth, he comes up again. His lips are hot against my skin, every touch making me throb with need.

I brush my hand across his incision site—a six-inch red line running diagonally just below his left ribs. "Is this okay?"

"Fine." He grabs my ass, pressing his hard cock against me, and kisses my mouth again. "And if it's not, I don't care."

He pushes me down onto the bed and I scoot backward to give him room. I tip my knees open and he kneels on the bed, his eyes roving over me.

"God, Kendra, look at you," he says. "You are so fucking sexy."

I feel a momentary pang of self-consciousness. Working out keeps me lean, but I've always hated how small my boobs are. "I'm probably not as, um, curvy as you like."

"Baby, no." He crawls on top of me and the look in his eyes leaves me feeling more naked than being undressed. "Your body is so beautiful." His hand slides from my hip, up my ribs, to cup my breast. "Absolutely perfect."

He groans, kissing down my chest. His tongue circles my nipple and my eyes flutter closed. He licks and sucks and grazes it with his teeth. I move my hips, trying to get him inside me, desperate for his cock. But he moves to the other side, his mouth unhurried.

As if he can sense my growing desperation, one hand slides between my legs. He sucks on my nipple and strokes my clit—and I'm ready to come unglued.

"Oh god, Weston, please fuck me."

"I need to taste you first," he says.

He kisses down my stomach and pushes my thighs open wider. His tongue brushes the sensitive skin outside my opening and my entire body trembles. Heat builds in my core, building with every lap of his tongue. He explores, teasing and testing me, until I'm writhing and clutching the sheets. An orgasm builds in a rush of heat and tension. I'm riding the peak, panting, my toes curling.

His low groan vibrates through me as he gently sucks my clit, his tongue moving in a steady rhythm. I've never felt anything like it.

"Weston... oh... that's... yes... I'm... oh god... gonna come."

Fingers dig into my thighs and his tongue is relentless. I roll my hips, reaching the summit, and burst apart into a thousand points of light. He doesn't stop, moving with me. I'm gasping for breath, the sweet agony of his mouth making me come again immediately.

When I finally come down off the high, he moves his way up my body, kissing me as he goes. He reaches into his nightstand for a condom and after tearing open the foil package, rolls it on quickly.

"Holy shit, what did you just do to me?" I ask between breaths.

His smile is intense and seductive as he settles between my legs. "Baby, you taste so good, I could do that all night."

"I want more," I say. "I want you inside me. I want all of you."

He hesitates, his cock pushing against my opening, and kisses my lips. He's surprisingly tender. "I'll give you all of me."

Our eyes lock as he slides his cock in. I gasp at his size, his thickness stretching me open, putting pressure in all the right places. He kisses me again—deep wet kisses while he slowly thrusts his hips.

"I'll give you everything you want." He kisses down my jaw, to my neck. "Everything you need."

He growls into my neck as he moves faster, his cock sliding easily through my wetness. I run my hands over his muscular back and wrap my legs around his waist. His gray eyes hold mine, his brow furrowed. He watches me as if he's fascinated, and time seems to slow, holding us captive in the heat of this moment.

"Weston."

He pushes in harder. "I love it when you say my name."

"Weston... yes... more..."

Faster. Harder. Deeper. He fucks me unlike anyone before. Like he's desperate. Like his life depends on it.

Intensity builds and he pins my arms above my head, holding me by my wrists. I'm completely in his control, drowning in the feel of him inside me. His taut muscles flex with every thrust.

His cock thickens, pulsing with the tension he needs to release. My pussy is so hot, every move he makes brings me closer to the brink. He kisses me again, dragging his teeth across my lower lip.

He groans, driving into me—hard. His body stiffens, his muscles clenching, and I feel him start to come. My body responds instantly, and that's when I realize...

The simultaneous orgasm is real.

I grab onto him for dear life, moaning as we come together. Each pulse of his cock makes my pussy clench harder, deep spasms that reverberate through my entire body. He keeps thrusting until my orgasm subsides and I'm left panting beneath him.

He picks himself up enough to look at me and brushes my hair off my forehead. It looks like he might say something, but he just kisses me again—soft strokes of his lips and tongue against mine.

Eventually he stops, and after a gentle kiss on my nose, he gets up to dispose of the condom. I'm so dazed, I can't move. I stay sprawled out on his bed, staring at the ceiling. He gets back into bed and pulls the sheets up.

I turn onto my side, facing him. I'm not sure what to do next. He doesn't strike me as a bed-sharer. "Should I go sleep in my room?"

He looks at me, his expression fierce. "No." He pulls me in close and wraps his arms around me. I settle in with my head resting on his shoulder, my arm across his chest. "Stay with me."

"Okay," I whisper, melting into his warm body, drenched in endorphins. "I'll stay."

21

WESTON

The light shining through a gap in the curtains wakes me. I blink my eyes open. Kendra is a few inches away, lying on her side, facing me. Her hands are tucked beneath her cheek and a tendril of hair is lying across her forehead. I brush it off her face and she takes a deep breath, but doesn't open her eyes.

I stare at her. I don't think I've ever woken up next to a woman and felt anything but impatience for her to leave. Maybe regret for letting her spend the night. But this? Waking up with this gorgeous woman next to me, her scent on my sheets, her hair fanned out over my pillow? I could get used to this.

My dick stirs at the memory of last night. Fuck, she was incredible. I'm no stranger to good sex—even great sex—but being with Kendra was something else entirely. I was completely immersed in her—in the feel of her body, in her taste, her smell. I've never experienced anything like it. Maybe it was simply the build-up—the weeks of wanting her, even before I admitted it to myself.

But I think it's something more. I actually *care* about her. And the list of people I can say that about is very short.

I've spent most of my adult life avoiding forming real relationships with anyone. I bet a shrink would have a field day with me. Dead mother. Emotionless asshole of a father. I'm sure they'd tell me I push people away before they can get close to me.

They'd be right.

I never thought I was missing anything. What more could I need? I had a reputable career. Plenty of money. I had no issues getting women and used casual sex to blow off steam. A relationship seemed like an unnecessary risk. Relationships end. People get hurt.

But now I'm watching Kendra sleep and the thought of waking up alone tomorrow—or the next day, or next week, or next month—fills me with dread. I want this—I want her—more than I've ever wanted anything before.

And it scares the shit out of me.

Kendra's eyes drift open and meet mine. A slow smile spreads across her face, puckering the tiny dimple near her lips.

"Are you watching me sleep? Creeper."

I smile at her. "I just like looking at you."

She reaches out and traces a finger along my lips. "Careful, big guy. Don't smile too much first thing in the morning. You might hurt yourself."

I grab her wrist and pull her on top of me. She giggles and rests her head on my shoulder while I put my arms around her, holding her close.

"You sleep with me now," I say, low into her ear. "I want you in my bed every night."

She holds herself up and meets my gaze, her eyebrows lifted in surprise. "Are you telling me what to do?"

"Yes."

She laughs again and rests her forehead against mine. "You are very persuasive."

I bring her mouth to mine for a kiss and her lips are like the oxygen I need to live. She shifts her hips, moving against my erection.

"Baby, I have to get to work." I kiss her again. "I have surgery this morning."

She groans with disappointment and nuzzles against my neck. "Are you sure?"

"Yes, but you're making it really hard to give a fuck about the patient who's going to be waiting for me."

"Okay, I'll let you go." She slides off me and lies on her side, her head propped up on her hand.

I lean in to kiss her one last time before I get up, wishing I could spend the day in bed with her. "I'll be back tonight."

MY SURGERY WENT WELL. I was worried about fatigue in my right hand, but so far I haven't had any issues. I spent the rest of the afternoon seeing patients and catching up on charting.

I look over an email from our accountant. I asked her to break down some of the credit card expenses; the balance seems to be running high. Apparently I need to tell Ian to get his spending under control. He's putting a lot of personal stuff on the practice's credit card. It's getting ridiculous.

My phone vibrates and I slide it across the desk to check. It's a text from Kendra. One corner of my mouth lifts. It's so weird how just seeing her name on the screen makes me smile.

Kendra: Hey you. When do you think you'll be home?

Me: Not sure. Pretty swamped here. Need something?

Kendra: Hmm, I can think of a few things.

She ends her text with a winky face. Emojis are the stupidest invention. But I do like the implication here.

Me: I'll hurry home, then. Wear your pajama pants. The striped ones.

My thumb hovers over the emoji button. Should I add a smiley face so she can see I'm teasing? God, when did I turn into a teenage girl? Screw this. I hit send.

Kendra: Oh. Okay.

Damn it. I should have used the fucking emoji. I'm terrible at this.

Me: Kidding, baby.

Kendra: LOL! I was going to say, you hate my pajama pants.

Me: I just hated not being able to rip them off you.

Kendra: In that case, I'll find my ugliest ones so you'll really enjoy taking them off.

I laugh. My girl is ridiculous.

My girl. I let out a long breath.

Fuck, I *am* turning into a teenage girl. I just sighed over a text message.

I put my phone in my pocket and grab my jacket. When I get out into the hall, I glance at Ian's office. His door is closed. I wonder if he's still here.

I knock on his door a few times.

"Yeah?"

"Do you have a minute?" I ask. "I'm on my way out."

There's muffled talking. Ian's voice, and a woman's. Who is he with behind a closed door? He doesn't see patients in his office. Oh for fuck's sake, he can't be—

The door opens and Ginny, one of our nurses, slips through. She bites her lip and smiles at me, her face flushing. "Hi, Dr. Reid."

I ignore her and push open the door to find Ian taking a seat behind his desk.

"What was that?" I sit across the desk from him. "Having an end of day meeting with one of the nurses?"

"None of your business."

By the look on his face, I can tell exactly what was going on. "It's absolutely my business. She's an *employee*, Ian. You can't mess around with the employees. Especially *here*."

"It's nothing," he says. "Not a big deal, so stop worrying."

"That makes her a walking lawsuit, asshole," I say. "You have her blowing you in your office now, but what happens if we need to fire her? You'll have a disgruntled little nurse on your hands with enough dirt on you to put your license in jeopardy."

Ian waves a hand, as if he can clear my argument from the air. "I have it under control."

"Like hell you do."

"Did you come in here to bust my balls?" he asks. "Because I get plenty of that at home."

I raise an eyebrow at him. "I can't imagine why."

He leans forward. "That is none of your fucking business."

I put my hands up. "Nope. Never has been. You do whatever the fuck you want."

"You're one to judge," he says. "You let some bitch get her claws into you, and now you get to have an opinion about my life?"

My nostrils flare and I clench my hands into fists. "Do not talk about her."

He laughs, shaking his head. "This is rich. *You*, with a girlfriend?"

"Yeah."

"I don't get it," he says. "You had it made; you were doing everything right. No ties. No commitments. You got more ass than any man I've ever known, and there was nothing stopping you. Why ruin a perfectly good thing?"

"Ian—"

"And for *that*? Fuck, man, you've had women who were ten

times hotter than her. At least get her to eat something. Maybe the weight will go to her tits."

I stand up in a rush, leaning over with my fingers resting on his desk. "Don't fucking talk about her."

Ian raises his eyebrows. "Calm down. I didn't mean anything."

"The fuck you didn't."

He puts up his hands, as if admitting defeat. "Okay, suddenly you're the protective type. Didn't see that coming." He closes his laptop. "I need to get out of here. Do you need something?"

"Yeah." I sit down. I'd love to break a few of Ian's teeth, but decide against it. For now. "I was looking at the credit card statements. Have you been going on vacations on the practice's dime? There's a shit ton of expenses on there."

"Oh, right," he says. "Yeah, sometimes I use the wrong card. I'll reimburse the practice."

"You use the wrong credit card?" I ask. "This is a business, not your personal bank account."

"I realize that," he says. "I understand how a business works."

He better not pull his *I started this practice when you were still chasing skirts in high school* bit.

"Then you should understand that we agreed not to use the business account for personal expenses," I say. "We aren't exactly swimming in money here."

"You don't have to tell me things are tight," he says. "But are you blaming me for that? Putting a few dinners on the company credit card isn't going to bankrupt us."

"It's a lot more than a few dinners."

He crosses his arms. "I'd say your bleeding-heart charity crap is having a bigger impact on our bottom line."

"Excuse me?"

"You're good at keeping it quiet, but I know about your

freebie surgeries," he says. "You're leaving tens of thousands of dollars on the table. Would you care to explain that?"

Fuck, I hate this guy. "I can choose to donate some of my time. That's not costing the practice anything."

"Like hell it isn't," he says. "Your time is worth money, Weston. A lot of money. Every time you scrub in for some pity case who isn't paying, you're costing the practice money."

"They wouldn't be patients at all if I didn't do it for free."

"No, but you could be operating on people who can fucking pay you what you're worth," he says.

"Maybe I want to be worth something more," I say, my voice heated.

Ian stares at me for a long moment. "I don't know what's gotten into you lately. I'm concerned."

"Concerned about what?" I ask. "That I'm not fucking random women every weekend? Or concerned that maybe I give a shit and want to do something more with my time?"

"Don't pull that holier-than-thou bullshit on me," he says.

"You can go fuck yourself." I stand and head for his door. "Better than letting the nurses do it in your office."

I don't wait to see if he replies.

22

WESTON

*K*endra is on the couch with her laptop, wearing her pig pajama pants, when I get home.

She smiles at me. "Hey."

"Hi." I put down my keys and take off my coat, then gesture to her pants. "You're right, those are definitely the worst."

She looks down, feigning shock. "What? What's sexier than chubby little piggies?"

"Almost anything."

She sets her laptop on the coffee table and I sit next to her. I lie down, facing her, and put my head in her lap. My arms wrap around her and I close my eyes, taking a deep breath.

"You okay?" she asks, running her fingers through my hair.

"Mm." The knots of tension in my back are already loosening. "Long day. Stressful."

She doesn't say anything, just slides her fingers through my hair, massaging my scalp and neck. My body relaxes, the strain melting away. God, she feels so good. She smooths out all my ragged edges—soothes the storm that's always raging inside me.

I nuzzle my face against her belly and pull up her shirt just enough that I can touch her bare skin.

"You're surprisingly adorable," she says.

I smile, but don't open my eyes. "I don't think anyone has ever called me that."

"Adorable?" she asks. "No, probably not."

I crack an eye open. "What?"

She laughs softly. "I'm sure Weston Reid has been called many things. Sexy. Brooding. Cocky. Mysterious, maybe. But adorable? I can see why you don't get that a lot. I don't think many people see you the way I do."

No one does, Kendra.

I'm getting so caught up in her, and I wonder if this is normal. Should I be thinking about her all the time? Missing her when we're apart? There's a piece of me that wants to shy away, like I'm reaching out to touch a flame. If I get too close, it's going to burn. But she's at the center of the fire, and right now I'm craving her heat.

I sit up and pull her beneath me so I'm lying on top of her. My mouth finds hers and I kiss her deeply, feeling the satisfaction of her body yielding to me. I move against her, gently pressing my cock between her legs.

"Too many clothes," she says between kisses.

"So greedy." I grind against her harder and she moans.

She already has the first few buttons of my shirt undone. I sit back on my knees and finish taking it off while she pulls her shirt over her head. I take her pants and underwear off and let them drop to the floor.

Her bra is black lace. I lean down and graze her nipples with my teeth through the thin fabric. She squirms underneath me as I release the clasp and reveal her perfect tits. I can't get enough of them. The contours of her body are so perfect—so beautiful. I gently pinch one nipple while I suck on the other. She arches her back and moans again.

"Weston, you're driving me insane," she says, her voice breathy.

I sit back again, on my knees in front of her, and unfasten my belt. She's breathing hard, her eyes half lidded. I unfasten my pants and let them hang loose around my hips, but don't take them off.

"I want to see you touch yourself," I say.

She bites her bottom lip and hesitates for a beat. Then she slides one hand down toward her pussy. Her fingers brush her clit.

"Show me," I say, my eyes locked on her fingers as she starts to move them. "I want to see how you make yourself feel good."

I grab my dick through my underwear and watch. She slips two fingers inside to get them wet and rubs herself, slow at first. She relaxes into it and moves faster. I caress her thigh with one hand and pull out my cock with the other.

"You too," she says. "Let me see you."

Oh Kendra, my dirty girl. I slide my hand between her legs and plunge two fingers into her pussy. She moans, her eyes rolling back, and gasps when I pull my fingers out. I spread her wetness onto my cock and with slow strokes, I pump my hand up and down my thick erection.

"How does that feel?" I ask.

"It feels like I want you inside me," she says.

I groan and stroke faster.

"I've done this before," she says. "Imagining you."

"Oh fuck."

"I laid in my bed and dreamed it was you," she says, moving her hand in a steady rhythm. "It was your cock inside me. Did you do it too? Did you make yourself come and pretend it was me?"

I groan again. "All the fucking time."

She bites her lip again and smiles. "And now you can have me."

I stop, my cock still clutched in my hand, and stare at her. I *can* have her. She's lying naked in front of me, vulnerable and defenseless. Holding nothing back. And I know Kendra. She doesn't give this to just anyone. This means something to her. Allowing me to touch her, kiss her, fuck her—giving me access to her most tender places—is such a fucking privilege.

"Come to bed with me, baby."

She nods and I help her up. I take her gently by the hand and lead her into my bedroom where she helps me pull the rest of my clothes off. My cock aches to be inside her, but I take my time, kissing and stroking her. Tasting her skin. I lay her down on her stomach and kiss up her spine. Nibble her shoulders and neck. Turn her over and kiss her tits. Licking, sucking, feeling her whole body with my hands and mouth. Reveling in the feel of her skin.

Nudging me onto my back, she smiles and licks her lips. Her mouth moves down my body, from my chest to my abs. She plants soft kisses around my incision, then moves lower. I groan when she gets to my cock and runs her tongue along the shaft.

She plunges down on me, suddenly aggressive, her eyes meeting mine. Her mouth is like silk. I put my fingers through her hair, but she's in charge. I give over to her and lose myself in the sensation. She moves up and down, my cock sliding through her wet mouth, her hand stroking the base. Watching her blow me is fucking unreal and in no time, I'm on the brink of coming down her throat.

"Baby, stop," I say, tightening my hands in her hair. "Stop, I need to fuck you."

She slowly releases my dick and as soon as I'm free, I grab her with rough hands and toss her onto her back. I curse the seconds it takes to get the condom on. I need her. I need her right fucking now.

Braced above her, I thrust my hips, my gentleness gone. I lean close so I can feel every inch of her skin and devour her mouth while I plunge inside her, over and over again. She clutches onto me, digging her fingers into my back, moaning into my mouth. I move faster, driving into her. She cries out with every thrust.

We're both gone, completely out of control. I'm fucking her so hard, but the deeper I go, the louder she gets. She's the only thing in the world—the only thing that matters. Her scent is all over me, the taste of her in my mouth. Her pussy feels like heaven and I can't get enough. I'll never get enough.

I growl against her neck as the pressure builds. She's so hot, her pussy clenching around me, her core muscles squeezing my cock. I plunge in hard and grind against her, holding where I'm as deep as I can go.

"Weston," she says, her voice tinged with urgency.

I lift my head so I can look at her. My dick pulses with the need to unload, but I wait, looking deep into her eyes. A feeling spreads through me, something I've never experienced before. It's warm and tender, and it has nothing to do with my dick buried in her hot pussy. I want to say something, but I don't have the words. I never have the right words.

So I kiss her, hoping she's feeling the same thing. Hoping this is enough. That I can show her that she means something to me. This means something to me.

Two more strokes and I feel her come apart beneath me. Her mouth releases my kiss and she cries out with the pulses of her climax. Instantly, my balls draw up and I explode inside her. I thrust my hips hard, burying my cock in her heat. The waves of ecstasy roll through me, so overwhelming I can't breathe. She feels so fucking good I can barely stand it. I drive into her until it's over, until I feel like I'm going to drop.

I stay on top of her, breathing hard, my face buried in her neck. My entire body trembles. I'm so overwhelmed, I can't even look at her yet. Her hands rub slow strokes up and down my back, her touch soothing the fire inside.

She whispers softly, her mouth next to my ear. "That was amazing."

I roll off of her and onto my side so I can hold her close. My arms envelop her, pressing her against me. I breathe her in, kiss her head. I don't know what to do with myself, so I keep my arms tight around her, feel the movement of her breath. She clings to me just as hard. It's as if we both need this—the assurance of each other. That this is real. That neither of us are going anywhere.

23

KENDRA

*M*ia's cat, Fabio, jumps up on the couch beside me. He sniffs my pants and seems to deem me worthy to grace his furniture, because he curls up and closes his eyes. I go to scratch his head, but Mia holds up a hand.

"I wouldn't do that right now," she says.

"Why?" My hand is still hovering in the air above his head. "He's going to sleep. He seems happy."

"Yeah, that's just to lull you into a false sense of security." She sinks onto the couch on the other side of Fabio, tucking her legs under her. "If he wants you to pet him, he'll let you know."

I put my hand down. "So how are all the wedding plans coming?"

"Having a destination wedding was the best decision I ever made," she says. "The resort is taking care of everything, and Shelby can't interfere. You should really consider doing something like this."

I arch an eyebrow and hold up my left hand. "Lacking a fiancé, Mi. Not exactly planning a wedding right now."

"I know, I know, I just mean *when* you're planning your wedding," she says.

"I love you for saying *when*, not *if*," I say. "Although, to be honest, I don't think I want much of a wedding."

"Really? I would have thought you'd want the whole shebang—church, big white dress, a dozen bridesmaids..."

I shrug. "Maybe I would have when I was younger. The fairy tale is pretty, but I've been in so many weddings. Don't get me wrong, I'm always honored to be a part of them. But I don't think that's what I want for myself."

"Well, you should definitely do what you want when the time comes," she says. "I learned really quick that people—as in my sister—have all sorts of opinions when it comes to a wedding. But at the end of the day, it's not about that. It's about the marriage, not the party."

"Have I mentioned lately how glad I am that you're marrying my brother?" I ask.

Mia rolls her eyes. "Stop. But me too."

Fabio gets up and stretches, then stands in front of me.

"He wants you to pet him now," she says. "And I am trying to be so patient and tactful, but you know I suck at that, so I'm just going to ask. How are things with Weston?"

I run my hand down Fabio's orange fur and he plops down with his head on my leg. I can't stop the smile from spreading across my face. "Good. No, not *good*. Amazing. And so surprising. Mia, it's crazy. I mean, we're—"

"Having a pants-off dance-off? Doing the mattress mambo? Tickling the fun bits? Doing the naughty?" she asks.

"What?"

"Sorry, the last book I read had all these hilarious euphemisms for sex," she says. "I can't get them out of my head."

"Well, that's not what I was going to say. But... yeah, that too."

She scrunches up her shoulders and lets out a little squeal. "But what were you going to say?"

"That we're really together. Like, dating. He introduced me as his girlfriend the other day."

"Ooh," she says. "That seems like a big step for Weston."

"I think it was," I say. "I don't know if he's ever had an actual girlfriend."

She gasps. "Oh my god, is he adorably terrible at it? Like, is he all awkward now because he doesn't know how to properly date a woman?"

I laugh. "A little, yeah. Sometimes he says things and I'm not sure if he's kidding. But for the most part, no. He's taken me out on some really nice dates."

"This is so great," she says. "And I know you said I could gloat if I was right about something happening between you two, but I'm too happy for you to gloat."

"Thanks," I say, "but don't get too excited. This is still so new. And it's still Weston."

"Yeah, I know it is," she says.

"The good thing is, we know each other pretty well already," I say. "You learn a lot about a person when you live with them. Even more when you take care of them after a car accident."

"I bet."

"He's..." I sigh like a love-struck girl. "He's so intense. He's still the same guy, but I feel like he's letting me see underneath the surface."

"Are you bringing him to the wedding?"

"I haven't asked him," I say. "Is it okay if I do?"

"That's what the little *plus one* is for," she says. "And yes, obviously it would be great if he came with you."

I smile. "Okay, yeah, I'll talk to him about it."

The front door opens and Alex walks in, dressed in a tank top and basketball shorts. "Hey, there's my two favorite girls."

"Kendra's shagging Weston," Mia blurts out.

Alex stops, his eyes on Mia, his mouth partially open.

"Mia, what the hell?" I ask.

She winces. "I'm sorry. I didn't mean to say that."

"I'm just going to go shower and pretend I didn't hear anything," Alex says.

I put a hand over my eyes and shake my head. "Oh, Mia."

"Sorry," she says, lowering her voice. "You know what's great, though? Alex really likes him. Or at least, he did before he just found out Weston's fucking his sister."

"You don't have brothers," I say. "I'm sure you can tell Shelby all about your sexual exploits. Brothers aren't so interested in hearing about their sisters' sex lives."

She giggles. "I know. I'm sorry."

"It's fine. Alex knows I'm a grown up."

"True," she says. "Well, let me know about the wedding soon if you can. We have to give the final guest counts to the caterer."

"I will. Thanks, Mi."

WHEN I GET HOME, I find Weston on the couch with his tablet. He pulls out his earbuds and smiles. "Hey."

Wow, I really love the way he looks at me. My cheeks warm and I smile back. "Hi. Sorry, I went over to Alex and Mia's for a little bit."

He shrugs. "It's no problem."

I put down my purse and hang up my coat. "I'm starving. Are you hungry?"

"Yeah, but I already ordered from that teriyaki place you like," he says. "I'll go pick it up in a few."

"Thanks," I say. "That sounds great."

"Oh, did you want some?" he asks. "I only ordered for me."

I look at him in surprise, my eyebrows raised.

He laughs while he gets up and walks over to me. "I'm

kidding." He slips his hands around my waist. "But you're cute when you're trying to decide if you're angry at me."

"You're an ass."

"You just realized this?"

I start to reply, but he shuts me up with a kiss. I really don't mind.

When he pulls away, I keep my arms around his neck and bite my lower lip. I want to ask him about going to the wedding, but suddenly I'm nervous. What if he doesn't want to go? What if going away together—to a family wedding, no less—is too much?

I can tell he knows I want to say something, but he doesn't press me. He just waits, giving me a moment to collect my thoughts.

"So, I wanted to ask you something," I say. "Obviously you know my brother is getting married soon. The wedding is down in Napa, so I'm going for the whole weekend. I was wondering if you'd come with me?"

"Of course," he says.

"Really?"

He kisses my forehead. "Yes, really. You think I'm going to let my girl go to a wedding alone?"

"Have I told you lately how much I love it when you call me that?"

"What, *my girl*?" he asks.

"Yeah."

He smiles again. "I love saying it. Now let me go get dinner. I'll be back in about twenty."

I smack his butt as he leaves and he winks at me.

The wedding invitation is in my little mail basket. I pull it out, write my name and a little plus one, then slide it into the return envelope.

Maybe it's silly to be so happy over this. But the fact that I'm not just bringing a date to this wedding—I'm bringing my *boyfriend*—is making me all fluttery inside. Being a bridesmaid for the ninth time won't be so bad, since I'll be there with Weston.

24

WESTON

"Maybe we should get up eventually," Kendra says, her voice lazy.

I take a deep breath and open my eyes. I wasn't asleep—just drifting in a post-orgasm haze. What was it I used to have against morning sex? Who the hell knows. Fucking Kendra first thing in the morning is a fantastic way to start the day. Especially when it's a weekend, and neither of us have anywhere to be.

I glance at the clock. It's closer to lunchtime than breakfast. Kendra has her head on my shoulder, her arm draped over my chest. One leg is bent, resting on top of mine. The sheets are kicked down to the bottom of the bed and her naked body molded against me looks fucking phenomenal.

"Don't move." I grab my phone, angling the camera so it gets more of her than me, and take a picture.

"Did you just take a picture of us? We're naked."

"That's why I took a picture," I say. "Your ass looks amazing."

"You're not keeping that, are you?" She lifts her head. "You can't have naked pictures of me on your phone."

I lift my phone again and take another. That one probably

has my dick in it, so I'll delete it later. But it's fun to get her riled up.

"Hey."

She grabs for the phone, but my arms are a lot longer than hers. I hold it out of her reach and kiss her.

"Fine," she says. "But don't let anyone see that. And don't accidentally text it or something."

"Trust me, baby, I won't let anyone see you." I grab her ass with my other hand. "This is mine."

"Oh, you think so?" she asks with a little grin that shows her dimple.

"Yes," I say. "All mine."

She takes a deep breath and moves her arm so she can rest her chin on her hand. "I guess I'll have to let all my other boyfriends know. But they're going to be so disappointed."

I drop my phone and grab her, flipping her to her back and pinning her arms down, my hands on her wrists. "You think that's funny?"

She smiles. "Yes."

I stare at her for a long moment. At her deep brown eyes. Her dark hair, fanned out across my pillow. "You know I'm not... that there's no one else, right?"

Her expression turns serious. "Yeah, I know. Me neither. Were you worried about that?"

I roll off her and lie on my side, resting my head in my hand, and she turns toward me. "No, not really. But I'm not always good at talking about things."

"You're not so bad," she says. "You don't need to chat about every little thing. But you say what's important, when it needs to be said."

"Well, this needs to be said." I reach out and brush my fingers down her cheek. "There's only you."

Her eyes start to glisten and she bites her lower lip. "Yeah. Same."

I lean close and kiss her forehead. "Good."

My hand slides down to her hip and I nudge her onto her back. I cup her breast and feel her nipple harden against my palm. I kiss her slowly, my mouth moving over hers, enjoying the feel of her soft skin.

Her phone dings and she groans. I pull away and glance at the nightstand.

"I should probably see who that is." She reaches over and grabs her phone. "It's Caleb. He's supposed to be off today, but he has to go in and he doesn't have anyone to watch Charlotte."

"I guess I have to let you get up." I palm her breast again and suck on her other nipple.

She moans, running her fingers through my hair. "Mm, I don't want to go."

"Text him back and tell him you'll be there in a little bit." I move down the bed and push her thighs open. She's pink and swollen, her pussy already wet again. "But I have to make you come again first."

I DIDN'T HAVE plans for the day, and with Kendra gone, I'm bored. I get a few things done and consider going into the office to catch up on charting. But I need lunch first.

The hinges on one of the kitchen cupboards are loose. It's crooked and feels like it's ready to fall off when I open it. I take a closer look. The screws are probably stripped. It would be easy enough to fix.

I glance around, thinking about all the little things Kendra's been meaning to fix around here. The loose hinges. Her bedroom door that won't stay shut. I know she wants to replace the light fixture in the bathroom; I think I even remember what the new one she wants looks like. And she keeps talking about putting up new curtains in the living room.

Who knows when she'll get to all that stuff. Owning an old home means there's always something to upgrade or fix. Kendra spends so much time working, not to mention helping everyone else, she never has time for this kind of thing. Today is typical; her brother needs her help, and she doesn't hesitate.

She's always taking care of other people. A thought hits me and I feel like a jackass for not thinking of it before—who's taking care of her?

I grab a quick lunch—leftovers she packaged neatly in the fridge. Like always, she left me a post-it note on top with my name and a little heart. Because of course she did. She's constantly making sure I'm fed. I've been getting so used to it, I haven't even thanked her lately.

I suppose a case could be made that I thank her in the bedroom—hard and fast, as often as possible. But I'm smart enough to realize that isn't enough.

After lunch, I head to the hardware store. I walk down the aisles, thinking of all the things the house needs. I'm sure there's more, but I get supplies for enough projects to keep me busy for the rest of the day.

Back at home, I get to work. I fix the cupboard and replace a few other loose hinges for good measure. I replace the light fixture in the bathroom. The new one fits perfectly and looks much better. She has good taste. The curtain rod in the living room is making the sheet rock crumble where it's attached, so I have to make another trip to the hardware store to get supplies to repair that. But once I do, the wall is good as new. It will need some touch up paint, but the new curtain rod is sturdy and looks good. I'm not sure if she'll like the curtains I got, but they match the couch, and she can pick something else if she wants. I'll just re-hang them for her.

The afternoon wears on, and I tinker with a few more things. Replace some outlets. Put a new doorknob on her bedroom door. I test it out a few times; it clicks closed on the first try every time. I add some WD-40 to the hinges on all the doors so they don't squeak. There's not much I can do about the squeaky floor. The hardwoods are old, and although they've been refinished so they look nice, they'll always be noisy. But I kind of like the way they creak. It's endearing. It's Kendra.

When she gets home, I'm back in the kitchen, tightening some of the pipes under the sink. I hear her come in, but I can't see her; I'm lying on my back with my head in the cupboard.

"What are you up to?" she asks, crouching down so she can look beneath the sink.

"You didn't have a leak down here yet," I say. "But some of the connections were getting loose. I replaced a piece here, and figured I'd make sure everything else was in good shape."

"Wow, thank you," she says.

I get up and put the wrench on the counter. "Sure. I did a few other things while you were gone."

"Really?"

"Yeah, come here."

I show her the cupboard, opening and closing it a few times. The curtains. The bathroom light. Her bedroom door. I point out a few other things I took care of as we walk through the house together.

"This is amazing," she says, her voice filled with awe. "I don't know how to thank you."

I shrug. "It's not a big deal. It needed to be done, so I did it."

She steps in and puts her arms around my waist. "It *is* a big deal. This stuff has been stressing me out for months, but I never seem to have time to deal with it. Thank you."

I smile at her and lean in for a kiss. My chest swells with

gratification. It feels amazing to do this for her. None of it was hard—just a couple of trips to the store and a few hours of work. But the payoff—seeing her so happy—is worth it a hundred times over.

It's a similar feeling when I successfully reconstruct a woman's breasts after she's had a mastectomy. Deep down, I know I do those for myself. Because I need to feel like I'm doing something worthwhile. And this—taking care of my woman, doing something that makes her life easier—it's like that times a million.

My phone rings from my bedroom. Kendra lets go and steps away, giving me another huge smile. I kiss her forehead before going to my room to answer it.

"Hello?"

"Hi Dr. Reid," a male voice says. "It's Mike with Robinson Construction. I'm just calling to let you know we completed work on your house. We got everything wrapped up this afternoon. We just need to have you come by for a final walk-through."

It takes me a second to respond. My house is done? That's right, it was supposed to be finished this week. "Right. Yeah, I can do Monday morning. Early."

"Great," he says. "Does seven work?"

"Sure," I say. "See you then."

I hang up and stand in the middle of my bedroom for a long moment, gaping at everything like an idiot. But it's not *my* bedroom. I was only supposed to be here for a few months. Just temporarily until my house was done.

Now it's finished.

I guess that means I have to move out.

I'm filled with a sense of dread. The thought of waking up anywhere else—without Kendra—feels so wrong. But we haven't really known each other that long. The time we've spent actually dating is even less. What am I supposed to do? Ask her if I can stay? Offer to have her come live with me? Obviously we're living together now, but we never decided to take that step. We just both lived here, and when it turned into more, it seemed silly to have her sleeping in the next room.

So what does this mean?

She appears in my doorway, a smile on her face. "Hey. Have you had dinner yet? I'm starving."

"No. I'm hungry too."

"Everything okay?" she asks, her voice light.

I pocket my phone. "Yeah, fine."

"You're all dirty, so let's just grab some takeout," she says. "I can go if you want."

"No, I'll come," I say. "I'd rather go together."

She steps closer and pops up on her tiptoes to kiss me. "Sounds perfect. I'll get my purse."

Fuck it. My house isn't going anywhere. I'll deal with it later. I follow Kendra out, smacking her lightly on the ass when she closes the front door.

25

WESTON

*T*anya pokes her head in my office. "Do you have a minute?"

"Sure, come in," I say. "I needed to talk to you, actually."

She sits down in the chair across from me. "Okay. What's up?"

"I need you to reschedule my appointments next Thursday," I say. "Kendra's brother is getting married down in Napa, and we're leaving that morning. I thought it would be Friday, but she wants to get down there a day early."

She nods, tapping on her tablet screen. "Shouldn't be a problem. I'll take care of it."

"Thanks. Did you need something?"

"Yes. Your four o'clock just canceled. Jenna at the front desk had me take the call. It was one of your mastectomy patients."

"Well, obviously we won't charge her a cancellation fee," I say.

"No, of course not." She shifts in her chair, looking down at her lap. "The thing is, the patient's husband called. He said that she... well, she died."

Her words hit me like a punch in the gut. "What?"

"She'd been told she was in remission, which was why she was going forward with reconstruction," she says. "Her husband didn't make it clear if this was a recurrence, or a secondary disease. But they got the news a few weeks ago that her cancer was back, and it was extremely aggressive. She was dead within two weeks. They'd forgotten she had this appointment, which is why they hadn't called sooner. I'm sure her family is just trying to pick up the pieces."

I stare at my desk, my stomach twisting. "Thanks for letting me know."

Tanya stands, but hesitates near the door. "Are you okay?"

I smooth out my expression and meet her eyes. "Of course. Just make sure Thursday is clear."

"Right," she says. "No problem."

Taking a deep breath, I rub my chin. Dead. Just like that. I bring up her appointment on my computer and find her name. Suzanna Holton. I don't know her, aside from having met with her for a pre-op consult. She was supposed to be one of two pro bono cases I was taking on this month.

And now she's gone.

Fucking cancer. Anger seeps in around the disquiet. They told me my mother was getting better too. Not that she looked it. After her surgery, she suffered through months of chemo-therapy. It made her sick for days on end. By the time the nausea and vomiting abated, she'd have to go in for another treatment. Her hair fell out. She wasted away to nothing but skin and bones. But she assured me it was making her better. That she would be all right.

I remember hearing people say *remission*. Looking back, I realize they must have been using that word mistakenly, or simply as a possibility. She never went into remission. The chemo beat the cancer back for a while, but it returned with a vengeance. Eventually, there was nothing more they could do.

She was so small. So frail. They shouldn't have let me see her at the end. I was too young to cope with how she looked. But it wasn't like anyone was watching out for me. I was shooed out of the way, punished for being where I shouldn't be. But no one was taking care of me.

I pinch the bridge of my nose, trying to banish the memories of my dying mother. People die of cancer every day. It's fucked up, and it isn't fair, but there's nothing I can do about it.

Tanya looks in my office again. "Sorry. Your father is here."

With enormous effort, I keep my face still. "Okay."

A few seconds later, my father comes in and closes the door behind him. He's dressed in his usual button-down shirt and slacks—expensive and custom-tailored. He's an imposing figure —tall, with straight posture and an air of arrogance that surrounds him like a cloud. His once dark brown hair is peppered with gray and his eyes are brown. I get my gray eyes from my mother, but otherwise, I look a lot like him.

"Weston," he says as he sits across from me.

"Dad."

"We need to talk."

Dread settles over me. That phrase never precedes good news. "About what?"

"I've been talking with Ian," he says. "About the finances."

"And?"

"Weston, if you're going to be a managing partner, you need to get your goddamn act together," he says. "Do you realize the size of the cash flow problem we have here?"

"I'm well aware," I say. "I talked to Ian about his spending sprees the other day. The guy acts like this place is his personal piggy bank."

"You and I both know that's not the problem," he says.

"Excuse me? How is that not the problem?"

"What is this about you doing free surgeries?" he asks. "Ian says you're doing a lot of them."

My back stiffens, but I try to maintain a casual air. I don't want to come across as defensive. "I do some pro bono work under certain circumstances. But that's not causing the practice's cash flow problem."

"Don't be an idiot," he says. "Of course it is."

I clench my teeth and take a breath. "As I already told Ian, these people wouldn't be patients if I didn't comp their surgeries. And I don't use any of the practice's money. If there are other costs they can't cover, I pay for it personally."

"What the hell are you doing?" he asks. "That's absolutely costing the practice money. You know how much we make on a single surgery. You work on someone who can't pay, you're neglecting a patient who can. That's costing us tens of thousands of dollars every time."

I lean back in my seat. "Then I'll do them on my own time; schedule outside my normal hours. But that doesn't change the fact that Ian is spending the practice's money on personal shit."

"Ian is not the one to blame here," he says. "Ian's patient roster is overflowing. He's done more surgeries than you in the last few months, by quite a lot."

"I was fucking injured," I say. "I spent a month recovering from a car accident. Or did you conveniently forget about that?"

"Regardless," he says, waving a hand, "you can't run a business by giving your services away for free."

"Dad, I've looked at the numbers," I say. "It has nothing to do with me doing a handful of surgeries on the side. There's a constant drain on the practice's funds and I don't know where that money is going. If Ian's using the credit card like his mommy gave it to him, what else is he doing with the practice's money?"

His face goes stony, his eyes narrowing. "Are you accusing Ian of stealing from his own business?"

"*Our* business, Dad," I say. "It's not his anymore. He was fucking it up well before I got here. So why would you think he's suddenly handling the finances well? Because you're involved? You don't think he'd screw you over?"

"No, he wouldn't screw me over," he says. "I've known Ian a long time. I trust him."

"You've known me my entire fucking life," I say. "But you don't trust me."

"I have been telling you since you were old enough to understand the lesson," he says, "trust is earned. Respect is earned."

"And I've done nothing to earn that from you?" I gesture to the framed diplomas displayed on my office wall. "None of that matters? Being one of the best plastic surgeons in the region doesn't matter? What the fuck do you want from me?"

"I want you to get your head out of your ass," he says. "You're running a business to make money, not a goddamn charity. You always were too much like your mother."

I clench my hands into fists and level him with a glare. "Do not talk about my mother."

He crosses his arms and lifts an eyebrow. "What do you think you know about her? You were a child."

"You're right, I was a child," I say. "But I was old enough to know you were cheating on her. Old enough to realize you abandoned her when she was sick."

"You don't know what the fuck you're talking about," he says, leaning forward and pointing a finger at me. "You have no idea what it was like."

"Yes, I do. Fuck, Dad, I was there. Not that you'd remember. You were off with whatever mistress you were fucking at the time while your wife was at home dying."

His face turns purplish-red and the cords in his neck stand

out. "You ungrateful little prick. This is how you talk to me? After everything I've done for you?"

"Then don't come in here and accuse me of causing the practice's financial problems," I say. "I'm not putting anything in jeopardy by donating some of my time. What's wrong with trying to do a little good in the world? You should try it sometime. It feels a lot better than being a narcissistic bastard."

"God, you do sound like her," he says. "You want to know the truth about your mother? She was weak. She never would stand up for herself. Let people walk all over her. Criticize my parenting all you want, I had a huge hurdle to get over to keep you from winding up the same way. And now look at you. If you can keep from running this place into the ground, you'll have it made."

I stare at him, unbridled hatred coursing through me. Feeling such rage toward your own father isn't natural. But hearing him talk about my mother with such disdain makes me want to rip his throat out. The fact that I don't want to spend the rest of my life in prison is literally the only thing keeping me on my side of the desk.

"Get the fuck out," I say, my voice cold.

"Excuse me?"

"You heard me," I say. "Out."

"You can't kick me out," he says.

"I just did." He opens his mouth to respond, but I cut him off before he can speak. "Get. Out."

I keep my eyes locked on his, my jaw clenched tight, until he stands. With one last hard look at me, he leaves, closing the door behind him.

It takes every ounce of self-control I possess to keep from trashing my own office. Anger rages through me, like hot steel coursing through my veins. I hate him. I fucking hate him for what he did to my mother. For what he did to me. And that bastard thinks he can come in here and lecture me? Accuse me of causing the practice's problems?

Fuck him.

I grab my keys and head out the back door so I won't have to talk to anyone on the way out. I'm so angry, I don't trust myself to speak. I get in my car and drive away, not paying attention to where I'm going. I just drive. I can't stop thinking about my mother. About Suzanna Holton. My bastard of a father. That fucking douchebag, Ian.

I'm wound up as tight as a spring, ready to snap.

26

WESTON

I'm still furious when I finally drive home, rage boiling in my gut. Kendra's car isn't in the driveway, and that pisses me off even more. Where the fuck is she? We have plans with her family tonight, and *I'm* late. She should be here.

I check my phone on the way inside, but I don't have any messages. I could text her to see where she is, but instead I stalk down the hallway to my room and toss my phone on the bed. It fucking figures she'd be late after the day I've had.

After changing my clothes, I head to the kitchen and down a glass of bourbon in two swallows. I pour another and get some aspirin out of the cupboard. Fucking headache.

The door opens and Kendra comes in.

"Hey," she says, closing the door behind her. "Sorry, I went to Costco with my dad. He has a hard time pushing those big carts around, but he's too stubborn to just let me do the shopping for him." She shrugs off her coat and puts down her purse. "Luckily it wasn't busy, but he doesn't get around very fast, so it took forever. But, now he has enough toilet paper for the next six months, so he has that going for him."

I don't say anything, just take a sip of my drink. I can't be mad at her for helping her dad, but I'm so fucking angry.

"Anyway, I know we're late. I already texted Alex and Caleb to let them know," she says. "But we should still hurry."

The last thing I want to do tonight is hang out with Kendra's brothers. I need to be alone. I take another swallow. "I'm going to bow out tonight. Stay here."

She comes into the kitchen. "Oh. Okay. Are you all right?"

"Fine."

"Sure, but how are you really?" She puts a hand on my arm, but I shrug it off.

"I said I was fine."

"Weston, what's going on?" she asks. "What happened?"

I take a deep breath. "My fucking father. The practice is losing money. He and Ian are blaming me."

"That's ridiculous," she says. "Do you know what's really going on?"

"Ian's bankrolling his fucking adultery on the practice's dime."

"Oh my god. Does your dad know that?"

I shrug. "He doesn't think it's the problem."

She pauses for a second, her eyes searching. "Does this have anything to do with the patients you help at no charge?"

I raise my eyebrows in surprise. I've never discussed this with her. "How do you know about that?"

Her forehead tightens and she hesitates for a second before answering. "Mia told me. One of the patients she's working with had you listed as the surgeon. So she kind of looked into it."

"That's fucking confidential," I say, my voice sharp.

"It's not like she gave me the patient's personal information," she says. "She only told me that you were doing the surgery for free."

"It's none of Mia's goddamn business."

"Okay, sorry. You don't have to get angry about it," she says. "Have you thought more about leaving the practice? Maybe it's time to cut ties with Ian, and your dad."

I down the last of my drink, slam the glass on the counter, and start walking to my room. "I don't need you telling me what to do."

"I'm not telling you what to do," she says, following me. "I'm just saying, you're not happy there. You don't like your partner, and it's obvious you don't like having your dad involved in your business."

I stop partway down the hall and turn to face her. "Do you know how much money I have wrapped up in that practice? I can't just walk away from that."

"Okay, but what's your happiness worth?"

"What kind of a question is that?" I ask.

"A good question," she says. "Working is about more than money."

"And you're just a shining example of that, aren't you?" I ask.

"What is that supposed to mean?"

"You quit your job to do what?" I ask. "Work twelve hours a day from your couch? How sustainable is that? Are you even making enough money to live on?"

"It's not easy, but these things take time," she says. "Why are you giving me shit about my job? Maybe it was irresponsible of me to quit when I did. But at least I'm being true to myself."

"I get it," I say. "You're overflowing with integrity. Maybe you were hoping some of it would wash off on me."

"What is that supposed to mean?" she asks.

"Nothing." I turn away again.

"Will you stop doing that," she says. "Turn around and fucking talk to me."

"About what?" I snap. "About my shitty father? About my

douchebag of a partner? How about my patient whose cancer came back and she fucking died last week?"

She touches her fingers to her lips. "Oh, god. Weston, I'm so sorry."

"Don't."

"Don't what?"

"Try to help," I say. "You can't fucking fix everything. You can't fix me."

"I'm not trying to *fix* you," she says.

"Aren't you?" I ask, the rage in my gut heating to a boiling point. "Isn't that what all this is about? You thought I was this wounded little puppy and you could nurse me back to health and maybe teach me to be a good boy. But I'm not, Kendra. There's nothing good about me. I'm a fucking predator, not a pet. You can't change who I am."

"I'm not trying to change you," she says, her voice rising. "How could you even say that?"

I know she's not. I know I'm fucking this up, but now that I've started, I can't seem to stop. "No? Then why do you keep bringing up my job? Carting me around to do shit with your family?"

"God, Weston, why are you doing this?" she asks. "I don't want to change you. Give me some fucking credit; I'm not that stupid."

"You sure about that?" I ask, my voice hard.

The stricken look on her face feels like a knife in my gut. Her lips part and her eyes flash with anger. "You know what your problem is?"

"I'm sure you're going to tell me."

"You're scared," she says.

"Fuck you," I say. "I'm done."

"Oh no you're not," she says, following me as I stalk down the hall. "You're so scared of letting anyone into your life, you treat people like shit so you don't have to care about them. You don't want to risk *feeling* anything. And it works pretty well, doesn't it?"

I stop with my hand on the door. I'm breathing hard, my back knotted with tension. "My life was fine before I moved in here."

"Yeah, I'm sure it was great," she says. "Fucking random women you don't give a shit about every weekend. That sounds very fulfilling."

I whirl on her. "What the fuck would you know about my life? I've been here a few months, and suddenly you're the expert? Maybe my life *was* better before."

"How can you look at me and say that?" she asks, her voice suddenly quiet.

Even in the dim light of the hallway, I can see her eyes glisten with tears. My chest feels like it's being ripped open, the pain worse than my car accident. It makes me angrier. I hate the way this feels. This is why I stay away from people. What the fuck was I thinking? How else was this thing with Kendra going to end?

"I'm moving out," I say.

She recoils, like I slapped her. Her eyes blink and she puts a hand on her stomach. "What?"

"My house is done," I say, my voice cold. "It's been done for a week. I should have left already."

"So that's it?" she asks. "You're just going to leave?"

"What the fuck did you expect, Kendra?" I ask. "I was never going to stay."

The pain in her face is killing me. I have to get away from her. Tears break free from the corners of her eyes and she stares at me, her mouth open.

"I would have stayed," she says, her voice breaking on the

last word. She turns around and walks away. A few seconds later, the front door opens and closes.

I lean against the door and dig my fingers into my chest. Why does this fucking hurt so much? I never should have put myself in this position. I let her get under my skin—let her in too deep.

My bedroom is a nightmare. The unmade bed, where we woke up together this morning. Some of Kendra's clothes draped over the chair. Her pillow with the light blue paisley pillowcase, the pattern standing out against my gray sheets.

Fuck this. I stayed out of relationships for a reason. This reason. To avoid these goddamn feelings. I'll get my shit out, move back into my house, and move on. Things will go back to the way they were before.

It's better this way.

27

KENDRA

*W*hen I get home a few hours later, Weston is gone. His room is empty. The furniture is there, but the bed is stripped, the dresser and nightstands bare. All his things are gone. I stand in the middle of his room—what was, for a little while, our room—and hold my hand over my mouth.

I want to collapse onto the floor and cry, but no tears will come.

I don't understand what happened. We got into an argument over... what? He was mad about his dad, and things at work. About his partner. And then suddenly he's accusing me of trying to change him? Where did that even come from?

And why did he leave like that? Without a single word. He hasn't tried to call. No texts. Is this it? It's over? We get in a fight, and he just bails? Moves out and moves on?

What the fuck did you expect, Kendra? I was never going to stay.

What *did* I expect? That Weston was going to stay with me? That for the first time in his life, he'd commit to someone? As if I'm so special. I should have known better. It was stupid of me to think I meant something more to him. If I did, he'd be here now. He would have waited so we could talk. Work this out.

But he didn't. He left. His absence sends a clear message: It's over.

Maybe this is for the best. I can't expect to build a life with someone who's going to bail as soon as things get hard. Weston does this to everyone. He doesn't just push people away, he shoves them as far as he possibly can.

The pillow I brought into his room from my bed is on the floor, just inside my bedroom door. I pick it up, but get a whiff of his scent on the pillowcase, and toss it into a corner. I'll have to wash it before I can stand to use it again. I won't be able to sleep if I can smell him. Maybe I'll just throw it away.

I consider texting Mia, but I'm not ready to talk. Plus, it's past midnight. After I left earlier, I canceled my plans with my brothers, telling them I wasn't feeling well, and just drove around. I didn't even want to come home, but I was running low on gas and didn't want to risk running out late at night. Now I just need this day to be over.

I get ready for bed, trying to ignore the quiet. The house is so still. I'm used to the little noises another person makes. But the only sounds are my own.

Curled up in my own bed for the first time in a while, the dam finally breaks. I cry hard, sobbing into my pillow, the pain of this loss overwhelming. I cry until my throat hurts and the skin around my eyes burns. By the time I pass out, I'm exhausted, my breath coming in ragged gasps.

"HERE," Mia says, handing me a mug.

"What is this?" I smell the hot liquid. "Did you put something in it?"

"Bailey's," she says. "Figured you could use something a little stronger than just coffee."

"Thanks."

She shoos Fabio off the couch and sits down next to me. "What happened? It seemed like everything was going great between you two."

"I know. He came home from work pissed off and somehow that turned into us having this huge fight," I say. "Honestly, I don't even know what we were fighting about. He was just angry, and the next thing I know, he's telling me he's moving out."

"And he really left?"

"Yep," I say. "I went for a drive to cool off, and when I got back, his stuff was gone. The furniture is still there, but he took everything else. His room was basically empty."

"Holy shit," she says. "That is bad."

"Yeah, he said his house had been finished for a week and he should have left already. Actually, he asked me what I expected, and said he was never going to stay."

"I'm sure he meant he was going to move back to his house," she says. "Not that he was never going to stay with you."

"I don't know," I say. "I think he meant me. Honestly, Mia, what *did* I expect? That I have the magical vagina that will make him want to stay, when he's never wanted to stay with anyone, ever?"

"Well, I'm sure your vajayjay is fantastic," she says, "but we both know you were more to him than that."

"I *don't* know that," I say. "Not at all. I thought so, but maybe that was me seeing what I wanted to see. I wanted it to be real, so I let myself believe it was."

"I'm sorry, sweetie," she says. "I hate this."

"I keep checking my phone, like an idiot," I say. "But sometimes when he had trouble saying what he meant, he'd text me instead. That was easier for him. But I haven't heard a word."

"Are you going to text him?"

I shrug and take a sip of my drink. The flavor is so nice, and the warmth is relaxing. "I don't know. I guess I'm afraid to. I can't decide what would be worse—if he tells me to leave him alone, or doesn't answer me at all."

"Silence is the worst," she says. "I was guilty of that with Alex, though. I feel bad about it now, but I didn't talk to him for a couple days after he tried to apologize. It wasn't that I wanted to hurt him or make him suffer. I just needed some time to get my head together. Maybe that's what Weston is doing."

"I suppose," I say. "I just don't want to start thinking like that and get my hopes up. The sooner I accept this is over, the sooner I'll feel better. Or maybe that's a delusion too."

"I'm sorry you have to be in a wedding in the midst of this," she says.

"No, don't," I say. "Actually, your wedding is going to be a bright spot. How can I not be happy when you're marrying my brother? And hey, maybe I'll meet a hot billionaire in Napa who will whisk me away to Tuscany for an ill-advised rebound fling. You're the one who's always saying those things can happen in real life."

She laughs. "Yeah, but if you met the hot billionaire, would you really run off with him?"

I sigh and lean my head against the back of the couch. "No. It would still feel like cheating, even though Weston left me."

"Uh-oh," Mia says. "It's worse than I thought."

"What do you mean?"

"You're in love with him," she says.

I close my eyes against the sting of tears. "Yeah," I whisper. "I am in love with him."

She takes the mug from my hands and puts it on the coffee table, then puts her arm around me. I lean into her, letting the tears fall down my cheeks.

"Love sucks sometimes," she says.

I nod. It doesn't just suck. It hurts. A deep ache that permeates my entire body. I can't remember the last time I felt so awful. But I guess that's what happens when your heart gets ripped out. An injury like that doesn't come without pain. And I know it's going to leave a scar.

28

WESTON

*M*y house is dead quiet.

There used to be the faint hum of nearby traffic, the noise of the city drifting in through the windows. But my new double-paned windows with extra insulation block out almost every sound. Just like I wanted.

I walk across the brand-new walnut floors. Look at the freshly painted walls, the custom cabinetry. Everything is exactly what I asked for. The designer I hired incorporated everything I wanted, creating a space that's precisely to my tastes.

I sit down in one of the huge windows; the windowsills are wide enough to almost be bench seats. The view is incredible. I bought this place for the view, knowing the house was going to need to be gutted and redone almost from the studs. This was what I paid for—the lights of the Seattle skyline twinkling in the darkness. I'm near the top of Queen Anne hill, the city stretched out beneath me.

That should make me happy. My house is perfect. Despite what it cost to remodel this place from floor to ceiling, I probably tripled the value. With a view like this, it will always be worth a shit ton of money. And it's perfect. Pristine. Quiet. Mine.

But it smells like paint. It's a sterile smell, reminding me no one has lived here in months. Kendra's house smelled like dried lavender and wood polish. It smelled cozy and lived in. It smelled like her.

And the silence—something that I used to value so highly—is distracting, rather than soothing. Closing my eyes, I try to soak it in. I love silence. It means no one is around to get in my space —no one to piss me off. But here, there's no sound of Kendra's fingers clicking on her keyboard. No water dripping through the coffee maker late at night, providing the caffeine she needs to stay awake and finish her work.

This is fucking stupid. I spend a few months living with her, and suddenly nothing is good enough? This house is everything I need it to be. And I'm going to sit here, pouting over the fact that I'm alone?

Well, that's one thing that's easy to change.

I get dressed to go out for the first time since before my accident, and consider where I should go tonight. I haven't been anywhere recently, so none of my usual spots have the problem of overexposure. The Terrace might be the best choice. It's classy, but still a hotspot for women looking for the same thing I am. I could try somewhere a little trashier—more chance of a sure thing—but I'm not in the mood for shitty watered-down drinks and groups of douchebags who think getting drunk off their asses on tequila shots is the way to party.

The bar is almost too crowded for my taste, but I go in anyway. There's no shortage of women. Some are with guys—boyfriends or dates. Others are in groups of friends, their eyes scanning the crowd. The lights are low, but it's easy to tell the ones who are here to stick with their friends, and the ones open to hooking up. I can see it in their body language—the way they angle themselves outward, like an invitation to the right man.

I order a drink and take up a position at the far end of the bar, where I can see most of the room. There's a blonde standing at one of the tall tables, her fingers resting lightly on her martini glass. Her short black dress clings to her curves, the neckline plunging low. Boobs look real—getting a big lift from her bra. Her friends are talking, but she's not paying attention. Her gaze is moving around the room, her posture relaxed, like she's bored.

Easy prey.

She meets my eyes, but I look away. Normally I'd hold her gaze for a long moment, then pretend I didn't see her. But as soon as we make eye contact, I feel sick to my stomach.

I take a sip of my drink, trying to pull myself together. This is fine. I'm going back to my life, and what else would I be doing on a Saturday night? Watching Netflix with Kendra? What was so great about that?

The blonde is looking at me again; I can see her from the corner of my eye. If she's the aggressive type, she'll probably come over here. What am I going to say to her if she does? Isn't that why I'm here? I could fill my bed with her tonight. Blow off steam by fucking her brains out. That's what I always did. Take out my stress on her body, make her scream, then send her home.

No complications. No feelings.

God, all these fucking feelings. She *is* walking over to me, and I'm hit in the chest with a shit ton of guilt. It almost makes me double over. What am I doing here? How could I do this to Kendra?

But Kendra and I are over. I left, moved out. We haven't talked. And I don't think we will. If she wanted to text me, she would have by now, wouldn't she? I haven't tried to contact her, but what the fuck do I say? I ruined everything. There's no going back now.

"Hi," the blonde says, sidling up next to me, and leaning her elbow on the bar. "Are you waiting for someone?"

"No." Suddenly my throat feels so dry. I take another sip. "No, I'm not waiting for anyone."

"Mind if I join you, then?"

"Sure."

She holds out her hand. "Mindy."

"Weston." I take her hand and shake it gently.

"Nice to meet you, Weston." She tilts her head a little. "Are you all right?"

"Yeah," I say. "Fine. Sorry. Been a long week."

She nods. "Then we have something in common. Want to talk about it?"

Fuck no. "I walked out on my girlfriend." Wait, what did I just say? Am I on pain meds again?

"Oh," she says. "Wow. I'm sorry to hear that. Was it serious?"

"Yes. I don't know."

"You seem pretty confused," she says.

"Yeah."

She runs her finger along the rim of her glass for a moment, seeming to consider. "Look, I've been there. My last relationship ended with spectacular drama. It took me a while to get over it. But do you want to know what helped?"

"Sure."

"Having lots of meaningless sex with a guy I didn't give two shits about," she says.

"That's... not what I was expecting," I say.

She laughs. "Sorry, my friends always tell me I'm way too forward. I can't help it."

"It's not necessarily a bad thing."

"I don't think so," she says. "It serves me well. A lot of men can't handle it, but what do I want with a guy who's intimidated by me? It weeds out the weak."

Holy shit. This woman is something else. I'm used to being the aggressor, so I'm not exactly sure how to respond to her. "I imagine it does."

"You don't strike me as weak, though," she says. "Hurt, maybe. I can see that. What happened with your girlfriend?"

I shake my head. "I don't know. I got mad. Said some stupid shit. Told her I was leaving."

"And you did?"

"Yep. Moved out."

"Ouch," she says. "Sounds like you guys had quite the blow up. I'm guessing it was a long time coming, though. These things don't usually just pop up out of nowhere."

"I guess."

"The thing is," she continues, "if you really wanted to be with her, you wouldn't have gone to all the trouble of moving out, would you? That's a lot of effort over something small."

"No, that's not... It wasn't a long time coming, actually. We were great. It wasn't even her fault."

"So, you're just an asshole, then?"

"Yes," I say, emphatic. "I'm an enormous asshole."

"Hmm." She taps a manicured finger against her lips. "Well, fortunately for both of us, I don't really care. You can be a grade A dick, and it doesn't make much difference to me."

"Excuse me?"

She smiles, her pink lips parting. "How long were you with this girl? Are you that out of practice? I'm trying to pick you up."

I don't answer and she laughs, running a finger down my chest.

"You're absolutely charming, do you know that?" she says. "I don't usually go for the sad and wounded thing, but on you it's irresistible. I wonder if you're doing it on purpose and the whole *I walked out on my girlfriend* bit is part of the act. If it is, well done. I bet it works like a charm. But like I said, I don't care.

You look good enough to eat and that's all I'm looking for tonight."

"Are you always this aggressive?" I ask.

"Does it turn you off?" she asks, but she doesn't wait for my answer. "No, I'm not. Sometimes I make men chase me pretty hard. But there is something about you. I don't know what it is. Maybe I want to see if I can fuck that sad look out of your eyes."

She moves in closer and licks her lips. "We both know how this works. We're supposed to exchange some witty banter. Have a drink together. Move somewhere more private. Do some more talking. Get increasingly flirtatious. Make out a little. Then you suggest we go to your place, or ask about going to mine." She runs her fingers up and down my chest. "But I'm so bored of all that. So I was thinking, maybe we can skip all the nonsense. You want to get lucky tonight? I'm your girl."

She is not *my girl*.

I step back, suddenly filled with revulsion. Not for her— Mindy is an attractive woman looking for a night of great sex. No judgment from me. I'm horrified at myself for being here. For thinking this was what I wanted.

Sure, I could take Mindy home and spend the night fucking her. A few months ago, that's exactly what I would have done, and I wouldn't have thought twice about it.

But I'm not the same guy I was then. I know Kendra didn't deserve what I said about her trying to change me. She wasn't *trying* to. But she did change me. She got into the core of who I am and left her mark there, and I'll never be the same.

I shake my head slowly, feeling bewildered. "Sorry. I have to go."

Without waiting for Mindy's response, I turn and walk out the front door. I don't feel any better. If anything, I feel a lot fucking worse. The ache of missing Kendra is overwhelming, and I feel like shit for what I was planning to do tonight.

I go back to my silent house and fall on the couch. Resting my hand on my chest, it's almost surprising to feel my heart still beating. Shouldn't the space inside my ribs be empty? Feels that way, like there's a huge gaping hole. A vast chasm that's swallowing up my life, leaving me with nothing.

29

KENDRA

*M*y hotel room is lovely. Big king-sized bed with crisp white linens and tons of pillows. Sliding glass door leading to a little balcony with a table and two chairs. Gorgeous view of the resort gardens.

I hang up my bridesmaid dress in the closet and put away a few more of my things, trying to focus on what is nice about the room. I can sit outside in the morning and enjoy the view over a cup of coffee. That will be great. Fresh air and quiet. Tomorrow night will be the rehearsal dinner in the restaurant downstairs, and I hear the food is wonderful. In between, I'll have time to lounge by the pool or take a walk. Maybe read a book.

Should be perfect, right?

Except all I can think about is how I was supposed to be here with Weston. And I'm alone.

It's been almost a week and I haven't heard a word. At first, I thought he just needed a little time to cool down. I kept expecting him to text me any minute. Maybe not an apology right away. But at least an opening. An *I want to talk* message. Something that would open the lines of communication between us again.

But nope. Nothing.

At first Mia encouraged me to text him. She argued that since I left the house first, maybe he saw that as me doing the leaving, and he was waiting for me to make the first move. I almost did, several times. And maybe I should have. But in the end, I couldn't bring myself to hit send. I was so afraid of what he'd say—or not say. If I texted him and got no response, it would be even worse than the silence I'm dealing with now.

After a few days, though, even Mia changed her mind. I think she's more angry at him than I am, now.

I kick off my shoes and flop down on the bed. It's comfortable at least. But so big. I don't need all this space to myself.

My phone dings and my heart leaps into my throat. It's probably Mia. I texted her when I got to the resort to see if she needed help with anything. But my hand still trembles as I pull my phone out of my purse.

Yep, it's Mia.

Mia: We're good for today. I told you, the resort is handling everything. Relax. We'll see you at the rehearsal tomorrow.

I let out a breath. I'm starting to regret coming a day early. I wanted to be around in case they needed my help, and I figured Weston and I could enjoy a little getaway before the craziness of the wedding. But now I'm here by myself with nothing to do.

After moping for about ten minutes, I decide this is ridiculous. I'm in a beautiful place and I don't have any obligations. I caught up on work before I came so I could take the entire weekend off. I didn't even bring any work with me, although now that seems like a mistake. But I should at least do something with my time, other than stare at the ceiling and wish I wasn't alone.

The weather is gorgeous—sunny and in the high seventies. Perfect for poolside. I change into a turquoise bikini and wrap a matching sarong around my waist. I put on some sunscreen—

because this Seattle girl can get a sunburn all too easily—slip on my sunglasses and sandals, and head to the pool with a book and a bottled water.

There are a few other people lounging around the outdoor pool, and a family playing in the water. I stretch out on a lounge chair in the warm sun and try to focus on my book.

There's a light breeze that keeps me cool, and my book is good. I read for a while, relaxing and enjoying the atmosphere.

A man dressed in a t-shirt and board shorts, with sunglasses on his face, comes to sit in the chair next to me. He gives me a nod in greeting and I smile back. He puts his things down next to the chair—a book, a cell phone, and a towel—and takes off his shirt. I glance up at him. He's tanned and fit, with a muscular back and arms. He tosses his shirt down with his other things and turns, revealing a broad chest and chiseled abs.

I look away quickly and go back to my book. But the warmth of the sun is making me sleepy and it's hard to concentrate.

"What are you reading?" he asks in a thick French accent.

"Oh, it's called *Agent of Enchantment*," I say. "It's an urban fantasy novel about a woman who's an FBI agent, but there's magic."

"Sounds delightful," he says.

"Yeah, it's good," I say. "What about you?"

"*The Dark Tower*," he says, holding up his book. "I've read it before. I like to read books in English when I'm in America. This helps me remember what to speak."

"Is that a French accent I hear?"

"*Oui*," he says.

"Where are you from?" I ask.

"I grew up in Lyon, but I live in Paris now," he says. "Have you ever been?"

"Yes," I say, wondering if I should admit to a native French speaker that I can speak the language a little. I'll probably butcher it. "I spent a semester in Nice."

"Ah," he says. "*Parlez vous francais?*"

"*Oui*," I say. "But I'm very rusty. It's been a while."

"I won't force you, then," he says. "Besides, my English needs practicing. I used to travel here quite often, but it's been about five years. I feel as if I've lost too much English in that time."

"I don't think so," I say. "You speak English remarkably well."

"That is nice of you to say. May I ask what brings you here? Are you in the region on business or pleasure?"

"My brother is getting married here on Saturday," I say.

"Ah, *felicitations* to your brother," he says.

"*Merci.*"

"And where do you live when your brother is not getting married?" he asks.

I pause for a second. I'm not sure if he's simply engaging in polite conversation, or if he's interested in me. If it's the former, I don't see any harm in chatting with him. Maybe he just wants to practice his English. But if it's the latter, I don't know how to feel about that.

"I'm from Seattle."

"That is a place I have not been," he says. "Do you enjoy living there?"

"Mostly yes," I say. "Around February it can get pretty dreary, and I start daydreaming about moving to the desert. But my family is there."

"You are close to your family?"

I nod. "Yes. Very."

"That is nice," he says. "I like this about you."

"Thanks. Are you close to your family?" I find myself hoping he says he has a wife.

"Perhaps not as close as I should be," he says. "Such is the life of the bachelor."

"Well, I'm sure you're very busy."

"Yes, this is true," he says. "Did you travel alone to this wedding? Or are you here with a husband? Or date?"

"No, I'm alone." As soon as I say it, I wish I hadn't. What is wrong with me? He just told me he's a bachelor, and he's asking if I'm single. I just swung that door wide open.

"This is lovely news for me. But I am getting ahead of things. I have not yet introduced myself properly." He reaches out a hand. "Louis."

I take his hand. "Kendra."

He brings my hand to his lips and kisses the backs of my fingers. "It is a great pleasure to meet you, Kendra."

Under different circumstances—specifically, pre-Weston—this would have been a dream come true. Louis is gorgeous. And who can resist a man with a sexy accent? He's obviously interested in me. What single woman wouldn't want to meet an exotic French stranger at a resort in California's wine country while she's dateless at her brother's wedding?

Me. Because no matter how shattered I am over Weston, I'm still in love with him.

It doesn't matter that we never said those words to each other, nor that I have no reason to believe he was in love with me. It doesn't change how I feel about him. I fell hard for that asshole, and I haven't even begun to pick myself back up again.

I take my hand back and pick up my book. "It's nice to meet you too, Louis. If you don't mind, I think I'll get back to my book."

"What if instead, I take you to lunch," he says. "We can drink some wine and get to know each other more deeply."

I take a breath. Would there be any harm in having lunch with him? There's no question I'm single. At this point, Weston has made it abundantly clear that it's over. I wouldn't be hurting anyone.

The little devil on my shoulder whispers in my ear that I *could* have lunch with Louis. Maybe take a few pictures of my meal and post them to Facebook—mention the pleasant company. Maybe even take a few pictures with Louis and post those. Weston's not big on social media, but he might see them. That could really get under his skin.

God, what am I thinking? I hate those kinds of games.

"That's really nice of you," I say. "But I'm afraid I have to decline."

"Are you certain?" he asks. "It is not right, for such a beautiful woman to be here alone."

"I agree with you there," I say. "But the fact that I'm here alone is someone else's fault."

"Ah, I see," he says. "A recent heartbreak, I presume?"

I nod.

"The French, you know, we understand how to treat our women," he says. "Whether it is just for one night, or for a lifetime. Our reputation as exceptional lovers is well earned. You could spend your weekend with me, rather than be alone. At the very least, I could ease the pain of your broken heart. Make you forget for a little while."

"I appreciate the offer, Louis," I say. "But I really can't."

He puts his hand to his chest. "I am saddened beyond measure. I think you and I would do very well together. You are very beautiful, and I could be pleasing you greatly."

I laugh and start gathering my things. "Thank you, that's very flattering."

He stands up at the same time I do and takes my hand again, kissing the backs of my fingers. "I am in room five-twenty-five if you should change your mind."

I slip my hand out of his. "Enjoy your visit, Louis. It was nice meeting you."

I walk away quickly before he can say anything else. It's not that I'm tempted. His offer to spend the weekend with me made it clear he never meant to simply take me to lunch. And I have no desire to jump in bed with anyone—not even a hot Frenchman with a sexy accent.

If anything, talking with Louis made me miss Weston even more.

I glance at my phone, but of course, no messages. I don't know why I keep waiting for him to text me. For all I know, I'll never hear from him again.

That thought makes me tear up and I hurry to the elevator, hoping it will be empty. I don't want to break down crying in front of anyone, and I'm not sure how much longer I can hold it inside.

30

WESTON

I knock on the door and wait. Caleb must be home; I saw his car downstairs. He might not let me in, and to be fair, I'm not sure what I'm doing here. But it's been almost a week since I moved out of Kendra's house and I'm starting to lose my fucking mind. I don't know what else to do.

He opens the door and I keep my distance in case he wants to hit me.

"What the hell?" he asks.

I keep my hands in my pockets and look at the floor. "I don't know, man."

There's a moment of silence, but he doesn't slam the door in my face. I just wait, letting him decide what he's going to do with me. If he tells me to leave, I'll go.

"Dude, you look like shit." He opens the door further and steps aside.

I come in and step around the suitcases sitting in the entry- way. Must be his bags to take to the wedding. I do look like shit. I haven't shaved and my hair is an unkempt mess. My clothes are rumpled. But I just don't care.

I sink down onto his couch, grateful he let me in.

Caleb goes into the kitchen and returns with two beers. He hands me one and sits in an armchair. "Charlotte's asleep. We don't have to be silent, but just be aware."

"No problem." I take a long pull from the bottle. "Thanks."

"So, what the fuck are you doing here?" he asks.

I take a deep breath. "I don't know."

"I guess this means you're not going to Napa," he says. "Didn't Kendra leave this morning?"

"She must have," I say.

"If you want to just sit here and drink a beer, that's fine," he says. "But my sister will probably murder me if she knows I let you in. I'm risking family loyalty here. I don't want to have to ask you a million questions to figure out what's going on. So either talk, or don't, but let me know what it's going to be so I don't waste my time."

I stare at my beer for a long moment. "I'll talk."

"Whenever you're ready."

"I don't know what she told you, but it was my fault. I got some bad news at work, and then my dad showed up in my office. He was being worse than usual. He said... it doesn't matter what he said. I went home in a shitty mood and I took it out on Kendra."

"So, what, you guys argued?" he asks.

"Basically," I say. "I was such an idiot. I laid into her about making me change and some other bullshit. And then I told her I was leaving."

"Okay," he says. "Then what happened?"

I shrug. "She left. So I packed up my shit and took it to my house. The remodel is done, so I guess I was moving out anyway."

"Huh," Caleb says after a momentary pause.

"What?"

"Well... is that it?" he asks.

"Yeah."

"So, what you're saying is that you came home in a pissy mood, got in a fight with your girlfriend, and said some things you regret," he says.

"Yeah."

"And in the midst of that, you moved out?"

I nod.

"When was that?"

"Last Friday."

"Okay, so what's the problem?" he asks.

"What the fuck kind of question is that?"

"Well, I mean, what happened then?" he asks. "Is she not responding to your calls or texts?"

I furrow my brow, looking at him like he's crazy. "I haven't called her."

"Not once? Not even a text?" he asks.

"No."

He gapes at me for a few seconds. "Are you serious?"

"What the fuck would I say to her?" I ask. "I screwed up. I ruined it."

"Well, you acted like a jackass," he says and ignores my glare. "But did you tell her you hate her?"

"No."

"Did you run out and bang some random girl?" he asks. "To get back at her or something?"

"Fuck no," I say, too loud. I lower my voice. "Sorry. No. God, no I didn't go out and bang some random."

"Good," he says. "But I think I'm missing something important, because this doesn't add up."

"What doesn't add up?"

"Why getting in one fight with her means you broke up forever," he says.

"What?"

He rolls his eyes. "Dude, this is what you get for avoiding relationships your entire adult life. Getting in an argument— even a really shitty argument—doesn't mean it's over. Do you really think people in long term relationships never fight?"

"No, I know they fight. I'm not an idiot."

"That's debatable," he says. "People fight. They say things they don't mean. It happens."

I shake my head. "You don't get it. This was worse than that. You didn't see the look on her face."

"Well, then you need to talk to her," he says. "Call her. Send her a text. Apologize."

"There's no way she'll talk to me."

"I guess you're fucked then," he says. "I don't know why you need my advice."

I glare at him.

"Do you want to know what I really think?" he asks.

"I don't know, do I?"

"You're sabotaging this," he says. "I don't know if it's fear of commitment, or a fear of rejection, or what. That's on you to figure out. But you're doing everything wrong, like you're trying to make it worse."

"The fuck I am," I say.

"Maybe you don't even realize it," he says. "There's nothing wrong with taking some space to calm down. But fighting with your girlfriend doesn't mean it's over, even if you say things you have to apologize for. Unless you move out and stop speaking to her. Then yeah, that's going to mean it's over."

I open my mouth to argue, but he's making a little too much sense.

"What do you want?" he asks. "That's what you need to figure out. Do you want to be with her? Then talk to her. Apologize. Tell her how you feel. I know that's not exactly your strongest skill set, but anyone can learn."

We sit in silence for a few minutes and I stare at the table, tapping my finger against the cold glass bottle.

"I want her back," I say, my voice quiet. "I never should have left."

"No, you probably shouldn't have," he says. "And you should have called her by now."

"You're right, I've done everything wrong," I say. "I don't think she's going to forgive me."

Caleb laughs.

"What?" I ask.

"Sorry, I was just remembering something," he says. "When we were kids, I put four pieces of chewed up gum in her hair when she was asleep. The next day, it was so sticky and tangled, our dad had to cut most of it off. She went from having long hair, all the way down her back, to this short little pixie cut. She was *so* mad at me."

"Your point is?"

"She forgave me," he says. "Well, at first she came at me like a feral cat. I think I still have a scar." He pulls up his sleeve and looks at his forearm. "But eventually, she did forgive me. Trust me, you can fix this."

"You think?"

"Yeah," he says. "It won't be easy. Every day that goes by makes it a little worse, to be honest. And she's in California until Sunday, so that's not working in your favor. But you should at least text her and let her know you want to talk when she gets back."

I let out a long breath. "Yeah. You're probably right."

"But Weston?"

"Yeah?"

"If you're not sure, you should just walk away now," he says. "Don't string her along. Kendra deserves better."

"Kendra deserves everything."

He meets my eyes and nods. "Exactly. You have to be willing to give it to her."

I put the half-empty beer on the table, pull out my phone, and start writing a text.

"Are you texting her?" he asks.

"No, Mia," I say.

"Mia? Why?"

I finish the text and hit send, almost afraid to hope. "Because I need her help and she'll know what to do."

"*Mia* will know what to do?" he asks. "I'm confused."

I stand and pocket my phone. "Yeah, me too. But thanks."

"Sure," he says as I head for his front door. "Where are you going?"

I pause and look over my shoulder. "I'm going to go fix this."

31

KENDRA

*A*lex and Mia's wedding is phenomenal.

The ceremony is outside in one of the resort garden areas. The smell of flowers fills the air and trees provide shade.

Shelby and I stand up front, dressed in our matching lavender dresses. The two nieces are flower girls—Mia's niece Alanna has to coax Charlotte up the aisle, holding her hand and whispering gentle encouragement. When Charlotte reaches the front, she dashes over to stand by Caleb, instead of staying by Alanna like she was supposed to. But no one minds.

Mia looks absolutely perfect in a simple strapless gown with a sweetheart neckline and a long, flowing skirt. The little bit of beading on the bodice catches the sunlight and makes her look romantic and almost ethereal. Alex is so handsome in his dark gray suit, his beard perfectly trimmed, and a constant smile on his face.

The ceremony is simple, but beautiful. They wrote their own vows, and there's hardly a dry eye when they finish. They're so in love with each other and it shines through in every look, every word, every touch they share.

Afterward, we all file to the reception. There's an indoor area with two sets of wide French doors leading to an outdoor patio. The photographer takes more pictures while the guests mingle, sipping wine and champagne and snacking on hors d'oeuvres.

My weekend started off leisurely—Mia loved hearing about Louis, who I haven't seen again—but since yesterday afternoon, it's been crazy. More people started arriving, so I helped people find their rooms and coordinated dinner for guests who wouldn't be at the rehearsal. Then we had the rehearsal and dinner afterward. That extended into a late night in the hotel bar. It was fun, and a little wine and a lot of laughs took my mind off Weston for a while.

Today started early, with manicures, hair and makeup, dresses, and making sure Mia ate and didn't get dehydrated. Then so many photos, my face hurt from smiling. Next thing I knew, I was watching my brother marry the love of his life.

Now I'm sitting at a table with a much-needed glass of champagne in my hand. I'm seated with Caleb and Charlotte, Shelby and her little family, as well as the bride and groom. Someone was kind enough to make sure there wasn't an extra place setting at our table, but I'm still aware of the space where Weston should be sitting.

Alex and Mia stand, and someone hands him a microphone. He signals for quiet and once the crowd has hushed, he says a few words, thanking everyone for coming.

He passes the microphone to Shelby, the matron of honor. She gives a teary speech about watching her baby sister get married, and how happy she is that Mia and Alex found each other. It's sweet and heartfelt, and earns a hearty round of applause from all the guests. Mia hugs her sister tight and has to take off her glasses to dab the tears from her eyes.

Caleb is the best man, and Shelby hands him the microphone. Charlotte crawls into my lap while her daddy stands to give his speech.

"Uh-oh," Charlotte whispers in my ear as her dad starts to talk.

"What's wrong, Bug?"

"My shoe fell off." She lifts the tablecloth and looks beneath the table.

"It's okay, I'll get it." I lean down to grab her shoe, then help her slip it back on her foot.

When I sit up, my breath catches in my throat. My eyes widen and my mouth drops open.

Weston is walking toward Caleb, picking his way between the tables. He looks devastating in a dark suit and matching tie. His storm cloud eyes flick to me once, and his brow furrows, but he keeps heading toward Caleb, just on the other side of my table.

Caleb finishes his speech to a hearty round of applause. I stare at Weston, my hands limp until Charlotte reminds me to clap.

"And now, I think there's one last speech tonight," Caleb says. He looks at Mia and she gives him an emphatic nod, gesturing toward Weston. Caleb hands him the mic.

"Is that Weston?" Charlotte whispers in my ear.

"Yeah."

"Good evening," Weston says, his deep voice amplified by the microphone. "First, I need to say thank you to Mia and Alex, for letting me crash their wedding tonight."

Mia smiles, scrunching up her nose, and gives Weston a double thumbs-up.

"I'm usually a man of few words," he says. "Someone I care about very much once told me that I don't need to talk about every little thing, but I say what's important, when it needs to be said. Tonight, I think I need more words than usual, because what I have to say is very important. And it absolutely needs to be said."

His eyes are on me as he continues. "Once in a while, a person is lucky enough to meet someone who sees them for who they are. Sees right through to their core. And not only do they see it," he says, glancing at Alex and Mia, "they love what they see."

He turns back to me. "I don't know if it means that person is your soulmate, or you're meant to be together. None of that really matters, because we're all human, which means we're basically idiots and capable of screwing up anything, even fate." He glances around at the tables of guests and his mouth turns up in a little smile. "Or maybe that's just me."

Everyone laughs and Charlotte shifts in my lap.

"The point is, we make mistakes. We say things we don't mean." He pauses, holding my gaze. "And sometimes those screw-ups have pretty shitty consequences."

Caleb nudges him.

"Oh—sorry, Bug," he says to Charlotte.

She puts a hand to her mouth and giggles and a murmur of soft laughter rolls through the crowd.

"Alex's sister Kendra is one of those rare people who shows her real self to the world," he says. "She is the most genuine, kind, caring person I've ever met. In fact, if you'd described Kendra to me before I had met her, I don't think I would have believed she was real. No one is that selfless. No one is that *good*. So, I have no idea what she ever saw in a man like me."

I swallow hard, trying to get rid of the lump in my throat.

"But she did see me," he says. "She saw through everything —saw something even I couldn't. And what she saw wasn't some romanticized version of who I could be. She simply saw me, on the inside. She understood who I am in a way no one else ever has. And the really miraculous part is that she liked what she saw."

"Is he talking to you?" Charlotte whispers in my ear.

I just nod.

"Kendra is sadly without a date tonight because I'm an asshole," he says and there's another murmur through the crowd. "Sorry again, Bug. But it's true. I'm one of those idiot humans who had something amazing—something really close to perfect—and I managed to screw it up."

Caleb quietly slips back into his seat next to me and takes Charlotte from my lap.

"I'm here, in front of all these people, making a scene at your brother's wedding, because I need to tell you that I'm sorry," he says. "I said some things I didn't mean, and I hurt you. And then I managed to make it worse. But you were right about me, Kendra. I did it because I was afraid."

He lowers the mic a few inches, his eyes still on me, and takes a deep breath.

"You told me on our first date—or maybe we're calling it our second date, we can argue about it later—that you were afraid to fall in love with me. You said it in French, so I didn't know what it meant at the time. But Kendra, *je n'ai pas peur de tomber amoureaux de toi*. I'm not afraid to fall in love with you."

More murmurs, louder this time. I gasp and hold a trembling hand to my lips.

"I'm *so* in love with you," he says. "Kendra, you're everything. You're the most amazing person I know. You make me want to be a better man. Not only that, you make me believe I can be."

He starts walking around the table toward me.

"I don't know if what I have to give is enough," he says. "You deserve a man who will make you happy—who will take care of you the way you take care of everyone around you. If you can find it in your heart to forgive me... and if you love me even half as much as I love you... I want to be that man."

He turns off the mic and sets it down on the table next to

Caleb. My eyes are locked with his, and I stand up slowly as he comes the last few feet toward me.

The rest of the room suddenly fades away, the hushed silence settling over us like falling snow. All I can see is Weston, standing in front of me with so much vulnerability in his eyes.

He cups my face with one hand and places the other on my waist. His eyes are fierce, but his voice is quiet. "I'm sorry. For everything. I love you."

I stare at him in awe for a few seconds before I can reply. "You had me at *I'm an asshole.*"

He breaks into soft laughter, his smile lighting up his expression. I try to keep a straight face, but I laugh along with him.

"I love you too, Weston. I love you so much."

He leans in and presses his lips to mine. The silence is suddenly broken by a room full of cheers and applause. But neither of us care. He pulls me close, holding me tight, and I wrap my arms around his neck. His mouth moves over mine, soft and tender. A tear trails down my cheek from the corner of my eye and it feels as if a million sparks are bursting inside me.

Music starts to play and the hum of conversation returns around us. Weston pulls away and kisses my forehead, then pulls up a chair next to mine. We both sit.

My heart feels lighter than air and I can't stop smiling. Mia and Alex come back to the table for dinner, and Mia gives Weston a big hug. Obviously she knew he was coming, and I can't believe she kept it from me. But I can't be even a tiny bit mad at her. My brothers shake Weston's hand and I hear Caleb tell him he's impressed. Even my dad shakes his hand and pats him on the back.

Weston holds my hand or touches me gently on my back or shoulder for the rest of the reception. He dances with me and feeds me bites of wedding cake. After we finish our cake, Charlotte climbs in his lap, surprising everyone—especially him. But he just smiles and holds her, rocking her back and forth to the slow beat of the music.

Mia and Alex come back to the table after mingling with their guests. She grabs her bouquet from the center of the table and tosses it in my direction, knocking over an almost-empty glass of champagne in the process.

"Oops," she says.

I catch it. "What's this about?"

"It's yours, K-law," she says with an exaggerated wink.

I roll my eyes with a laugh and glance at Weston. I hope he doesn't think this means I expect something. But he watches me with an enigmatic look in his eyes, his arm resting on the back of my chair. His mouth twitches in a hint of a smile and he takes another drink of his champagne.

It's late when the reception finally winds down. Charlotte is asleep with her head on Caleb's shoulder. I offer to help him get her up to their room, but he says he's fine. The rest of us send Mia and Alex off to their honeymoon suite in a swirl of bubbles at the door. She trips on the hem of her dress, so Alex picks her up and carries her to the elevator while she laughs and waves goodbye.

Weston gets his bag from the concierge and we head upstairs to my room. Our room, now. My feet are killing me and I'm so exhausted I can barely keep my eyes open. He helps me out of my dress and hangs up his suit.

We crawl in bed together. He pulls me in tight, my back to his front, and kisses my shoulder and neck. I want to tell him I'll wake up if he wants me to—we haven't been together in a week and his thick erection presses into me—but I'm already falling asleep.

But Weston simply holds me. I snuggle into his warm body and drift off to sleep.

32

KENDRA

The feel of Weston's lips on the back of my neck wakes me. I arch my back, pressing my ass into him, my body coming alive before I'm fully awake.

His hands tighten on my hips and he rubs his erection against me. He groans into my neck, a low sound in his throat. "Baby, I need to be inside you. Right fucking now."

I roll onto my back while he puts on a condom. I'm hot and throbbing for him already. He settles between my legs and kisses me, his mouth hungry, while he slides in. The feel of his cock filling me makes me shudder with pleasure.

He plunges all the way in and stops. "Oh my god, Kendra, I missed you so much."

"I missed you too."

Our bodies move together, slow at first. I cling to him, my hands running up and down the flexing muscle of his back. He kisses me deep, like he can't get enough. Our pace increases, the intensity building. I need more of him. I wrap my legs around his waist and grind against him, trying to get him in deeper. He moves faster, thrusting his hips, driving into me. The steady rhythm brings me to the brink. My core muscles clench, releasing bursts of electricity that radiate through my whole body.

He rests his forehead against mine. His cock pulses, so hard and thick. I'm breathing hard, teetering on the edge. He feels so good, I'm completely consumed.

Two more thrusts and I shatter into a million pieces beneath him. He comes in me with fury, pushing me higher up the bed. I dig my fingers into his back, crying out with the waves of bliss.

After we both finish, he holds me tight, still inside me. The feel of our bodies locked together, his hot skin pressed against mine, is overwhelming. I keep my arms wrapped around him while we catch our breath.

He kisses me again, a slow, sensual caress. "Good morning."

"Good morning," I say with a smile. "I like it when you wake me up like that."

"I tried to let you sleep, but that ass was driving me crazy," he says.

He gets up to deal with the condom while I pull the sheets up and rest my head in my hand. He lies down next to my legs and rests his head on my thigh.

He's silent for a long moment, but I can tell he's thinking about something. I wait, knowing he'll talk when he's ready, and enjoy the warmth between my legs.

"I brought you something," he says.

"What?"

Still lying on his stomach, he leans over the edge of the bed and grabs something out of his bag. Whatever it is, he keeps it covered so I can't see. Looking down at his hands, he slowly moves them, revealing a small box.

My tummy feels like I just went over the drop on a roller coaster. "Wait a second. Is that what it looks like, or is it something else? You better tell me because I need to know if I should be freaking out or not."

His beautiful mouth parts in a huge smile. "This is exactly what it looks like."

"But... it's... that's a..." I sputter, suddenly unable to find any words.

"I know," he says, still smiling, and he laughs. "This is all wrong. It's way too soon. I guess normal people date for months, or even years, before they do this. But Kendra, I don't want to date you. Don't get me wrong, I want to take you out. Give you beautiful things. Spoil you rotten. And if you need time, I can put this away for a while. Maybe this isn't the right way to do it; I should probably be in a suit in a fancy restaurant. Maybe I should have learned how to ask in French. But at the very least, I want you to know I have this, and I plan to give it to you."

"Are you being serious right now?"

"Completely serious."

I stare at him, my heart racing. "Why? What made you decide to do this?"

"You deserve someone who is going to fight for you and never let you go," he says. "And I mean *never*. I knew if I came down here, I had to be all in. This isn't something I want to try for a while and see how it goes. That's not what you need, and that's not what I want. I have to be in, or out, and baby, I'm in. No matter what."

"Really?"

"Absolutely. I'm going to marry you, Kendra Lawson. The *when* is up to you, but that's what's going to happen." He pauses, biting his bottom lip. "Do you want to see it?"

My eyes dart back to the box. I'm tingly all over, my tummy doing little flip-flops. I meet his eyes and give him a quick nod.

He smiles again and slowly opens it.

Inside is a gold ring with a pale blue opal surrounded by small, sparkling diamonds in a halo around the pearlescent stone.

"This was..." He hesitates and looks down at it, then meets my eyes. "It was my mother's."

My hand flies to my mouth and my eyes sting with tears. "Oh, Weston," I breathe.

"I know that when she wore it, it wasn't the symbol of a happy marriage," he says. "But it was hers and that means something to me."

A tear leaks out the corner of my eye. "You kept her wedding ring?"

"Yeah," he says. "I don't have much that was hers, but I ended up with a small box of her things. Never could bring myself to get rid of it."

"And you want to give it to me?" I ask, my voice barely a whisper.

"It's already yours," he says.

"Yes, Weston," I say. "Ask me now."

He raises his eyebrows. "Are you sure?"

I nod and sit up, holding the sheet over my chest. "Right here. In English. I don't want fancy or a suit or any of that. Now is perfect."

He takes the ring out of the box and sits, moving so he's right in front of me. Our eyes meet and his voice is soft. "Kendra, will you marry me?"

"Yes, Weston," I say. "I would love to marry you."

He smiles and a few tears fall unchecked down my cheeks. He takes my trembling hand and slips the ring onto my finger.

"Oh my god," I say.

He rubs his thumb in a slow circle around the ring. "It looks beautiful on you."

"Thank you," I say. "I love it so much."

"I love you so much." He leans in for a kiss, his mouth soft against mine.

When he pulls away, I look down at the ring again. I almost

can't believe this is happening. Is it too soon? Maybe. But I know he's right, deep in my soul. He *is* going to marry me. It doesn't matter that this is fast, or that we've already had some ups and downs. We'll have more. That's the way love—and life—works.

"Weston," I say, wiping the tears away, "we're going to get married."

"Yeah. And we can do whatever you want. I'm clueless about wedding stuff, so you just tell me where to be and when to show up. You can have anything you want."

"Anything?" I ask.

He shrugs. "Sure. Anything."

"What if I said I just want to go to the courthouse," I say. "No big wedding."

"Is that really what you want, or are you looking for my reaction?"

I laugh. "No, that's really what I want. I don't want a wedding. I guess we could do something to celebrate with my family. Weddings are nice, but, I don't know, I've been in nine and only four of those couples are still together—including Alex and Mia who've been married less than twenty-four hours. I'd rather *get married*, and then go on an amazing honeymoon."

"I swear to god, you're a fucking unicorn." He pushes me to my back and kisses me hard. "In that case, when do you want to do this? Is Friday good?"

"What?" I ask through my laughter. "You want to get married this Friday?"

"Baby, I said I'm all in. I don't like to fuck around."

"You're so sexy when you're decisive."

He smiles and kisses me again.

"This is crazy," I say. "Are we crazy?"

"Yeah," he says. "But I wouldn't have it any other way."

EPILOGUE
WESTON

I pull open the door to the clinic and hold it for a guy who's on his way out. He thanks me and I walk in, nodding to Jenna at the front desk. She stares at me while I head into the back, like she knows something is happening.

Tapping the manila envelope against my hand, I go straight for Ian's office. I know he's in—I had Tanya text me when he arrived. I didn't want to have to wait around for him to show up or get out of an appointment.

I knock on his partially open door and let myself in.

He looks up at me from a stack of paperwork as if he's dazed. His mouth hangs open and he blinks a few times, like he's confused.

I hesitate, clutching the folder in my hands.

"I just got served with divorce papers," he says.

Maybe if I wasn't basically an asshole, I'd feel bad for him right now. But I don't.

"Why do you look surprised?" I ask.

"What?" he asks. "We've been married over twenty years."

"How long have you been cheating on her?"

He gapes at me, apparently without an answer.

I'm about to make his day considerably worse, but I'm hard pressed to feel even the slightest regret. He made his bed. He can lie in it.

I toss the manila folder on top of his divorce papers.

"What's this?" he asks.

"It's a buyout agreement," I say. "I'm leaving the practice."

"Are you fucking kidding me?" he asks. "You know I don't have enough liquid capital to buy you out. I'll have to close down."

"Not my problem."

"After everything I did for you, this is the thanks I get?"

"The guilt trip thing isn't going to work," I say. "I know you've been skimming money from the practice. You've been doing it for years. I have to give you credit, you hid it well. But I found all of it—the secret apartment where you've been taking your flings, the mistress you keep down in San Diego, the expense account you're not supposed to have. My lawyer wrote up all the details in the packet there, but the gist of it is, if you buy me out now, I won't turn you in for fraud."

He narrows his eyes and crosses his arms. "What does your father think about all this?"

I shake my head. He's really reaching—trying to bring the fear of daddy down on me. "Do you think I give even the slightest of fucks? I'll be honest, Ian, I hope you refuse my offer. Because I'd love to turn you in and see you both go down. The thanks you want? It's in that envelope. I'm giving you a chance to walk away. Take it or leave it."

He stares at me, his mouth hanging open.

I turn and move toward the door, but pause and look over my shoulder. "By the way, I'm the one who told your wife."

He coughs, making a harsh choking sound, but I walk away without looking back.

"So how did it go with Ian today?" Kendra asks.

I flick on the blinker and turn right, heading up the hill. "About how I thought. He wasn't happy, but he doesn't have a leg to stand on."

"Do your employees know yet?" she asks.

"Yeah, I sent an email explaining what's happening. I'll have jobs for some of them, and I'll pay the people I can't hire a good severance package. Everyone will be taken care of."

"That's good," she says.

I pull up outside my house and the motion activated flood-lights wink on. Kendra and I get out of the car and she follows me inside.

It's quiet, and I flick on a few lights.

"Wow," she says, looking around. "It's really nice. Looks like you."

"Thanks," I say. We stop in the living room, and I glance around with my hands in my pockets. "It did turn out really well."

Kendra walks over to one of the big windows, the city skyline sparkling in the darkness. "This view is amazing."

It's strange that I haven't shown her the house yet. I guess I've already stopped thinking of it as mine. It didn't seem all that important.

"Yeah, it is," I say, gazing at her. "I figured you'd want to see it before I sell the place."

"Sell?" she asks. "You're selling your house? You just remod-eled it."

I shrug. "Well, we can live here if you want. But I like your house better."

"Better than this?" she asks, gesturing around her. "My house is old and creaky. And small."

"It is, but it has character," I say. "And it's on a flat street with a bigger lot. This place doesn't have a yard at all. Besides, with this view I'll make plenty of money on the sale to pay for the addition."

"Addition?" she asks. "What addition?"

"Your house is only a two bedroom," I say. "We'll need to add on."

"How many bedrooms do you think we need?" she asks.

I shrug again and give her a little smile. "I don't know, how many kids do you want?"

Her lips part and she stares at me, her mouth moving like she's trying to say something, but no sound comes out.

I step in and brush the hair back from her face, then lean in to kiss her.

Kendra was serious about not wanting a wedding, but we didn't get married the week we returned from Napa. She wanted to wait until Alex and Mia got back from their honeymoon. So we waited an extra week.

We decided to make it a surprise, so we made plans with her family, telling them to meet us downtown. We gave them a time and an address, nothing more. They arrived to find me in a suit and tie, and Kendra in a flowing ivory dress. It was just reminiscent enough of a wedding dress that it took no time at all for her shocked family to realize what we were doing.

After we explained ourselves, everyone hugged for what felt like an eternity—this family hugs over everything—and we went into the courthouse. Mia bought Kendra a bouquet of flowers from a guy selling them outside the door. And there, in the presence of her dad, her brothers, her sister-in-law, and her niece, in a ceremony that took all of five minutes, Kendra gave me what would have been my dream wedding, had I ever dreamed about it before that day.

Short. Sweet. Perfect.

Afterward, I took everyone out to dinner to celebrate. I was happy Kendra got to share the experience with her family; I know how much they mean to her. Truth is, they mean a lot to me too. But for me, the thing that mattered the most was her. My girl. My wife.

I'm creating a life with Kendra that I thought I didn't want. But really, I was just afraid to try. Afraid to be the sort of man who could love a woman this way.

I look at her now, her beautiful face silhouetted by the twinkling city lights through the windows. Fortunately for me, she made it easy. "I love you."

"Who are you and what have you done with Weston?" she asks.

I just laugh.

"Wait, be serious though," she says. "We're going on a very extravagant honeymoon in New Zealand. You just left your job, and you're about to open your own practice. We can't afford to build an addition on my house anytime soon. You mean in a few years, right? Five? Maybe ten?"

"*Our house,* now," I say. "And no, we can get started on it when we get back. Or wait, it's up to you. But I have plenty of money."

"You do?"

"Of course," I say. "Didn't I ever tell you about my mother?"

"What about her?"

"Her parents were wealthy," I say. "Extremely wealthy. Probably why my dad married her. But the joke was on him. Before she died, she took her entire inheritance and put it in a trust for me. My dad was never able to touch her money."

"Are you serious?"

"Yeah," I say. "It's how I got through med school with no debt, bought this place, bought into Ian's practice. Trust me, money is never going to be an issue."

Kendra shakes her head slowly. "All this time, I was a gold digger and I didn't even know it."

We both laugh, and I kiss her forehead. I show her around the rest of the house, but in the end, we both agree that her little house is our home.

After I drive us home, Kendra changes into a pair of her ridiculous pajama pants—which is fine, because I know I'll get to take them off her later. We get comfortable together on the couch and turn on a movie. I wrap my arms around her and kiss the top of her head.

It's a strange thing, to feel such a deep sense of contentment. I can't remember a time in my life before Kendra when I was actually happy. But with her, I am. And knowing she's mine— she's my wife—melts some of the ice that used to encase my cold heart. It beats for her now, and I wouldn't have it any other way.

DEAR READER

Dear reader,

So what'd you think of Weston?

Did he piss you off in the beginning? Did you love him by the end? Yeah, me too.

The core ideas for this book came from a few different places. I already had Kendra lined up to be a heroine—after writing Book Boyfriend, clearly Kendra needed her HEA. I also wanted to do a roommate story. There's something so tantalizing about that version of forced proximity. And it gave me the admittedly cheeky title of Cocky Roommate.

But who was the hero?

Here was where I set myself up with a challenge. Actually, it's more like the challenge was hurled at me (although the *hurling* of it wasn't intentional) by my friend Nikki. She said something to the effect of, "I'd love it if you wrote a hero who was a champion asshole."

So, of course I had to do it.

I loved the challenge of making Weston a dick in the beginning and finding ways to redeem him by the end. I knew it was possible. I've read some great books with asshole heroes who you grow to love. But it required careful attention to his motives, his backstory, his decisions, and his thought processes.

Believe it or not, I had a harder time making him an asshole than I did making him lovable by the end. Probably because I knew why he was that way. There always has to be a really solid *why*, particularly if I'm giving a character undesirable traits (or traits that make it difficult for them to get to the HEA). Understanding where Weston was coming from made it easier for me to dig beneath his asshole armor and find his good side.

Weston broke when his mom died. He didn't have anyone to care for him, so he quickly grew accustomed to being swept out of the way. Between spending so much of his childhood without anyone who was the least bit nurturing (arguably when he needed it most), and the pain of losing his mother, he becomes an adult who intentionally pushes people away before they can get close to him. But deep down, he craves the connection he's been working so hard to avoid.

Kendra came alive for me in Book Boyfriend. She was straightforward and sassy with her brothers, but also very supportive. Alex might have been the one doing the heavy lifting for their dad financially, but Kendra was always there, quietly getting things done.

So why throw a guy like Weston at a sweetheart like Kendra? Well, I knew she could handle him.

Kendra isn't about to take Weston's shit. But she also believes that most people are generally decent, and from the beginning, she tries to see the good in Weston. And when he's hurt, and she realizes he literally has no one else to help him, she doesn't really see it as a choice. Of course she's going to take care of him. To her it's not an amazing feat of generosity; it's just what she does.

And that's kind of the heart of it. This isn't a story about a woman trying to show a man how to be different. Kendra isn't trying to change Weston. She just goes on doing what she always does. And that's what starts to unravel Weston's assholedom.

Kendra doesn't seduce Weston with her sex appeal (although he fully admits she has it). It's how she treats him, and the people around her, that gets under his skin. He can't help but begin to care about her. She makes it impossible not to. She cares about him, and she doesn't try to hide it. Because again, to her, it isn't anything extraordinary. Of course she remembers what kind of pasta sauce he likes. Of course she packages up leftovers and leaves a little note. Of course she knows he loved her lasagna. That's just Kendra.

But Weston has never been the recipient of that kind of care and consideration. As a child, he should have, but his parents were unable or unwilling to give it to him. As an adult, he doesn't let anyone in his life; he stops them by being a jerk before they can begin to care for him. Kendra gets the chance to show him what it feels like to be cared for, and to care for someone in return. And it's life changing.

Writing Weston through that transformation was really satisfying. I loved him in the middle, when he's confused and frustrated. I joked more than once about poor Weston and all his damn FEELINGS. He didn't know what to do with himself for a while there. I like it when characters really have to struggle against their flaws—when their view of the world is turned upside down. They have to reorient themselves and figure out what it all means, and who they really are.

I hope you enjoyed the book! And if you're hoping for more from the Lawson family, I'm happy to say you're in luck. Caleb and little Charlotte also have a story to tell.

Thanks for reading!

CK

ACKNOWLEDGMENTS

A big thank you to everyone who continues to help, love, and support me while I make shit up in my head and write it down.

Thanks to Elayne for cleaning up my manuscript and telling me hilarious and semi-relevant stories in your comments.

Thanks to Nikki for inspiring me to write an asshole. I hope Weston's assholery made you happy.

A huge thank you to my readers who keep coming back for more CK. I've said it before, and I'll say it again, you crazy people are why I do what I do. I love you.

And thanks to David for... all the things.

ALSO BY CLAIRE KINGSLEY

For a full and up-to-date listing of Claire Kingsley books visit www.clairekingsleybooks.com/books/

For comprehensive reading order, visit www.clairekingsleybooks.com/reading-order/

How the Grump Saved Christmas (Elias and Isabelle)

A stand-alone, small-town Christmas romance

The Bailey Brothers

Steamy, small-town family series. Five unruly brothers. Epic pranks. A quirky, feuding town. Big HEAs. (Best read in order)

Protecting You (Asher and Grace part 1)

Fighting for Us (Asher and Grace part 2)

Unraveling Him (Evan and Fiona)

Rushing In (Gavin and Skylar)

Chasing Her Fire (Logan and Cara)

Rewriting the Stars (Levi and Annika)

The Miles Family

Sexy, sweet, funny, and heartfelt family series. Messy family. Epic bromance. Super romantic. (Best read in order)

Broken Miles (Roland and Zoe)

Forbidden Miles (Brynn and Chase)

Reckless Miles (Cooper and Amelia)

Hidden Miles (Leo and Hannah)

Gaining Miles: A Miles Family Novella (Ben and Shannon)

Dirty Martini Running Club

Sexy, fun stand-alone romantic comedies with huge... hearts.

Everly Dalton's Dating Disasters (Everly, Hazel, and Nora)

Faking Ms. Right (Everly and Shepherd)

Falling for My Enemy (Hazel and Corban)

Marrying Mr. Wrong (Sophie and Cox)

Flirting with Forever (Nora and Dex)

Bluewater Billionaires

Hot, stand-alone romantic comedies. Lady billionaire BFFs and the
badass heroes who love them.

The Mogul and the Muscle (Cameron and Jude)

The Price of Scandal, Wild Open Hearts, and Crazy for Loving You

More Bluewater Billionaire shared-world stand-alone romantic
comedies by Lucy Score, Kathryn Nolan, and Pippa Grant

Bootleg Springs

by Claire Kingsley and Lucy Score

Hot and hilarious small-town romcom series with a dash of mystery and suspense. (Best read in order)

Whiskey Chaser (Scarlett and Devlin)

Sidecar Crush (Jameson and Leah Mae)

Moonshine Kiss (Bowie and Cassidy)

Bourbon Bliss (June and George)

Gin Fling (Jonah and Shelby)

Highball Rush (Gibson and I can't tell you)

Book Boyfriends

Hot, stand-alone romcoms that will make you laugh and make you swoon.

Book Boyfriend (Alex and Mia)

Cocky Roommate (Weston and Kendra)

Hot Single Dad (Caleb and Linnea)

Finding Ivy (William and Ivy)

A unique contemporary romance with a hint of mystery.

His Heart (Sebastian and Brooke)

A poignant and emotionally intense story about grief, loss, and the transcendent power of love.

The Always Series

Smoking hot, dirty talking bad boys with some angsty intensity.

Always Have (Braxton and Kylie)

Always Will (Selene and Ronan)

Always Ever After (Braxton and Kylie)

The Jetty Beach Series

Sexy small-town romance series with swoony heroes, romantic HEAs, and lots of big feels.

Behind His Eyes (Ryan and Nicole)

One Crazy Week (Melissa and Jackson)

Messy Perfect Love (Cody and Clover)

Operation Get Her Back (Hunter and Emma)

Weekend Fling (Finn and Juliet)

Good Girl Next Door (Lucas and Becca)

The Path to You (Gabriel and Sadie)

ABOUT THE AUTHOR

Claire Kingsley is a #1 Amazon bestselling author of sexy, heartfelt contemporary romance and romantic comedies. She writes sassy, quirky heroines, swoony heroes who love their women hard, panty-melting sexytimes, romantic happily ever afters, and all the big feels.

She can't imagine life without coffee, her Kindle, and the sexy heroes who inhabit her imagination. She lives in the inland Pacific Northwest with her three kids.

www.clairekingsleybooks.com